I0705830

EX MARKS THE SPOT

TEACHERS' LOUNGE
BOOK 3

HAZEL JAMES

COPYRIGHT

AUTHOR'S NOTE

The idea for this book dropped out of the sky and into my brain as I crossed the parking lot at Walmart. I've always strived for authenticity in my books and this idea brought with it two massive hurdles:

- I'm not an international traveler, and
- Up until that point, I'd never seen an episode of *The Amazing Race*.

What followed was hundreds of hours of research about incredible places and cultures. (If I ever win the lottery, I'd love to follow Court and Hartley's itinerary . . . just maybe not on the same timeline.)

The locations I mention in this book are real, and I've tried my best to get it right. The same goes for the logistics of filming an international reality TV show.

If I missed something, please accept my sincere apology and know it was either an honest mistake or a careful exercise of creative liberty in the fictional world I built.

I had a blast traveling with Team Hartbreak, and I hope you do too.

All my love,

Hazel

CHAPTER 1
HARTLEY

Day 1—Dallas, Texas

There's an eighty-four percent chance I'm going to murder Courtland Mueller in the next twenty-one days.

For starters, he's ruining the first thing I've done for myself in half a decade. And secondly, he was supposed to turn into an ogre after college. How dare he barge onto my favorite TV show with his annoyingly perfect hair and magazine-cover body looking like the new-and-improved version of the man who tossed my heart into a meat grinder six years ago.

The *audacity*.

And the worst part is, my only shot at winning a million dollars rests in his hands. Scratch that. The worst part is being required to stay within twenty feet of him for the next three weeks while trying to win a million dollars. Screw him for auditioning, and screw the jerk in casting who paired us up. I'm sending a strongly worded email to that department as soon as I'm allowed to have my phone again.

What do I hate most about Court? The obvious answer would be him dumping me with an explanation that reeked of bullshit, though I suspect it had something to do with the bachelor party he'd attended that weekend. But it turns out our breakup was the product of a larger problem: Court Mueller is the lyingest liar who ever existed.

1

At least I'd gotten some good artwork out of it.

I'd ended up ditching everything I'd prepared for my senior capstone and submitting a new series called *The Evolution of a Lie* that I'd created in a weeklong breakup-induced state of mania.

Seven pieces of varying mediums—charcoal, pastels, acrylic paints, even a watercolor done with wine—to represent each month of our relationship, with the final piece being a blank canvas because I was so emotionally spent that I'd had nothing left to give.

Until Gallery Night anyway.

An hour into my capstone exhibition, I watched Court walk through the packed gallery with a woman hanging on his arm as if he wanted as many witnesses to my humiliation as possible.

The.

Freaking.

Audacity.

Red (and crimson . . . and scarlet) clouded my vision and my fist begged for a meeting with his face. Instead, I punched a hole in the center of the blank canvas at the end of my series. Naturally, every head snapped in my direction, so I smiled, took a bow, and thanked the guests for attending my performance of *The Evolution of a Lie*, then spun on my heel and left the gallery.

That was the last time I saw Court.

"Miss? Is everything okay?"

The taxi driver's voice brings me out of my thoughts, and I realize I'm shooting daggers out the window at the man in the matching Central Tennessee State College shirt. He's standing beside a row of hedges with a few other contestants, laughing at something one of them said. My stomach clenches at the sight of his smile.

"Sorry, I've just never seen a statue of an eyeball before." I grab my back-pack and slide out of the taxi into the heart of downtown Dallas, Texas. "Thanks for the lift," I add before stepping aside so a member of the crew can pay the driver.

Along with no cell phones, contestants on Xtreme Quest aren't allowed to bring cash from home, credit cards, cameras, or smart watches. Everything we are allowed to bring must fit into a backpack that we'll carry while we're competing.

This season features eleven teams of two people who graduated from the same college. To make it easier on the crew and viewers at home, the show sent us shirts from our alma matter to wear on the first leg of the race. Some teams already knew each other and auditioned together, and the rest, like me, auditioned by ourselves knowing we'd be partnered with a fellow alum.

If only I'd had a crystal ball.

But at least I have one thing on my side right now—Court hasn't seen me yet. That means he didn't witness my moment of panic when I discovered who my partner would be, and more importantly, that means I'll get to witness his.

Petty? Yes.

Satisfying? Also, yes.

A woman with an iPad and an earpiece greets me on the sidewalk. "Welcome to Xtreme Quest. I'm Fiona."

"Thanks. I'm Hartley Billings." My mouth forms its first smile since arriving at the Giant Eyeball, a thirty-foot-tall sculpture plopped at one end of an Astroturf lawn the size of a city block, its massive blue iris staring back at me. I haven't done much with sculpting, but maybe it's worth exploring. I could gather junkyard treasures that remind me of Court and shape them into an enormous pile of poop. Working title: *The Shit He Says*.

For now, I focus on what Fiona is explaining.

"The race itself won't start until early this afternoon. In addition to getting multiple takes of Paul talking with the contestants, we'll get shots of each team before the race starts. You can choose your own poses and expressions—some teams keep it light and others prefer to stay serious—but keep in mind this is what will appear in the opening credits, as well as still shots for promo. When we're done with that, we'll sit you down for a quick interview for the first episode."

What's the best way to stand beside a man I wouldn't spit on if he was burning alive? Is wringing his neck suitable for primetime TV?

"Your partner is already here. Let's get you two—" Fiona swipes her finger across the iPad screen. "Ohhh." She tries (and fails) to hide a snicker. "You're the exes. Looks like introductions aren't necessary."

A light knock on the front door interrupts the romantic comedy my roommates and I are watching.

Corrina looks at me and waggles her brows. "Your stripper is here."

"For the bajillionth time, he's not a stripper and this is strictly an assignment for Hodson's class." I toss my throw pillow in her direction and hop off the couch.

"He's coming here to take his clothes off in your bedroom. Sounds stripperish to me," Megan says around a mouthful of popcorn.

Since I'm out of pillows, I flip her the bird on my way to the door.

A few weeks ago, I asked friends if they knew any guys who'd be willing to sit nude for a charcoal drawing. My only requirements were punctuality and not being a sexual predator.

Megan's boyfriend mentioned his chemistry lab partner who is, and I quote, "not ugly and doesn't smell weird." The next day he showed me a photo. The clunky plastic goggles blocked most of the guy's face, but he had a nice smile and more importantly, he agreed to sign a release in exchange for a (meager) model fee and the promise of snacks. Win-win, right?

I open the door prepared for the usual blast of setting sunlight, so it takes my eyes a moment to adjust to the tall figure blocking the golden rays. When they do . . .

Whoa.

If this is Megan's boyfriend's version of "not ugly," I'd like to be his version of "not poor." Seriously. On a scale of one to ten, the man on the welcome mat has a preliminary score of twenty. His face is a masterclass on the golden ratio—dark brown eyebrows, a straight nose, a squared jaw, and a perfectly angled chin that would make Fibonacci himself weep—but it's his beach-glass eyes that steal the show. The left one is seafoam green and the right is cornflower blue.

"Was that a good whoa or a bad whoa?"

It was supposed to be a private whoa, but apparently my mouth didn't get the memo. "A good one because . . ." I glance around, desperate for a plausible excuse, and spot the watch on his wrist. Bingo. "You're on time." I hold up my own watch as proof.

His lips—full and luscious—purse together in an obvious attempt not to smile. "Are most of your models late?"

"I've never done this before. You're my first."

Now he's grinning.

"Private model, that is. Not my actual *first . . ." My inward groan comes out as a long breath through my nose. Where's a freight train when you need one? "Let's try this again. Hi. I'm Hartley. You must be Court." I extend a hand like a normal person.*

He slides his palm against mine and gently squeezes. "It's nice to meet you."

I gesture for him to come inside and shut the door behind him as he toes off his shoes. "I hope you don't mind working in my bedroom. It's basically the only available space in this matchbox-sized duplex." And only available, I might add, because I disassembled my bed frame and flipped the mattress against the wall earlier this afternoon.

He shrugs. "I'm all yours for the next four hours. Just tell me where to go and what to do." His eyes hold mine for a beat and then he smiles again. Unlike the one in the chemistry lab photo, this one holds a spark of mischief that my brain interprets as, "I follow directions in the bedroom."

Nope.

Nope, nope, nope.

I quietly clear my throat and lead him through the galley kitchen and around the corner into the living room. As soon as my feet hit the carpet, Channing Tatum comes to life on the TV, peeling his shirt off and grinding across the stage to the beat of "Pony" by Ginuwine. Megan and Corrina cackle like traitorous hens and high-five each other.

"Court, these are my soon-to-be former roommates." I shoot them a playful glare as I snatch the remote from Megan's hand and hit the red power button. "Formal introductions aren't necessary because I'm murdering them after you leave."

He laughs and lifts his palm in a wave. "Nice to meet you."

"Guess that means I don't have to clean the bathroom tomorrow." Corrina steals the remote back with an evil grin. "It's lovely to meet you, Court. I'm Corrina and that's Megan. Rest assured, you're in great hands with Hartley."

If he heard Corrina's emphasis on the word hands, *he doesn't let on. Megan did, though, and she makes a terrible attempt at covering her laugh with a cough. For the past year, my mathematically inclined roommates have been conducting a quasi-formal study on the proportional relationship between a man's hands and his . . . yeah.*

And Court?

Massive hands.

"Oookay, let's get to work." I spin him around and point to my bedroom. "Second door on the left."

Movement in the corner of my eye catches my attention. I glance back to Corrina and Megan, who are flailing dramatically on the couch and mouthing, Oh my god!

I don't bother hiding my smile when I mouth, I know! *before heading into the hallway.*

Court enters my room two steps in front of me. I flip on the light and watch his jaw fall slack as he turns in a full circle, taking in the blue, yellow, and white swirls sweeping from one wall to the next.

"Wow," he whispers.

"*I take it that's a good wow?*"

"*That's an incredible wow. Van Gogh would be seriously impressed.*"

My lens of self-criticism rarely allows me to accept compliments at face value—there's always something that didn't transfer correctly from my head to my hand, and my first instinct now is to highlight those flaws. But the quiet wonder in Court's voice encourages me to see my room through his eyes.

"The Starry Night *has always been my favorite painting. When I was a kid, my parents took my brother and me to New York City. We went to the Museum of Modern Art, and I remember standing in front of the display and telling my mom to be careful because if you looked at the swirls long enough, they'd carry you away to the village in the painting. It's the first time a piece of art made me feel something. I already loved art class in school, but that was the day I decided to be an artist when I grew up.*"

My lips form a soft smile at the memory of seven-year-old me gaping up in wide-eyed wonder at van Gogh's greatest masterpiece.

"*Then I started studying art history and learned that van Gogh painted* The Starry Night *while he was at an asylum in France. The landscape is based on the view from his window. I mean . . . to create something as beautiful as that when your mental health is at its lowest point . . .*" *I release a breath and let my eyes drift over the life-sized swirls. "It's like looking at fragments of his soul on a canvas.*"

Court tilts his head, studying the wall. "I never thought about it that way, but it makes sense."

"*Yeah, but I tend to get carried away. Sorry for nerding out on you.*"

"*There's nothing wrong with being passionate. Like your roommates said, that just means I'm in good hands tonight.*"

I immediately glance at his crotch. In related news, Megan and Corrina can kiss my classically conditioned ass.

"*On that note, let's get started.*" *After trapping my rebellious chestnut waves in a hair tie, I twist on the floor lamp beside my easel and kill the overhead light. "Our prompt for this project is 'rearview mirror.' We can draw whatever comes to mind, but I'm obviously taking a literal approach.*" *I cross the room, flip the switch on a small nightstand lamp, and position myself in front of the freestanding mirror I set up earlier.*

"*You'll stand like this with your back facing me so I can see your reflection. I taped two lines on the carpet as a mark for your feet when you're ready for a break. With the way I've angled your position and the lighting, I won't be able to see any of your . . . front.*"

Which is a damn shame.

"Also"—I point to the quilt I tacked over the lone window to prevent rogue shadows and sidewalk voyeurs—"I've triple-checked from every angle and no one can see in from outside."

"Sounds easy enough." He grips his T-shirt at the back of his neck and tugs it over his head, revealing a body that's no stranger to lifting heavy things.

I was so captivated by his face (and, subsequently, his hands) that I didn't notice his physique until this moment. It's a crime I atone for now. His chest and abdomen are an intoxicating blend of ridges bathed in light and shadow from the floor lamp. If I was a photographer, I'd tell Court to freeze in this exact pose—hair askew, arms slack, and shirt hanging from his right hand—to capture it all.

He folds the shirt and sets it on my dresser, then unbuttons his jeans. It's like watching Michelangelo's David *undress, if* David *was six-two and wore denim . . . and deliciously form-fitting black boxer briefs.* Whoa. *Whoever gets to see this view every day is—shit!*

"I should've asked before, but do you have a partner? Or anyone else who might be upset at the idea of you sitting nude for me?" I quickly add, so it doesn't sound like I'm asking for personal reasons, which I'm (mostly) not. "Because if you do, I'd be happy to talk with them to explain my idea and ensure there are no issues—"

He stops me with a shake of his head. "No girlfriend . . . or anyone else."

Relief washes over me. "That's good. Not that it's any of my business what you do or who you do it with." I pause, cringing. "Also, I didn't mean 'do it with' like that. Well, sort of, but . . ." The rest of the sentence dies along with my pride.

Thankfully, Court offers an amused smile instead of looking at me like I've lost my mind. "I understand what you meant. But what about you? Do I need to worry about any jealous lovers coming after me?"

My brain short-circuits watching the word lovers *come out of his mouth. Or maybe it's from him rising to his full height after removing his socks, wearing nothing but the aforementioned boxer briefs.*

"I am also single," I finally manage, the words dropping onto my tongue one at a time like I'm brand-new to speaking English.

Kill.

Me.

Now.

"That's good," he parrots, smirking. He slides his thumbs under the waist-

band of his boxers, which, coincidentally, is the exact moment I remember to double-check the supplies on my easel.

Graphite pencil for sketching, assorted charcoals, kneaded eraser, chalk, paper towels . . . yep, all right where I left them earlier today.

"It's safe to look now."

It's worth repeating that although Court is my first private model, I've used male models in class before. I've also previously seen naked men during recreational bedroom activities. But none of those experiences have prepared me for what I see when I peer across the room.

Court Mueller is the most gorgeous human being I have ever laid eyes on.

And for the next four hours, he's all mine.

"Have you talked to him since the breakup?" Fiona asks as we pass through a gate onto the artificial grass.

"The last time we spoke was the day he walked out of my bedroom."

I drop my backpack under a pop-up canopy aptly named Backpack Drop-Off and continue toward the small cluster of castmates near the hedges. When we get close enough to hear his voice, the part of my brain reserved for bad ideas and self-destruction shouts, *Maybe he's changed!*

Nope.

Nope, nope, nope.

Court Mueller is the human equivalent of shrimp—my favorite food until the day it almost killed me.

And as with most allergies, he can't hurt me again if I don't let him in.

CHAPTER 2
COURT

Day 1—Dallas, Texas

The women from Holbrooke University have been eye-fucking me for the past fifteen minutes. Based on the number of times they've mentioned how close they are and that they don't mind sharing their supplies—*"after all, that's what friends are for" *insert flirtatious smirk*—* I'm pretty sure I have a walk-on role in a threesome.

I pretend to like it, or at least be intrigued by it, because only an idiot would sabotage his chance at laying groundwork for a future alliance on a show with a million-dollar prize. See, that's the thing about Xtreme Quest: the competition starts long before the race actually begins.

For instance, after my second callback from the audition team six weeks ago, I dove into memorizing each country's flag because the show is notorious for tossing in a test on the last leg. When I got the official invite four weeks ago, I broke in a pair of new shoes and cross-referenced past race routes with average temperature charts to create a packing list. I even stepped up my cardio to make sure I was in peak shape for running.

Sure, it's probably overkill—previous seasons have been won by far less prepared teams—but I can't take any chances. If I don't win this race, I'll be forced to return to Green Valley and accept my lot in life. And by lot, I mean the literal parking lot at Studs N Suds.

Technically speaking, I'm the manager of a business owned by my best friend, Rhett. In reality, I work in the office of a car wash. Does it matter that my idea of creating a mobile detail team increased our revenue by thirty percent last year? Or that I helped bring in four thousand dollars in our most recent fundraiser? Not really, and neither does substitute teaching. I'm pretty sure the only ones who would miss me at Green Valley High School are the thirsty single moms.

Basically, I have an unused psychology degree, a burning desire to put Green Valley in my rearview mirror, and no resources to actually make that happen. I'm a twenty-seven-year-old man with an impressive cache of failed occupations and one shot at changing it all.

"Hey man, I think your teammate is here," the guy (Oscar, I think?) from Auchenbach State College says.

I follow the direction of his finger and cough out a strangled gasp.

No.

My head swivels side to side.

Please tell me the woman I gave up everything for isn't walking toward me.

She stops a few feet away, crosses her arms, and fillets me with a glare. "Hello, Courtney."

Shit.

I can't move. Or breathe. Or think. I am a statue, and the Astroturf is now a two-for-one special of body parts: the Giant Eyeball and the Giant Asshole.

Possibly Oscar scoffs. "Your name is Courtney?"

"Is Court a nickname or your full name?" Hartley asks as she perches on her stool.

"It's short for Courtland."

She gives an impressed nod. "That sounds so . . . distinguished. Is there an 'esquire' at the end?"

I envision the park ranger uniform my dad wore every day, the elementary school my mom teaches at, the modest three-bedroom house I grew up in, and the station wagon my parents have been driving since I was ten. They keep a roll of duct tape in the glove box at all times. "Not that I'm aware of."

"And I don't need to bow in your presence?"

I smirk at her reflection. "I mean, you can if you want."

She playfully rolls her eyes. "So, what kind of modeling have you done?"

"None. This is a first for me too."

Her head pops up from the easel. "Really?"

"Why do you sound surprised?"

"I just figured you would have with . . ." She waves a hand up and down in my direction. Wait, is she blushing?

"With what?" I glance down and pat my torso, then find her eyes in the mirror again. "A body? I suppose that would be helpful in a modeling career."

Her quiet laughter sparks an unexpected blast of warmth in my chest. "I meant the muscles."

"These things?" I flex the arm facing her, relishing her sharp intake of breath. Damn, she's cute. "I picked them up at the model store before I came over tonight. I'm lucky they had my size."

On the word size, Hartley's gaze drops several inches. She clears her throat and starts inspecting a stick of charcoal. "And when you're not modeling with store-bought muscles, what do you do with your time?"

"Work, mostly. I'm in a toxic relationship with my car so I'm saving for a new one. Well, newer one, anyway." Hence me being here tonight. A hundred bucks to stand naked for four hours seemed like a no-brainer. I've certainly done far more for far less.

"Where do you work?"

"Shucks."

Her eyes go wide. "I love that place! Megan, Corrina, and I go there for brunch on Sundays. I've never seen you there though."

"I'm a cook, so I don't get out of the kitchen much."

"Maybe that's why I keep coming back for corn cakes every week."

I make hundreds of corn pancakes during my weekend shifts, so she's probably right. "I don't want to brag, but I'm pretty sure I'm the reason Shucks was voted number one in the county's non-chain-restaurant category."

"And yet you're so humble," she says, chuckling.

I lift my hand and let it fall to my side. "What can I say? It's a gift."

"Are you working this Sunday at ten a.m.?"

I nod.

"Then I expect nothing short of Gordon Ramsay-level corn cakes."

"Please," I scoff, hoping it hides my excitement at knowing I'll get to see her again in two days. "Gordon Ramsay wishes his corn cakes were as good as mine."

She gives me a look that says, "We'll see about that," then turns her attention back to the easel. "So, what's the best thing that's happened to you this week and why was it the best?"

That's easy—tonight, because what started as an easy modeling job for Jace's girlfriend's roommate turned into meeting a girl who's as beautiful as *she is talented, which is saying something considering her portfolio on Instagram. But how do I say that without it sounding like a smarmy pickup line?*

"That's an . . . interesting question," I hedge.

"I already know your campus police information, so I figured I'd jump into something meatier."

My brows bump together. "My campus police information?"

"From your model release. Court Mueller, twenty-one, junior, psych major," she says, ticking the facts off her fingertips. "Those are things anyone could learn about you in a ten-second conversation at the grocery store."

"Don't tell me you're anti-small-talk. And here I was thinking we could be friends." *I shake my head in mock dismay.*

Hartley's shoulder bounces in a half shrug. "Life is so much more interesting when you take time to see the details."

Unwilling to pass up an easy opportunity to make her blush again, I arch a brow, smirking. "What I'm hearing you say is that you want to see my details?"

Her eyes zero in on the lower half of my body. "That's, uh . . ." *She diverts her gaze to the ceiling, the wall, the floor, and finally, the hem of her shorts.* "I just meant . . ." *As she shifts on the stool, her foot slips off the bottom rung and connects with the easel, sending it flying. I pivot on instinct and dive for it while Hartley chases her drawing through the air.*

The next few moments play out in slow motion: I catch the easel and perform a half bellyflop onto the carpet. Hartley trips on my leg and lands face-first on my ass. I panic and flip over, subsequently rubbing my penis across her chest and neck. The paper floats down and settles next to the dresser.

I'm lying frozen—which is probably not the best considering the proximity of my genitals to her chin—when Megan pounds on the door.

"Is everything okay?"

"Yep," *Hartley croaks, rolling to her back beside me.* "We're good."

"What happened?"

"I accidentally kicked the easel and it fell."

Megan pauses, then loudly whispers, "If that's code for your stripper was trying to take advantage of you and we need to bust in there with a steak knife, cough once."

I bark out a laugh as Hartley smacks a palm over her face.

"No steak knives needed," *she says from under her hand.* "You can go back to watching Channing twerk."

"All right. We'll keep an ear out though," Megan says before retreating down the hallway.

The room falls silent. I turn my head in Hartley's direction to ask if she's hurt and instantly regret it. From a socially acceptable bubble of two to four feet, her mossy green eyes, messy brown waves, and plump lips are beautiful. From eight inches away, it's an exercise of self-control not to reach over and touch her. It doesn't help that we're horizontal in a dimly lit room and I'm naked. Or that my dick wouldn't mind—

Nope. Uh-uh.

Now is not the time for a boner. I abandon all thoughts of touching Hartley and shift my gaze to the ceiling. The very dark, very blank ceiling. A perfect canvas.

"You should put some glow-in-the-dark stars up there," I say like we're two people hanging out on a completely normal Friday evening. "Maybe you could do some van Gogh swirls."

"Hmm. I never thought about it, but that's not a bad idea."

"You know what was a bad idea?" I pause for a beat, then say, "Diving for that damn easel."

More silence.

Then, laughter.

So much laughter.

My face hurts and my sides ache and I can honestly say I haven't had this much fun in a long damn time.

When I finally catch my breath, I sit up and hug my left knee for strategic coverage. "There isn't a good segue for this part, so I'll just say I'm sorry for the . . . detailed view of my details."

Hartley rises and mimics my position. "Don't worry about it. It was an accident. I just hope me landing on you didn't hurt your details."

I glance down. "I can confirm my details are intact and unharmed."

She clamps her lips between her teeth but loses the battle and surrenders to a smile. "Good to know." Her eyes move to the easel, and she lets out a quiet breath. "Should we get back to work?"

"Hang on, you've got some charcoal . . ." I point to a black smudge on the side of her face.

She swipes the back of her hand over her cheek. "Did I get it?"

"Mostly."

She tries again. "Better?"

Yes, but I lie and shake my head because now I have a perfectly plausible excuse to touch her. I reach out and gently sweep my thumb across soft skin dusted with freckles. Her thick, dark lashes flutter at the contact and she leans into my hand, igniting a spark of electricity in my blood. My fingers itch to yank out her hair tie and sink into her I-just-had-sex-and-now-my-hair-is-a-mess waves.

As if she can read my mind, her gaze slides down to my mouth and back up.

"All set," I rasp, leaning back. Damn, when did it get so hot in here? I clear my throat and push to my feet, careful to keep my backside facing her.

"Um . . . thanks. Want some water?" She hops up, snags a bottle off the dresser, and passes it to me without waiting for an answer.

Not yet trusting my voice, I nod in appreciation and twist off the cap. It's not the bucket of ice I need, but it'll do for now. I take a long pull as Hartley reassembles her workspace, starting with the easel. When she bends down, her green cotton shorts ride up, up, up the back of her tan, shapely legs.

Damn.

Wanting to plunge my fingers into her hair is nothing compared to the growing desire to grab her by the hips and sink deep inside her. I groan inwardly, but my mouthful of water doesn't get the message in time and floods my windpipe, sparking a long string of coughs.

Hartley is at my side instantly. "Are you okay?"

My head bobs once and then I'm back to hacking up my wet lungs. She tries to raise my arms over my head, but the ten-ish inches I have on her doesn't help.

"Get your hands off her, you asshole!" Corrina rushes into the bedroom with a baseball bat at the ready. Megan is on her heels wielding a knife.

Hartley turns, eyes wide and mouth agape, and shoves her hands out. "Stop! I'm fine. He's the one coughing."

Dying is more like it. I suck in a strangled breath and expel more water. The floor starts to sway. My vision swirls and my body suddenly feels a hundred pounds lighter. Before I hit the carpet for the second time, Hartley is back in front of me, lifting my arms up.

"Breathe."

I slowly inhale, relieved that my lungs are tentatively cooperating.

"Good. Again."

I end up coughing more, but the room finally stops moving and I no longer feel like I'm going to float away. Well, not from lack of oxygen anyway. From the woman blinking up at me? That's a different story.

"Better?"

I nod and lower my arms.

"Sorry, for trying to kill you," Megan says, hiding the knife behind her back.

"Yeah, sorry," Corrina echoes, wincing.

Taking one more deep breath, I turn my head toward my would-be assassins. "I've never been that close to being beaten, stabbed, or drowned before—especially all at the same time—but I admire your dedication to Hartley's safety."

"More like their dedication to true crime documentaries," Hartley mutters. "But now that we've established no one is being assaulted, it's time for us to get back to work. I'll see you two later." She ushers her roommates toward the door. I swear I hear them whisper something about hands along the way.

———

The monitor above the stove flashes with an incoming order.

Corn cakes x3, custom: Gordon Ramsay

The last two pixelated words on the screen have me more awake than the two shots of espresso I downed at the start of my shift.

She's here.

Alice, a fiftysomething waitress who takes her role as work-mom-of-college-students seriously, pops into the kitchen. "The trio of young ladies at table sixteen assured me you'd know what they meant."

I hide my shit-eating grin with a fake yawn, but Alice's smirk tells me she's not buying it.

"Which one is she?"

"Which one is who?"

"The girl making you smile like it's 'buy one, get a hundred free' day at the candy store."

I peek through the doorway into the dining room. Hartley and Corrina are listening to Megan's animated monologue about a large fish, if I'm correctly interpreting her wild gestures. They both laugh when Megan mimics an explosion. I can't hear them from across the room, but the sound of Hartley's laugh echoes through my head anyway.

The rest of Friday night went much smoother than it started. Specifically, everyone remained upright and there were no more threats of death. My only complaint is that four hours went by way too fast. I bought another twenty minutes with her by insisting that I help reassemble her bed before I left, but time has dragged more than a one-legged elephant since then.

As if she can feel my gaze from the kitchen, Hartley turns her head and locks eyes with me. A shy smile emerges on her face as she lifts her hand in a tiny wave. Seeing the gesture, Megan immediately pauses and follows Hartley's line of sight. Her smile is much bigger. Corrina's too. Megan says something and playfully nudges Hartley, who bites her bottom lip and ducks her head.

"She's pretty," Alice says beside me.

And smart. And talented. And so damn funny.

Alice laughs and guides me back to the stove. "Get to work, Gordon. I'll be back in a few."

I'm putting the finishing touches on Hartley's plate when Alice returns. Corn cakes are normally served stacked with ramekins of whipped cream and blueberry syrup on the side. I arranged Hartley's in a row, spread the whipped cream across the tops, and added van Gogh swirls of blueberry syrup. Not gallery worthy by any means, but an honest effort from a psych major who specializes in stick figures.

Alice takes one look at the plate and grips me by the shoulders. "Open the door for her, don't leave her on 'read,' and for Pete's sake, use a condom."

My mouth hangs open. "We're not—"

Her pointed look silences me.

"Yes, ma'am."

Confident I've absorbed her instructions, she transfers the order onto a tray and starts for the dining room.

"Wait!" I rush to the wall of lockers to retrieve a small package. "Give this to her?" I ask, setting it beside Hartley's plate.

"Oh, Court." Alice shakes her head and laughs all the way to table sixteen.

I move to the doorway and watch Hartley's hand fly to her face when she sees her breakfast. She looks back and forth between me and her plate, then removes her hand to mouth Thank you *while Megan and Corrina practically ooze out of their chairs.*

I smile back, my heart feeling like I just summited a mountain.

When Alice delivers the package, Hartley's eyes find mine again and she raises her brows. I'm just about to motion for her to open it when Megan grabs her by the arm and tells her the same thing.

Laughing, Hartley slides her fingers under the tape and removes the grocery store paper bag wrapping in one piece. She reads the note and holds up the package of glow-in-the-dark stars. And then she's beaming—at me, her roommates, her breakfast, and the family one table over. But most importantly, she's nodding.

Which means I officially have a date on Friday to hang stars on Hartley Billings's ceiling.

"Courtney over here is already lying to us," Possibly Oscar says to the Holbrooke girls and the guy from Dixon State. "He didn't even tell us his real name."

"Courtland is my real name. I go by Court. She calls me Courtney when she's mad at me."

"But you said you were on a strangers team, so you *are* lying to us," Holbrooke Girl Number One says. She adds a dramatic finger point like she just uncovered the last clue in a cold case.

"I thought I was. They *told* me I was," I clarify.

Hartley turns to the woman from the crew. "Is that why there were so many questions about my college relationships in my callback? Were they planning this all along?"

She shrugs. "I don't work in that area, but anything's possible on Xtreme Quest." With that, she heads toward a tent, leaving me to face four skeptical competitors and one very pissed off ex-girlfriend.

Fuck.

Me.

CHAPTER 3
HARTLEY

Day 1—Dallas, Texas

"Can I speak with you in private?"

One of the female competitors mumbles, "Awkward," under her breath as I stomp away from the hedgerow. Court wisely follows.

When we're out of earshot, I spin and narrow my eyes at him. "I'm going to make this crystal clear. If you purposely screw this up for me, I will murder you, dismember your body, and feed it to the starving wildlife of whatever continent we're on."

His Adam's apple bobs once. "That was oddly specific for an impromptu threat."

"Please. I've fantasized your demise for years. I even painted it once. The title was *Dying, in Detail*. I used melted red wax to represent the blood oozing from the gaping wound on your p—"

"Very creative," he says, casually draping his hands over his groin.

"If you like that, you should've seen the performance art I did with sausage and a blender. So therapeutic."

I stifle a laugh when he mimics the sound of a dying accordion. Remembering every inch of that man's *details* had been a curse until I realized I could destroy a replica of it any time I wanted. Megan encouraged me to profit off my heartbreak by displaying my collection as *A Sadist's Paradise*. I still wonder if I should have.

"Central Tennessee State, you're up in five for promo photos," a guy calls from across the turf.

I wave, letting him know we heard him, then turn my attention to Court. "Ground rules: you will not touch me unless it is required to win a challenge, we will not speak unless it is directly related to this race, and if anyone from the show asks you why we broke up, the acceptable answer is, 'Because I'm a horrible human being.' Got it?"

He nods. "I want to say one thing, though."

"Fine." I look to my right and focus on a team of crew members attaching a massive blue-and-orange Xtreme Quest curtain to a set of trusses.

"Hartley."

"What?" *Are they going to hide something behind that?*

Court breathes out a frustrated grunt and takes my chin between his thumb and finger, forcing me to look up at him.

I absolutely do not savor the familiar waft of woodsy cologne, and I refuse to acknowledge the spark that sizzles down my neck and across my chest. "I thought I told you—"

His blue-green eyes flash with heat. "No touching or speaking unless it's about the race. And this is."

"Then let go of me and spit it out."

He crosses his arms, giving me a front-row seat to a wall of biceps and pecs. Has he been carrying cinderblocks for the last six years?

"This isn't a game to me. I need to win this race. It's—" He peers off in the distance, lips pressed thin, and releases a long breath through his nose. When his gaze settles on me again, the heat in his eyes has been replaced with . . . sadness?

Whatever. I don't care.

"I'll make you a deal," he continues. "I won't sabotage this for you as long as you don't sabotage it for me as a method of revenge."

I cross my arms and match his stance. "You think I'd willingly give up my share of the prize money just to make sure you don't win either?"

"Would you pay for a chance to get back at me? Possibly. Especially considering you wouldn't be giving up your own money and you'd get to add more countries to your passport while you're at it."

Okay, so he has a point. But still. "I came here to win. Being forced to work with you doesn't change that."

"Good." He unfurls his arms and extends a hand. "Let's make a pact. No sabotaging each other."

I breathe out a harsh laugh. "You might as well put that thing away. Your promises mean nothing to me."

———

"Just do what comes natural," Shanna says from behind her video camera.

I turn to her, eyebrows raised, and smile brightly. "I can knee him in the balls?"

The handful of crew members milling around us chuckle as Court puts another foot of Astroturf between us.

"I like the enthusiasm, but I don't think the network would go for that. How about a back-to-back shot instead?"

I wrinkle my nose. "Physical contact is a no-go."

Mack, the photographer, gestures to where Court and I were standing moments ago. "What about repeating that little face-off y'all did with your arms crossed?"

Shanna's mouth ratchets into a sly grin. "Oh, I like that."

In the spirit of compromise, but mostly because my other ideas also include violence, I give in. "Okay. Let's get this over with."

Shanna and Mack briefly demonstrate their idea and then Court and I take our respective places on the artificial lawn. It takes us a few tries to get the timing down, but we manage to get several clips of us walking toward each other, crossing our arms, then turning our heads toward the camera.

The still photos are another story.

Mack stations us a few feet apart and tells us to cross our arms again. "Now hold it right there." He steps back and fires off several shots. "Court, you're perfect. Hartley, I need you to look up."

I slide my gaze from the letters spanning Court's chest to the top hem of his T-shirt.

"I meant look in his eyes."

Oh, for fuck's sake. That's the last place I want to be looking.

"Good, now a little less murderous please."

"The quicker you cooperate, the quicker we'll be done," Court murmurs.

"Shut up," I mutter back. Not the most mature or eloquent response, but it's hard to think straight when he uses his Sexy Voice. Or when I'm required to stare into those beach-glass eyes that have captivated me from day one.

There are a few more lines around them now, forged in the years I thought we'd spend together, and isn't that a punch in the damn gut?

"You're scowling again."

"You're scowling again," I parrot.

"I'm just trying to help you out."

"You could drop out," I simper. "I'm sure they have backup contestants on standby."

"So you *are* capable of smiling at me."

"Only when I'm imagining your demise."

His brow arches up and his stupid, stupid lips curve into a smirk. "What I'm hearing you say is that you're fantasizing about me right now?"

"Don't even start with that."

"Or what?"

"Or I'll—"

"Okay, I think we got it," Mack says from a million miles away.

Blinking out of my Court-induced stupor, I realize we've uncrossed our arms and we're now standing toe-to-toe. My face is flushed and my blood is buzzing in ways I've long forgotten about.

"I've missed that fire," he rasps, eyes raking over me.

His confession is a blast of ice-cold truth that snaps me back to my senses. "Yeah, well whose fault is that?"

———

After a five-minute break in which I woosah'ed my heartrate back to a normal level while a crew member outfitted me with a lavalier mic and a battery pack, I plop down in a canvas chair to film the interview they'll play in the intro of the first episode. Court's chair is a foot to my right, but at least I don't have to look at him this time.

A producer named Wendell smiles from his seat beside the camera. "This shouldn't take long. Just be yourselves and try to answer your questions in full sentences. Hartley, let's start with you. What's your current profession?"

"I'm a painter." I leave out the part about my medium being houses instead of canvases because the less Court knows about my life, the better.

"And what about you, Court?"

After a brief pause, he says, "I'm a substitute teacher."

"Interesting, because here on your application it says you work at a—"

"Yes, I'm also a COO for a startup in the automotive industry," Court says, shifting in his seat.

My quiet snort doesn't go unnoticed by Wendell. "What do you think about his jobs?"

"I think it sounds like he runs a chop shop and doesn't want to admit it on television so he's using the teacher thing as a cover."

Court rolls his eyes. "It's a perfectly legitimate company."

"So are businesses in the mafia," I say, shrugging.

"At least I don't rip off my customers. You can't say the same for yourself."

"Excuse me? I've *never* ripped off a customer."

"Then what do you call the twenty-seven dollars and twelve cents you stole from me?"

Oh yeah. I can't believe I forgot about that. "You purchased something from me. I mailed it. That's not stealing."

"I purchased a five-by-seven art print. You sent me a crappy version on regular paper from a cheap home office color printer that needed a new ink cartridge."

A zing of satisfaction ripples through me. I laughed all the way to the post office that day. "Again I say: You purchased something and I mailed it. It's not my fault that you don't understand my art."

He huffs a laugh and mutters, "You're ridiculous."

"No, what's ridiculous is you having the gall to contact me through *my* online business in a shitty attempt to assuage *your* guilt."

"What made you reach out to Hartley?" Wendell asks Court.

He sighs and rubs the space between his brows. "A couple of years after we broke up, a mutual friend sent me a screenshot from Hartley's social media. She'd posted some memory thing of a picture of us when we were dating. The caption talked about her biggest regret being the time she wasted with me. I'm not big on social media, so I bought a print from her website and wrote in the note section that I'd like to talk and hoped she was doing well."

"And I take it you didn't like that idea?" Wendell asks me.

"I would've rather massaged a porcupine than talked to him."

"I see." I expect another follow-up question, but instead he flips through his notecards and says, "Let's move on. This is the first time Xtreme Quest has had a team of exes. How do you feel about it, Hartley?"

That's easy. "I feel like I can't wait for it to be three weeks from now so I never have to see him again."

"Can you tell me about the breakup?"

I have no idea what Court said during his audition, but I'm not sugar-coating anything for his benefit. "The breakup was worse for me than it was for him. I guess it helps to have another woman from back home waiting on the side."

Wendell glances at Court and lifts his brows.

"There was never another woman."

"Enough with the lies! I saw you parading her around the gallery during my showcase." I press a dent in the armrest with my thumbnail. Better that than Court's eyeball.

"I didn't cheat," he says pointedly to Wendell. "The rest of it is . . . complicated."

Complicated? Ripping my heart out and then showing up to the biggest night of my college career with another woman on your arm seems straightforward to me.

"Do you feel bad about what happened?" Wendell asks him.

The full weight of Court's gaze settles on me. Probably because he's about to admit he has no soul and wants to see my reaction.

"Of course. I hate that she was hurting because of me."

"*Seriously?*" I seethe, adding another dent in the wood. "You are *unbelievable.*"

"What makes you say that?" Wendell probes.

I turn and glare at Court. "That's like saying, 'I feel bad she got a bruise because I punched her.' You *broke* me. You don't get to feel bad about something you purposely caused."

His jaw clenches as if he wants to say something—perhaps another explanation for ripping my heart out six years ago—but of course he never does. Instead, he takes a deep breath and focuses on Wendell again.

"Breaking up with Hartley was the right decision, but I don't see the benefit in rehashing ancient history. I'm sure we'll manage to be civil throughout the race."

My armrest has three more dents by the time I'm done rolling my eyes.

"Do you agree?" Wendell asks me.

Hardly, but my desire not to let Court paint me as the scorned ex is greater than my desire to level him with a comeback. "Court's right. I came to Xtreme Quest ready to work with anyone. The fact that it's him has no bearing on my strategy to win. I hope the other teams are ready for the fight of their lives." I'm careful to say all of this with my best millions-of-people-are-going-to-see-my-resolve face.

"Let's talk about that," Wendell says. "What made you want to audition for Xtreme Quest?"

"I've wanted to travel the world since I was a kid, but never got the chance. I can't think of a better opportunity than combining my biggest dream and my favorite show." This time my smile is genuine.

Court, however, looks like he just got punched in the gut.

"What do you mean you never got a chance to see the world? You went to Italy after college," he says, his voice strained.

"Actually, I didn't."

"Then where'd you go?"

"Not that it's any of your business, but home, Courtney. I had to go home."

CHAPTER 4
COURT

Day 1—Dallas, Texas

She *what?*

Questions bombard my brain, and I spit out fragments of each one in rapid-fire succession—"How did . . . ? Weren't you . . . ? When were . . . ?"—before landing on an exasperated, "*Why?*"

Hartley crosses her arms and stares straight ahead. "Plans change."

"But you had the perfect opportunity on a golden platter!" I hold my palms out for visual reference of said platter because seriously, *what the hell?*

"I'm well aware of what I lost," she retorts before pressing her lips into a thin line.

"Did the breakup play into your decision not to go to Italy?" Wendell asks.

We both reply with an immediate, "No," which puts me in Wendell's crosshairs again.

"What makes you so sure of that answer, Court?"

I draw a long breath and release it before speaking. "Hartley's one of the most determined people I've ever met. She's also a super-optimist. To her, the glass isn't just half full, it's overflowing with sparkling water and served with one of those paper umbrellas. I knew if I pushed her away enough, she'd go over there and then realize I'd done the right thing. But apparently, I gave up everything for nothing," I add with a derisive snort.

It's quiet for approximately three seconds.

Then Hartley swivels her head and pins me with a murderous look. "You *what?*"

One thing is on my mind when Hartley's name pops up on my phone: Bachelor camping trips are infinitely better than regular bachelor parties. Especially when they involve a luxury cabin with a mammoth game room and a hot tub that comfortably seats twelve.

"No girls allowed, Mueller!" Rhett shouts from across the pool table.

"You know the rules," Nick adds, pointing to the Cone of Shame, which is just an ugly lampshade he found in the hall closet that I'll have to wear once I'm off the phone.

I respond with a good-natured middle finger, then pass my pool stick to Wade and head to an adjacent bedroom where it's quieter. "Hello?"

A weird, not-quite-static noise greets me.

"Hartley? You there?"

The noise continues for several seconds, then stops and I hear a muffled female voice say, "—you're choosing him over Michelangelo. I'd like to go on record and say you're a dumbass."

Sounds like Hartley's roommate Corrina based on the Southern accent.

"And I'd like to go on record and say you watch too many legal shows," Hartley's distant voice replies.

Ah, now it makes sense. Also, there's no way in hell I'm wearing the Cone of Shame for a butt-dial. Nick can kiss my ass.

I'm about to end the call when Corrina says, "Seriously, Hart. This is a once-in-a-lifetime opportunity. Don't just throw it away for a guy."

Wait . . . what? I crank the volume and close the bedroom door.

"You know he's not just a guy. And besides, I already have a job lined up at the campus gallery."

"A job that pays minimum wage, and they won't even let you feature your own work until you've been there for six months."

"Hold up. You were excited for me when I got that job."

"Of course I was. But this is Italy."

A door slams, and then I hear Megan say, "Hey, I got your 911 text. What's wrong?"

"Do you remember the undergrad abroad program Hartley applied to last year?"

"Yeah."

"Do you remember how gutted she was when she didn't get in and they waitlisted her for the paid internship?"

"Yeah."

"Look what came in today."

Papers rustle, and then Megan presumably reads, "Congratulations, Hartley. We are pleased to extend an invitation to the Immagiano Museum's . . . holy shit. Holy shit! You got in! That's— wait. Why aren't we happy dancing right now?"

"Yes, Hartley. Tell our roommate why we aren't breaking out the Two Buck Chuck from Trader Joe's."

"Because I'm not going."

"What? Why? You wanted this so badly last year."

"I did, but I can always apply to other programs."

"What about traveling to see your brother and his family?"

For the first time since I picked up the phone, I know what they're talking about. Hartley's older brother, John, married a woman in the air force. They're stationed in Germany and she's pregnant with their second daughter.

"I can still fly out there and see them."

"So you're really not going?" Megan asks.

"I don't want to leave Court."

I don't want her to leave either, but I don't want her to miss out on this.

"Have you two talked about what happens after you graduate?" Megan continues.

"He knows I'm staying here to work at the gallery."

"I mean in the future. It sounds like you're planning long-term. Is he ready to settle down?"

"We haven't talked about it specifically, but things are going really well. I mean, you guys know him. He's a great guy. I've never loved anyone the way I love him."

"He is a great guy, but if he really loves you, he'll understand what an opportunity like this means to you and your career," Corrina says.

"Fair point," Megan replies. "But I kind of see where Hart's coming from too. What about trying a long-distance relationship? The program's only for a year, right?"

"With the possibility of an extension or job offer," Corrina adds. "And you've seen her portfolio. You know she wouldn't come home next summer."

"Guys, I appreciate what you're trying to do, but please stop. I've already made up my mind."

"Why don't you wait to do that until after you get Court's input?" Megan asks.

"Because there's no point. This is my decision."

"Just do us a favor and give yourself a few days," Corrina says.

After a long pause, I hear a resigned, "Fine."

"Good. Now . . . regardless of what decision you make, I really think we need to celebrate you being accepted to one of the most prestigious art programs in the entire world. Megan, pour the wine. I'll grab the emergency stash of cookies from my nightstand."

I end the call and immediately pull up a search for "Immagiano Museum internship." After scanning through the results, I tap a link that takes me to a short collection of testimonials from past participants. Phrases like, "I owe everything to this program," "the greatest experience of my life," and "exponential growth in my art" stand out—and that's just from the first review.

The knots filling my stomach draw tighter when I tap on a link to a picture gallery and see people touring world-renown museums and bringing canvases to life while sitting in front of architecture from the Roman Empire.

It could be Hartley in any one of these pictures.

Or rather, it should be.

Because as much as it kills me to admit it, Corrina's right. If Hartley stays with me, she'll be forced into a life of mediocrity while I finish my undergrad and get my master's degree. And a long-distance relationship means she'd be tethered to time zones and video dates instead of going out and having fun. As an accomplished artist who wants to advance her career, Hartley deserves to experience Italy in Technicolor, not black and white.

With a heavy sigh, I lean my elbows on my knees and grip my hair while selfishly wishing I'd followed the rules and turned my phone off.

Wade finds me in the same position when he knocks on the door a few minutes later. "Everything okay?"

Nope. Not even close.

I sit up and swallow around the lump in my throat. "If Sophia had a dream career, would you support it?"

"Of course."

"Even if that dream meant you'd have to make sacrifices?"

He studies me for a moment, then says, "I'm sure there's a deeper discussion to be had, but simply put, Sophia is my person. I can't think of anything I'd have to give up that would be more important than seeing her happy."

I sigh and nod. "Figured you'd say something like that. Guess that's why you're the one getting married."

"Sorry, man. I can always send Bobby in." He hooks a thumb over his shoulder toward the game room, where Mr. Chronically Single is singing a drunk and curse-filled karaoke version of "I'm Too Sexy" by Right Said Fred.

I offer up a weak smile. "Getting relationship advice from him is about as smart as taking a bath with a toaster."

"Sad but true, my friend. How about we skip philosophical discussions and toasters and get you drunk instead."

He extends a hand and pulls me off the bed. I follow him back to the game room, where Nick is waiting with the ridiculous lampshade.

"Rules are rules, dude."

There's one thing on my mind as he crowns me with the Cone of Shame: I refuse to let Hartley choose me over Michelangelo.

Dread and preemptive regret have blanketed the drive home. I only took a few shots last night because breaking up with Hartley will be hard enough without dealing with a hangover on top of it. As it is, my stomach is already churning when I maneuver my car into a visitor's space in her lot. The only silver lining in this shitstorm is the no-phone rule working in my favor today. I told her I'd call when I left the cabin, so she still thinks I'm unavailable and hasn't tried to contact me.

I thought about calling my sister, Ella, on my way home. She's the actress in the family and could probably give me pointers on drafting a script for what I'm about to do, but I don't feel like explaining myself to anyone, blood or not.

Pulling in a few deep breaths, I exit my car and focus on my upcoming performance as I cross the pavement. After a few quick knocks, Megan answers the door and thrusts two twenty-dollar bills at me. "Oh. Sorry. I thought you were the delivery guy." She steps back and waves me in. "Hart's on the couch. We'll have plenty of pizza, so you're welcome to have some if you want."

"Thanks, but I won't be here long."

Just long enough to rip out your roommate's heart.

And mine too.

My first gut punch comes in the form of Hartley's face lighting up when she sees me round the corner. "Hey! I didn't think you'd be back until tonight. Did you have fun?"

"Yeah, but we should talk."

"Um . . . okay?" She casts an uneasy glance at her roommates as she slowly rises from the couch.

Unable to look at the damage I'm already causing, I retreat to her bedroom like a coward. One of her senior capstone canvases is sitting on her easel, with two others propped against the legs. She's spent months on these pieces, and I've been looking forward to seeing her show them off next month. I guess that makes Gallery Night another casualty of what I'm about to do.

Hartley closes her door with a soft click but doesn't say anything until she's sitting on her bed, knees crossed and fingers twisting in her lap. Her eyes meet mine briefly before dropping back to her hands. "What do you want to talk about?" she asks in a small voice.

My mind races with answers I can't give, like my immense regret for answering my phone this weekend, how I don't mean anything that's about to come out of my mouth, and how I already know I'll never completely get over her.

Leaning against the dresser, I release a quiet breath and start with the words I practiced on the drive home. "Being at the bachelor party and hearing Wade talk about his future with Sophia forced me to open my eyes about our relationship. When I sat down and looked at everything objectively, it became clear that we're at two very different points in our lives. It doesn't make sense to keep wasting our time on something that won't work long-term."

I've shocked us both—me, that I was able to get through it, and her, that I said it in the first place.

Hartley moves her head back and forth. "Wh-what are you talking about? We're both in college. That doesn't put us at two different points."

"You're getting ready to graduate, and I still have a year left. I don't even know where I'm doing graduate school or where I'll end up after that."

"I thought we'd figure that out together."

So did I.

"I don't want to hold you back. If we stayed together, you'd put your life on pause for who knows how long and you shouldn't have to do that."

Hartley's brows bunch together. "Court, where is this coming from? What happened at that bachelor party?"

I answered my goddamn phone! *I shout in my head. Outwardly, I release a heavy sigh and cross my arms against the rubber band forming around my chest. "Nothing happened, other than me taking a good hard look at reality. You deserve a life I can't give you."*

That, at least, is the truth.

But she's not buying it.

"Uh-uh." She shakes her head. "Everything was fine on Friday before you left, and all the months before that. There's no way you went from 'I love you, babe. See you Sunday,' to 'I've had an epiphany about my life and it doesn't include you anymore.' Something happened at that bachelor party."

Before I can respond, her eyes go wide and her mouth falls slack. "You were with someone." It comes out in a whisper, like she's testing the words before giving them a voice.

I did the same thing on the way home—thought that maybe I'd just tell her I got drunk and hooked up with an exotic dancer or a bartender or someone from high school—but the thing about crafting a convincing lie is using as much truth as possible. For example:

"There's no one else."

"I don't believe you."

"Well then I can't help you."

"I'm not asking for help."

"What do you want then?" I push away from the dresser and pace the carpet. "I told you nothing happened. I can't make it any clearer than that. Why are you making this so difficult?"

She's off the bed in a flash, flinging her arms out wide. "Why am I making this so difficult? Pardon the hell out of me for not understanding why the man I was considering spending the rest of my life with would throw everything away for a weekend fling and then lie about it. Quit acting like a coward and at least have the goddamn decency to tell me the truth."

I am, I am, I fucking am!

My lungs choose this moment to malfunction, and my stomach threatens to follow suit. I didn't practice a closing speech on the way here and really, there's nothing left to say anyway.

So I leave.

I walk out of her room and out of her apartment and out of her life.

I make it halfway across the parking lot before retching on the cracked concrete.

Wendell swings his gaze to the ball of anger simmering beside me. "How do you feel after hearing Court's explanation?"

"I feel stabby."

I swear I see the corners of his lips twitch.

"And why's that?" he continues.

"Because if he's even telling the truth, his explanation means he doesn't respect my ability to make decisions on my own. I didn't need Captain Caveman to barge in and decide my future for me."

"I wasn't barging in. I was trying to keep you from sacrificing a once-in-a-lifetime opportunity."

"Don't you get it?" Her arms fly out as she whips her head toward me. "*You* were my once-in-a-lifetime opportunity, Courtney. Me choosing not to go to Italy was the easiest non-sacrifice I'd ever made, which you would've known if you'd actually talked to me."

I stare ahead and force myself not to react to the sting of her words.

"And besides, his explanation leaves out one very important detail," she says to Wendell.

"And that is?"

"The woman he brought to the gallery."

"I already told you that's not—" I release a long sigh though my nose. "You know what? Never mind. It's not like you're going to believe anything I say anyway."

She fires a contemptuous smile at me. "Finally, something we can agree on."

CHAPTER 5
HARTLEY

Day 1—Dallas, Texas

They weren't kidding about doing multiple takes before the race started. The last few hours have been a craze of booms and jibs and Steadicam shots from every angle imaginable. Thankfully, I didn't have to talk to Court for any of them.

The other bonus is that I've had a front-row view of Xtreme Quest's extremely hot host, Paul Rutherford. Corrina joked that getting to meet him was the only reason I applied for the show. She's not entirely wrong.

"Good afternoon and welcome to downtown Dallas, Texas, and season seventeen of Xtreme Quest!" Paul says to the contestants and the crowd of onlookers flanking the lawn of the Giant Eyeball. Everyone cheers, but this time there's an undercurrent of excitement buzzing through the atmosphere because it's the last take. When he says "go," the race will officially start.

"In just a few moments, you'll begin an international race across thousands of miles for a chance to win one million dollars. But to do that"—he gestures to a massive Xtreme Quest curtain about a hundred feet down the Astroturf—"you'll need your first clue."

The curtain opens, revealing eleven waist-high plexiglass cubes filled with multicolored plastic balls. For obvious reasons, this is the only part we didn't shoot earlier during filming.

"Each ball pit contains one thousand plastic footballs." Paul accepts an example ball from a crew member and holds it up. "Nine hundred ninety of them say Xtreme Quest, and ten of them have the name of your university or college. When I say 'go,' one person from your team will run down and climb into your assigned box. When you find a football with your school's name, bring it to me in exchange for your clue."

"It's too bad they won't let me keep the football and leave you with Paul instead," I say to Court through a camera-worthy smile.

"You mean leave me *and* the football and take Paul instead, right?"

"That works too."

Paul lifts his arm. "Good luck, have fun, and I'll see you at the first checkpoint. Go!"

Court surges forward as soon as Paul's arm drops and quickly takes the lead, vaulting into our ball pit several seconds before the other teams. I want to be irritated that he took off without discussing it with me first, but one, that seems to be his MO, and two, the ball pit looks to be about four feet high so sending the tallest teammate in is the logical option.

While he hunts for our football, I grab our backpacks and move up closer to Paul. Less than a minute later Mitchell from Dixon University hollers, "Found it!" and sprints back up to the starting line. His teammate, Kennedy, meets him with his pack, and after a quick detour to Paul, they run off to the side with their film crew to read the clue.

Worry doesn't set in until the fifth team turns in their football. By the eighth team, I'm livid. The remaining alums are still shouting encouraging messages to their teammates, but all I can muster is, "Use your eyes, Courtney!" and, "Did you forget how to read?"

That one makes the sound guy laugh.

Just as I'm about to go down there and force him out of the box so I can take over, his fist shoots in the air. "Got it!"

"Took you long enough!" I don my backpack and shove Court's into his chest when he gets back to the Giant Eyeball. "Are you blind?"

"Shut up. That was a lot harder than it looks."

"So's your head," I mutter as he slings his pack over his shoulder and exchanges our football for a clue. Per our earlier instructions, we move off to the side and read it aloud together.

F LY TO S AN J OSE , C OSTA R ICA . W HEN YOU ARRIVE , MAKE YOUR WAY TO J UAN S ANTAMARIA P ARK TO FIND YOUR NEXT CLUE .

. . .

For one millisecond, we pause our feud to share a smile because HOLY CRAP THIS IS IT! And then I remember I'm stuck with him twenty-four hours a day for the next three weeks and mentally curse the casting department all over again.

"I'll hold on to the clue," I say, hand outstretched. I'd practically squealed when I'd discovered my backpack came with a waterproof fanny pack that clips to the top when you're not wearing it. One thing I've learned as an Xtreme Quest superfan is to always keep your passport and clues on your person. Sounds paranoid, but Victoria from season nine and Max from season fourteen are proof of the consequences.

"It's okay, I've got it." Court swings his pack around and shoves the envelope into the main compartment.

"It wasn't a request. I have a safe spot for it."

"So do I." He pats the backpack.

"And what happens when you leave your backpack somewhere or it gets stolen, and we lose the clue and our travel money?"

He has the audacity to sigh. "I'm not going to leave it, and no one can take it if I'm wearing it. Now let's go."

As we begin to jog toward the fence, the team from the Rockville Institute of Technology and their crew fly by us in a streak of purple and black, respectively. That's when I notice the Holbrooke team diving into a cab out on the street. When the hell did they get past us?

"Seriously? We're last now, thanks to you."

"I'm not the one who overreacted about where to store a clue."

"That's called logic, not overreacting."

He ignores me in favor of beating me to the sidewalk to hail a taxi, except all the oncoming traffic is now stuck at a red light a block down the street.

The Rockville team has the same problem, so they opt for running to the cabs parked in front of a hotel farther down the road.

"Let's follow them," I say.

"We don't have time to go down there."

"But we have time to wait on a red light?"

"It'll change in a second."

"Oh, now you control traffic signals? What other magical powers do you have?"

Before he can reply, the light flips to green. Court shoots a smirk at me and lifts his arm. "You were saying?"

Ugh! I hate him so, so much. It's too bad I can't push him in front of the bright yellow sedan that rolls to a stop in front of us. I duck my head to see the driver through the open passenger window. "Can you take us to the airport?"

"Which one?"

"There's more than one?" I look at Court. "Did you know that?"

He shrugs. "I've never been to Dallas."

"What does your ticket say?"

"We don't have them yet. We're buying them at the airport," Court says.

The driver spots the cameraman maneuvering to my side. "This is for TV?"

"A travel documentary," I reply, sticking to the rules of the NDA we signed.

"Where are you flying to?"

"Costa Rica."

"Okay. DFW." He puts the car in park and pops the trunk.

Finally.

After stowing our bags, we sardine ourselves into the back seat—Court behind the driver, me in the middle, and the sound guy behind the cameraman, who's sitting in the front passenger seat.

As we pull away from the Giant Eyeball and pass the hotel down the street, Court nudges me and points out the window. Rockville's cab is stuck behind an SUV unloading what looks to be an entire household onto several luggage carts.

"We're not in last place anymore."

I ignore his cocky grin and keep my attention on the view from the windshield instead.

———

I'm in deep shit.

The deepest of shits.

The Mariana Trench of Stench if you will, because our thirty-minute drive to the airport sparked an unexpected internal battle between biology, psychology, and physics.

Basically, my traitorous body has either forgotten what Court did or absolved him of it and is now fully on board with the Law of Attraction.

It didn't help that I was practically sitting on top of him in the back seat. Or that he had to rest his right arm behind my head to make room for the left half of my body. Or that on at least three occasions, his fingertips brushed the back of my neck, thus causing a biological response that thoroughly tested the limits of my lightly lined sports bra.

So yeah.

Deep shit.

"Are you okay?" comes a sweet voice from the sink to my left.

I blink and discover a bewildered version of myself in the bathroom mirror. I'm far, *far* from okay, but at least my mini breakdown wasn't being filmed.

Shoving all thoughts of Court aside, I smile and say, "Sorry, I must've zoned out there for a second."

I finish rinsing the soap from my hands and press them against my flushed cheeks before pulling a paper towel from the dispenser. "You're Haylee, right?"

She nods. We didn't get much time to chat earlier between her interview, my interview, and my subsequent cool-off period after Court's asinine display of martyrdom. I plan on using our pre-flight downtime for intel gathering so I can write notes on the plane.

So far, I've talked to:

Treva, a self-proclaimed "crunchy" mom (whatever that means) on a strangers team from Aspen Creek University. Her partner is Boyd, who loves Egypt and is desperately hoping we'll make a stop there this season. He even has a basenji named King Muttankhamun, AKA: King Mutt. His reason for being on the show is to prove to his ex-boyfriend that he's not a homebody who's incapable of being spontaneous. Treva dubbed them Team Kick Asspen, but I think that's just her way of trying to boost Boyd's confidence.

Team Loud and Proud is a friends team from Auchenbach State College. Despite his loud Boston accent and type A personality (I heard, "I'm a real go-gettah" about six times in less than five minutes), Oscar's handshake was akin to a holding a limp fish. His teammate is Janessa, who went in for an unex-pected double-cheek kiss during our introduction to "prepare for Europe," although I think it was an excuse to sort-of kiss Court. She's been covertly checking him out ever since.

And lastly, friends Alexis and Gianna from Holbrooke University, who have been openly checking him out too (along with Paul Rutherford, a couple of other competitors, and a handful of crew members). Of course, both women have bleach-blond hair, amazing eyelashes, and killer bodies, but something tells me they're leaning into the stereotype. Team Bombshell is definitely worth keeping a close eye on.

"Is anyone else freaking out yet, or is it just me?" Haylee's teammate Kadeeja asks as she joins us at the sinks.

"I'm right there with you," Haylee says, laughing. "I wonder when it'll hit us that we're actually on the show."

"My guess is about two weeks after the last leg," I reply, tossing my paper towel into the trash. "Also, I think you two take the record for cutest day one outfit."

They pause in front of the full-length mirror to admire their handiwork—blue crab earrings, knee-high Maryland flag socks, and black-and-gold tutus that match their Chesapeake Bay University shirts. Not surprising they're Team Old Bay, on account of the actual jars of Old Bay seasoning they brought with them.

As for me and Court, shortly before our interview ended, Wendell declared us Team Hartbreak. That's fine with me since it just reinforces the crap Court put me through.

"Took you long enough," the devil himself says as we exit the bathroom. "Are you constipated?"

"Au contraire. The only one full of shit is you, Courtney."

Haylee and Kadeeja laugh and lead the way back to our gate.

It turns out, it didn't matter who was in last place on the way to the airport. There are two flights going to Costa Rica tonight. The first left fifteen minutes ago with two teams. If they manage to make the thirty-minute connection and successfully change planes, they'll land in San Jose at 8:15 tonight. The rest of us are on the nonstop flight that gets in at 9:07.

Court pushes off the wall and we follow the girls around the corner and down the concourse. When we pass by the sundry shop, he quietly snorts to himself.

"What's so funny?"

"Nothing."

"Something, otherwise you wouldn't have smirked."

Holding my gaze, he arcs a brow and points to a display of rubber duck keychains near the entrance.

Oh.

Oh.

Asha plucks two flutes of champagne from a passing tray and gives one to me. "I'd bet half of the people in this room could use hundred-dollar bills as toilet paper and never make a dent in their bank account."

"True, but someone's sponsoring the open bar, so I don't mind."

"Well you know what they say—one man's drunken bid is another school's treasure."

"Cheers to that." I clink my glass against hers.

Proceeds from Central Tennessee State College's eighth annual New Year's Eve gala will go to public schools in the Green Valley area with struggling arts programs. Last year, they raised a little over a million dollars thanks to the pay-it-forward premise: everything, from the swanky hotel ballroom itself, to the catered food, to the items up for bid in the silent auction, was donated. That's where Asha and I (along with a dozen other students) come in—she created two designer dresses, and I painted four canvases. We won't see any money from the auction, but it's a hell of a confidence boost to see the current bids for my art running at least seven thousand dollars higher than the rest.

Although I think Court might have something to do with that.

For the last hour, he's meandered through the crowd of patrons mingling near the pop-up gallery saying things like, "Don't you just love the way Miss Billings captures the essence of longing for one's inner potential?" and, "Her brushstrokes and use of texture are absolutely illuminating." I know this because I was standing next to him trying not to laugh. Eventually, I gave up and excused myself while he continued schmoozing art aficionados for the greater good.

"Have you found your midnight kiss yet?" I ask Asha.

I'm surprised no one has approached her yet, but that could be because this is the first time she's stood still all night. Objectively speaking, she's freaking gorgeous—flawless skin, a million-dollar smile, and cheekbones for days—but her heart is equally beautiful and she's one friend I hope to keep up with after we graduate.

Lips curving into a sly grin, she says, "I have my eye on a couple of prospects."

"And they are . . . ?"

Before she can reply, my phone buzzes. I set my half-empty champagne glass on a nearby table and open my clutch to find a text from Court.

You are absolutely breathtaking.

Asha reads the message over my shoulder (an easy task given that she's nearly six-feet tall) and fans herself through a swoon. "If he has any brothers, please send them my way."

"Just a younger sister," I reply with a conciliatory smile.

"Figures. Guess that means I should narrow down tonight's choices before it's too late."

I wave her off with a laugh and turn my attention to my phone.

Me: You're pretty sexy yourself. You should wear a tux more often.

Court: I'm actually looking forward to taking it off. Along with that little black dress of yours.

He'd said the same thing when he picked me up earlier this evening. Well, it was more like, "I can't wait to peel off this dress later tonight." Naturally, I'd considered turning around and making a beeline for my bedroom to get a head start on later tonight. *Instead, he'd reminded me that the evening's cause was important, and my dress—a sequined number with an open back and a thigh-high slit—was worth showing off.*

But later tonight *is* technically *now, which means it's time to go. But first, I need to find Court.*

Me: Where are you?

Court: Turn to your left.

I do as I'm told.

Court: Now look up.

Warmth spreads through my chest when I spot him leaning against a column on the mezzanine, where we'd mingled during the cocktail hour. He truly is the most beautiful man I've ever seen. And although I'm not a fan of possessiveness in relationships, right now a part of me—a large part, if I'm being honest—revels in the knowledge that Court. Is. Mine.

He holds my gaze for several moments, then taps out another message.

I'm going to duck you so hard.

A giggle bubbles out of me, gathering a few curious looks from people standing nearby. Confused, he checks his phone and slaps a palm over his face.

I'm grinning as I reply with a GIF of a rubber duck.

Now he's shaking his head, but at least he's smiling when he types,

All ducks aside, I still want to duck you.

"Ladies and gentlemen, the New Year's countdown begins in just a few minutes. Please use this time to place your final bids for our silent auction, which ends when the clock strikes midnight," the emcee says over the speakers.

Most of the attendees head toward the displays, but I return my phone to my clutch and aim for the stairs instead.

"Hiding among the shadows?" I tease when I reach him.

"Just admiring the view."

"Unless someone goes crazy down there, I'll be the highest grossing artist tonight." I deposit my clutch on an empty high-top and snake my arms around his waist. "Thanks for that."

"I'm glad to help. I feel like I should thank you for wearing this dress," he adds with a mischievous gleam in his eyes.

"It was my pleasure."

His fingertips graze the exposed skin on my back as he leans in, bringing his lips to my ear. "Miss Billings, your pleasure hasn't even started yet."

My entire body shivers, and I exhale a soft moan when his parted lips glide from my jaw to the crook of my neck.

"That sounds promising," I finally manage to say.

"I think you'll find I'm full of promises." With that, he grips my ass and walks me deeper into the shadows, past several cocktail tables and a server's station, until my back is pressed against a wall in the far corner of the mezzanine.

His hands slide around my hips and up my sides, coming to a rest just below my breasts. Not one to be left out, I unbutton Court's tuxedo jacket and untuck his dress shirt to find . . . more fabric. Seriously? How many layers is this man wearing?

A low, quiet laugh rumbles in his chest as I yank his undershirt out of his pants.

"Impatient?"

"I just need—" My fingers finally meet the hard, warm skin of his back. "There."

"Do you have any idea how torturous it's been not to be able to touch you all night? Or kiss this pretty, red mouth of yours?"

I lift my chin and arch into him. "You are cordially invited to do both of those things right now. Please and thank you." My voice is breathy and full of need, but really, can you blame me?

"Tempting," he murmurs against my neck, "but I must regrettably decline the last portion of your invitation." Before I can object, he continues with, "Because the last thing I want is for you to walk out of here with smeared lipstick. Also, red's not my color."

Okay, he has a point. "I should've skipped the lipstick."

"I disagree. I have plans for that lipstick when we get home."

"I thought you said red isn't your color."

"On my face? No. On my dick while you're wearing these heels? Yes."

Sweet mother of Claude Monet.

"But in the meantime," he says, palming my breasts, "I have other options."

Yes. Options are good. Great, even. Big fan of options. Except for when they involve Court taking three steps back.

"Wait, where are you going?"

One side of his mouth kicks up in a devilish smirk. "Nowhere." He slides his arms out of his tuxedo jacket, drapes it over a stack of chairs next to the server's station, and rolls up his sleeves.

I repeat, HE ROLLS UP HIS SLEEVES.

With nothing to hold on to, I press my fingernails into the textured wallpaper and brace myself for the man who's pinning me with a gaze that can only be described as primal. Is this what an animal feels moments before it's eaten?

Because I'm pretty sure I'm about to be eaten.

This assumption is confirmed when he closes the short distance between us and kneels, skimming his palms from my ankles to my hips and back down again, this time with my thong. Seconds later, it's in his pocket and my leg is draped over his shoulder. He digs his fingers into my flesh and strings a line of biting kisses along my inner thigh but stops several painful inches from where I need him most. I'm just about to voice my protest when he trails his free hand up the inside of my other leg and glides his finger over my wet center.

His name comes out in a moan.

"Shh," he says, bringing that same finger to his lips. Then, with his eyes locked on mine, he lowers his head to carefully and completely devour me.

My back arches and my hands trade the wallpaper for tufts of his dark brown hair, holding him in place while he traces hot swirls around my clit with his magical tongue.

Downstairs, the emcee announces the start of the official countdown to midnight. Without slowing his pace, Court arches a confident eyebrow as if to say, "Challenge accepted."

"I mean you're good, but I don't know if you're that *good," I tease, mostly because my body is already on fire and begging for release. If he can get me there in ten seconds, I'm all for it.*

He responds by plunging his fingers inside me and hooking them forward, expertly massaging my G-spot to the rhythm of his tongue. I try to stay quiet. I really do, but I'm powerless against the exquisite burn building inside me.

I cry out when the crowd reaches "Eight!" and feel more than hear Court's growl of approval as he inches me closer and closer to the edge.

"God yes, right there." I'm shamelessly grinding against his face, and he welcomes it with eager licks and encouraging squeezes on my ass with his free hand.

"Four!"

His fingers move faster.

"Three!"

He sucks my clit.

"Two!"

Yes, yes, yes!

"One!"

My climax slams into me everywhere, all at once, robbing me of my breath and my bones and my ability to form words. I sag against Court and surrender to every delicious bolt of lightning coursing through my body as the rest of the attendees welcome the new year.

By the time they shift into "Auld Lang Syne," he's slowing the pace of his fingers and praising me between kisses on the inside of my thigh.

"You're so beautiful."

"I love making you come."

"I can't wait to fuck you when we get home."

"Don't you mean 'duck me'?" I rasp. "Because I was really hoping to see what that's all about."

———

Every now and then, I get what I call a "universe moment" that makes me feel like I'm on the right track. For example, a few years ago, my mom was watching an obscure movie I'd never seen while I worked on a commissioned piece. Nothing I did was right, and after going through three canvases, I was ready to give up and return my client's payment. Mom told me not to worry because everything would work out and went back to watching her movie.

Near tears and out of supplies, I drove to the craft store and what did I hear? The theme song from Mom's movie. I chalked it up to coincidence but was forced to change my tune two days later when I heard the song again, this time while waiting for the puck to drop at a Carolina Hurricanes game. I finished the painting a few days after that and wound up with a handwritten thank-you letter and three referrals from my client. But the weirdest part? I haven't seen Mom's movie or heard that theme song since then.

I've come to appreciate these universe moments for their quiet reassurance that I'm doing the right thing at the right time.

And currently, the universe is encouraging me to murder Court.

In my defense, I didn't wake up with murder on my mind, just the need to pee. Except Court has been in the bathroom for the last forty-five minutes. I've banged on the door in five-minute increments, and each time he's said, "I'll be out in a few."

The obvious solution would be to venture out of our hotel room and find another bathroom, but one, that's the equivalent of letting him win, and two, the crew takes the twenty-foot proximity requirement seriously.

With no television in our room and no technology to serve as a distraction, I opened a blank page in my notebook and started doodling the many ways I could kill him. I'd just completed my third sketch (where I commandeered our shuttle and ran him over) when I experienced another universe moment in the form of a crew member knocking on the hotel door to deliver breakfast.

Chorreadas, to be exact.

Translation: Costa Rican corn pancakes with fresh whipped cream.

As if he hadn't hogged the bathroom all morning, Court saunters out in a shirt and athletic shorts and says, "Who was that?"

I ignore him in favor of finally relieving my bladder but run smack into another problem as I pass him in the tiny entryway.

He smells so. Freaking. Good.

This realization is made worse when I lock myself in a cloud of Eau de Court in the bathroom. Where he was likely standing naked mere minutes ago. Naked and wet. And smelling like God's gift to anyone who's attracted to penises.

Exceptttt Court's penis is attached to a man who completely upended my life without even discussing it with me first, and no amount of voodoo witchcraft cologne is going to change that. But just in case, I mutter, "Behave yourself," to my crotch before finishing my business and washing my hands.

That's when I notice his unzipped toiletry bag beside the sink—more specifically, the glint of silver inside it.

No. Freaking. Way.

With curiosity vastly outweighing my conscience, I peek into the bag and extract the weighty handle of the safety razor I bought Court. I'd gone to the mall to buy a pebbled leather crossbody purse I'd been drooling over, but had gotten distracted when I'd passed by what can only be described as an upscale beauty boutique for men—artisan soaps, lotions, colognes, shaving supplies . . . and all of it packaged in expensive-looking boxes with sophisticated labels.

The display of old-fashioned razor sets reminded me of a picture Court had shown me of him as a three-year-old pretend-shaving with his grandfather, who'd promised him the razor after he passed. When that time came, his grandmother couldn't bear the idea of not seeing it on the bathroom counter anymore, so Court said he didn't mind letting her hold on to it. That's just the kind of guy he was, though—thoughtful and selfless even when it meant he had to wait longer to get something he wanted. In that moment, foregoing my purse to get a new safety razor set for Court had been an astonishingly easy decision.

And right now, it's just as easy to put the razor back and pretend I never saw it because I don't have the emotional time or energy to sort through the fact that he still has it six years later.

Court's halfway done with his breakfast when I grab my plate and return to my bed. The slight flare in his nostrils tells me he knows exactly what we're eating, so of course I quietly moan and say, "These are the best corn pancakes I've ever had," when I'm finished with my first bite. It's not quite a true statement, more like Court's are the best American version and these are the best international version, but I still enjoy watching him release his annoyance when he stabs his next bite of food.

Boosted by a dose of petty satisfaction, I continue with, "We need some ground rules."

"Um . . . okay?"

"First, you can't hog the bathroom in the morning. It's not fair to those of us who need to take care of bodily functions. What were you even doing that took forty-five minutes?"

His gaze drops to my chest for a split second and then he says, "I was also taking care of bodily functions, but fine."

Holy shit. Did he . . . ? Was that . . . ?

Was he having bodily functions about me?

"What else?"

"Huh?" I blink and nearly miss putting my fork in my mouth. Thankfully Court is looking at his plate and didn't see it.

"You said ground rules. That implies you have more than one."

Oh. Right. Well, forbidding him from wearing voodoo cologne would be great, but I can't say that without providing an explanation. Also, when did bare feet become sexy? Is that a thing? Are other strangers teams embracing the intimacy of walking around their hotel room in bare feet?

Probably not, ergo my next rule is, "Socks."

Court's brow furrows. "Socks?"

"Do you want athlete's foot taking you out of the race?" Ha! I mentally pat myself on the back because that was a pretty good save.

His focus falls to my chest (again) and then to my feet. "I see you still haven't figured out how to work a sock drawer."

I frown, not because of the remark itself but from the memories it brings to the surface. Memories of Court and I doing laundry together. Of him teasing me because I always wore mismatched socks. Of him attempting to organize my sock drawer but getting distracted by the thongs I kept in there, then requesting a topless fashion show so I could model each one. For obvious reasons, his favorite was the pair with a rubber duck print, but we are NOT going there again.

For the record, I ducking hate him *and* my stupid stomach, which is now abuzz with warm waves of anticipation. Needing something to do that doesn't involve sitting three feet away from Court, I abandon the last of my breakfast and dig today's outfit and my toiletry bag out of my backpack. "I'm taking a shower." A cold one.

"Wait."

"What?" I say with a frustrated sigh.

He sets his plate on the nightstand and leans back on the bed, resting his arms behind his head and crossing his dumb bare feet like he's a model for athletic wear. "What about my rules?"

Oh, for heaven's sake. "Fine, Courtney. What are your rules?"

His jaw moves to one side in contemplation and his gaze intensifies as if he's challenging me to see which of us looks away first. Jokes on him, though. I'll stand here all morning, starting time be damned.

"I haven't thought of any yet, but I'll let you know when I do." And then he loses his own game with another glance at my boobs.

"I can't wait."

The good news is the bathroom has aired out a little, but I still make a mental note to shower before him as much as possible. Ladies first and whatnot.

Plan in place, I set my supplies on the counter and flip the lock. That's when I see the splotch of whipped cream in the center of my shirt. Which means Court wasn't looking at my chest, he was looking at a damn stain.

Hot prickles of delayed embarrassment creep up my neck and across my cheeks as I start the shower.

I'm such an idiot. Of course he wasn't checking me out. Why would I even think that?

And furthermore . . . why am I disappointed?

CHAPTER 6
COURT

Day 2—Costa Rica

I'm in hell.

Brown-haired, green-eyed, five-foot-five hell.

Do you know how hard it is to remain outwardly unaffected when Hartley Billings is sitting on your lap in a cramped backseat? Or when she changes into a sleep shirt and shorts that are neither sexy nor revealing, but your brain runs a slideshow of what's underneath? Or when you wake up with morning wood that rivals the sequoias out in California?

Exactly.

So yes, I hogged the bathroom this morning. I had to. It was the only place I could escape to without breaking the proximity rule. The added challenge came when she asked what I'd been doing in there that took so long. After our interview yesterday where she'd thrown the lies I'd told in college back in my face, I made a promise to myself to be truthful for the duration of the race. Of course, I haven't told her about that because she's made it abundantly clear that she trusts me about as far as she can throw me. (Side note: the death doodle she drew this morning of her throwing me out our seventh-floor window was my favorite.)

Anyway, the fact remains that I'd made a promise, so when she mentioned bodily functions, I ran with it. I mean, jacking off is technically a bodily function, right? But before you judge me for being a creep, let me ask you which is worse: tending to my physical needs in the privacy of the shower, or having a visible boner in my gym shorts on national TV?

That's what I thought.

Thankfully, today's sound guy is about six inches shorter and forty pounds lighter than yesterday's, so that should reduce the overcrowding if we end up in a taxi. For now, I'm enjoying some extra space in our minibus as we make our way toward La Fortuna.

We were the ninth team to make it to Juan Santamaria Park last night. When we got there, we learned we'd take a shuttle to our first challenge today. Each shuttle holds two teams, and rides departed the hotel in twenty-minute increments. That means we're an hour and twenty minutes behind the first group and twenty minutes ahead of the last group. Not ideal, but not terrible.

There's a thirty-ish-year age gap between Padma and Bobby, the other team on our shuttle. He graduated from Stephen R. DePriest College in the mid-nineties and the ink on her diploma is still drying, making them the oldest and youngest competitors this season. Bobby joked that they should be Team Niles, as in "senile" and "juvenile," and the name stuck.

According to the clue we got this morning—which is "safely stored" in Hartley's dumb fanny pack—we're looking for the four-hundred-year-old tree when we get to Arenal Volcano National Park.

That's it. Go to the park and find the tree. It's on us to figure out where it is and how to get there once we're dropped off. But according to our driver, Eduardo, the park has a map and decent signage so I'm not worried.

"How'd it go last night? Was it weird rooming together?" Padma asks Hartley.

"Aside from Courtney snoring and monopolizing the bathroom, it was fine. I'm just glad we had two beds."

That was something I hadn't thought about until we checked into our hotel. Every team will either share a room if there are two beds or have separate rooms if there's only one bed. I think the only thing Hartley and I can agree on right now is the hope for single occupancy tonight.

Also, she's lying.

"I don't snore."

She rolls her eyes. "It must've been the *other* annoying ex-boyfriend in our room."

"You should get that surgery," Bobby says, gesturing to the length of his nose. "Best thing I've ever done. My wife says she finally gets a full night's sleep."

"I don't think he has a deviated septum. His problem is how far his head is shoved up his ass. His butt cheeks interfere with the oxygen flow." Hartley demonstrates her point by smooshing her palms to her own cheeks (on her face, not her butt), drawing laughs from everyone but me on the shuttle.

I tune them out in favor of something far more important—gawking at the volcano coming into view out my window. When we boarded the shuttle this morning, Eduardo said the region was enjoying a *veranillo*, which translates to "little summer," and that we should have a full view of Arenal.

He was right.

Majestically, gloriously, holy-shit-I'm-looking-at-an-actual-volcano right.

Hartley catches on and peers out her window. "Hey, Eduardo. You said this is an active volcano?"

"Si, señorita."

"You afraid of an eruption while we're up there?" Bobby asks her, shifting slightly in his seat.

"No, I'm just wondering if they'll let me throw Courtney in."

We see three teams leaving the park when Eduardo deposits us at the reception station. Big Mike from Stone Ridge College slows his jog long enough to say, "There's a shortcut to the tree. Don't take the first right, take the second."

His teammate, DeAngelo, quickly whacks him in the arm and whisper-shouts, "Why'd you tell them that?" as they continue to . . . somewhere. I guess we'll figure that out soon.

"What do you think?" Padma asks as she connects the chest clip of her backpack. "Do we listen to him?"

"No," I reply at the same time Hartley says,

"Yes."

She narrows her eyes. "Why not?"

"I have my reasons." *None of which I want to discuss in front of another team*, I add through a long blink and a pointed look.

"Whatever." She flings her arms out and lets them slap against her legs. "Let's go."

She starts walking, but I take up a jog and quickly pass her. "Come on. We've got time to make up."

"That's not a bad idea," Padma says.

Hartley begrudgingly follows, and Bobby does his best to keep up with us. A few minutes later, we stop at the entrance to Sendero Las Coladas—the Las

Coladas trail—to study a giant wooden map of the park. I can't help my smug smile when Hartley realizes Big Mike's "shortcut" to Sendero El Ceibo adds at least another kilometer to our route.

"Did he think we wouldn't see the huge tree on the huge map?"

"He was probably hoping we wouldn't stop to look at it since we already had his directions," Padma says, frowning.

I agree, because while Hartley chatted up other teams at the airport and on our flight, I quietly observed them and came away with a few notes.

First, Big Mike is an ass. About thirty minutes before we started boarding, an elderly couple arrived at the gate. Seating was limited, and rather than offer up the two seats he and his backpack were occupying, Mike slouched down and stretched his legs out to claim as much space as possible. Thankfully a flight attendant saw the whole thing and brought wheelchairs over to them. DeAngelo was facing the other direction, talking to Marcail and Stephanie from Southeast Alaska University and didn't see the couple walk up. I haven't completely made up my mind on him but so far, he seems like the nicer half of Team Wise Guys.

As for Team Alaska, Stephanie's family runs a charter fishing company near Juneau and Marcail is a bush pilot, so they'll be strong competitors in any challenge involving hiking, boats, or planes.

Team High Tech, comprised of Homer and Ji-ho from Wisconsin Tech, is another one to watch. I overheard Ji-ho talking about teaching land navigation to his son's Boy Scouts troop, so he'll have an advantage in wayfinding. Homer told anyone who would listen about his undefeated college record for home runs (an impressive ninety-two, hence the nickname). After college, he opened a microbrewery called Big Tater Brewing—apparently potatoes have a different meaning in baseball?—and has won a handful of awards for his craft beers. Translation: he thrives on competition.

It's even more of a reason to pick up the pace as we start down Las Coladas. The trail is lined with towering green grass that soon gives way to a dense rainforest and the most beautiful symphony of wildlife I've ever heard. How was I sitting at a worn wooden desk ordering soap and spray wax three days ago? And how in the hell am I supposed to return to that life after the show's over?

Although after three weeks with Hartley, maybe I'll be begging to go back.

A few hundred meters in, we cross paths with Janessa and Oscar, who raises his arms and says, "I feel like I'm back home! They have birds in here that sound like car alarms!" Except it comes out like *cah alahms*, which makes Hartley and Padma laugh. Unfortunately, Bobby's doing more heavy breathing than laughing, and soon he and Padma fall back while Hartley and I continue running toward the tree.

When we reach Sendero El Ceibo, howler monkeys on either side of the trail launch into a lively conversation. Hartley waits a few seconds, then shoots a disingenuous smile at me and says, "Hey Courtney, what are they talking about?"

"How good looking I am," I reply without missing a beat.

"Huh. I didn't know howler monkeys needed glasses."

I roll my eyes in the camera, which the camera guy is holding backward while he runs in front of us like he's taking a casual stroll through the park. It's no wonder that the crew members look like they could eat a triathlon for breakfast. As I make a mental note never to complain about the weight of my ten-pound backpack, we round a bend on the trail and catch our first glimpse of the soaring four-hundred-year-old ceiba tree.

Oddly, it doesn't look that big at first. It's not until we're right up on it that I grasp the actual scale of this thing. For starters, the roots (which look more like walls than standard roots) are three times my height, and I'm six-two. The vines spiraling around the trunk are as thick as my body and—holy shit. Is that a toucan?

"I think I see a toucan."

Hartley ignores my pointed finger and instead aims hers at the clue box ten feet ahead. "Focus, Courtney."

"But it's a *toucan*. The only other time I've seen one is on a box of cereal."

She tosses a thumb over her shoulder and says, "Weren't you the one who was all, 'We have to make up time' a few minutes ago?"

"Okay, one, I don't sound like a douchey gym bro. And two, I highly doubt taking five seconds to admire an exotic bird is going to make or break our current standing."

"Fine," she huffs. "Take your precious five seconds."

I make a show of crossing my arms and gazing up at the branch I pointed to . . . which is now empty, but I keep pretending all the same. After a slow count of five Mississippis, I unfold my arms and pull in a deep breath of hot, damp rainforest air.

"Are you done now?"

"I am. Thank you for asking."

"Good. Because the damn bird is over there now." Hartley gestures to an adjacent tree and plucks a clue from the box.

I stand over her shoulder while she reads it aloud.

. . .

GO TO MIRADOR COLADAS AND ANSWER A QUESTION TO RECEIVE YOUR NEXT
CLUE.

"I saw that on the map," she says, adding the clue envelope to her fanny pack. "It should be easy. We just keep going on this path and make a right."

———

We arrive at the volcano lookout point out of breath and dripping with sweat. Turns out the "easy" route involved another two kilometers of trails, a couple of steep stairways, and rocky lava flows from the explosion in the early nineties. The only thing working in our favor is the lack of rain. How many ankles have succumbed to Mirador Coladas?

"You have a question for us?" Hartley asks between deep gulps of air.

A man holding a small stack of Xtreme Quest clue envelopes nods. "What does ceiba mean in English?"

Shit. I squeeze my eyes shut and try to recall the sign posted next to our clue box, but all that comes to mind are the numbers. "It's four hundred years old and thirty meters tall. That's all I remember."

Hartley chews on her bottom lip. "It started with a *k*. Kapua, maybe?"

When I shrug, she repeats her guess to the man, who shakes his head.

"*Dammit.*"

I hate that I'm about to say this, but, "We have to go back."

"I'm aware of that," she snaps, pushing past me. "Maybe if you hadn't been staring at an invisible bird, you would've been paying better attention to the sign."

"How is this my fault? You were there too, and you don't remember either."

"Because I was too busy trying to keep you on task and read the clue!"

"I'm sorry for trying to briefly admire the country we're in."

She makes a weird growling noise before muttering, "I hate you so much."

"Feeling's mutual."

Neither of us speaks again until we see Bobby and Padma approaching.

"Don't tell them why we're running back. With any luck, they won't know either and they'll have to do the same thing," I say.

"Or we could ask them if they know, and if they do, we can run back with them and keep some of our lead on the other two teams."

"If we're going to make an alliance, it should be with a strong team. I don't see the Niles lasting more than a few legs."

"I was talking about sharing information, not forming an alliance."

"You realize that's literally the point of an alliance, right?"

"Don't talk to me like I'm stu—"

I interrupt her with a hearty, "Woo!" as we get within hearing distance of Padma and Bobby. "Raise your hand if you already need a shower." I wave both arms in the air like an idiot, but I don't mind because it works. Bobby's too out of breath to say anything and Padma's too busy chuckling and raising her own arm to ask questions about what Hartley and I are up to.

After they pass, Hartley whacks me across the chest.

"Ow! What was that for?"

"Stop. Making. Decisions. For. Me," she seethes.

"I wasn't making a decision for you. I was taking the lead on choosing the most logical option for this situation."

"Whatever you say, Captain Caveman."

CHAPTER 7
HARTLEY

Day 2—Costa Rica

The summer after I graduated high school, I flew to New York City with my three best friends. We were in our Meg Ryan era and spent a week traipsing across the city to see where some of our favorite Meg movies had been filmed. We hit almost two dozen locations while we were there, with my personal favorites being the top of the Empire State Building (from *Sleepless in Seattle*) and the Brooklyn Bridge (from *Kate & Leopold*—one of her more underrated films, and also what kick-started my crush on Hugh Jackman).

But anyway, my point is, I've been on the eighty-sixth floor of a skyscraper, and I've walked across New York City's most iconic bridge with nary an issue, so imagine my surprise when I nearly shit myself in the middle of Mistico Arenal Hanging Bridges Park.

Our clue at Mirador Coladas (ceiba means kapok, by the way) told us we'd find the next clue on one of Mistico's six hanging bridges. What it didn't say was how much those damn things moved. I'd gotten about five steps onto the first one—which was suspended a staggering hundred and forty-seven feet in the air—before immediately returning to solid ground.

Courtney, of course, was less than thrilled because we'd fallen to tenth place and Moe and Randall from the Rockville Institute of Technology (with the highly original nickname of Team Rockville) had just come up the trail, putting us at risk of dropping to eleventh. Personally, I think his attitude was because his two brain cells couldn't understand that my newly discovered aversion to being on things that moved *and* were high in the air was not the same as flying.

In a fit of frustration, I'd shouted, "Bridges aren't supposed to move!"

Moe, some sort of engineer with an inability to read the room, had piped in with, "Actually, bridges are designed to shift to some extent," before I cut him off with a glare and my assurance that his mansplaining was unnecessary.

Once they'd left, I told Court that because he was so good at making decisions for me, he could choose whether to go through the park on his own—and subsequently earn us a time penalty for breaking the rules—or study the map with me to strategize a route that would (hopefully) save us time and (more importantly) reduce the number of bridges we'd need to cross. His poor, lonely brain cells finally showed some intelligence, and he went with option B.

Based on past seasons of Xtreme Quest, I knew the clue wouldn't be at the first or last bridge. My guess was the Heart of Palm Bridge in the back of the park, which we could get to by backtracking and crossing the Guan Bridge. And by crossing, I mean sliding my feet in a weird ski-shuffle while gripping the sides like my life depended on it even though the bridges were only forty-six feet and twenty-six feet up, respectively. America will probably make fun of me when this episode airs, but I was right and that's all that matters.

I may have gloated all the way to the helipad.

That's right. A helipad. Because the clue dangling from the side of the death bridge told us to take a helicopter to Sarchí, an artsy town northwest of San Jose.

I spent the first part of the flight trying to memorize the landscape so I can paint it when I go home. Then I started thinking about my parents. My mom swore she had everything covered and told me I wasn't allowed to worry or feel guilty while I was gone. I promised I wouldn't, but despite three years of therapy, I still have moments where my inner voice tells me I'm the reason my parents almost died.

As soon as the wheels meet the runway, I take my phone out of airplane mode and text my mom.

Landed. I'll meet you in baggage claim.

My original plan of driving home for a short break before returning to campus to work at the gallery changed to me selling my car (and most of my possessions) and flying home for the summer before moving to Italy for my internship. Marchella, my coordinator, arranged for me to arrive two weeks before the program starts to acclimate and sightsee. I was not upset about that.

I'm hoping I'll be able to get up to Germany to visit my brother, John, too. His wife was just put on bedrest for placenta previa, and it's been almost a year since I've seen my four-year-old niece.

"Thank you again, dear. I can't tell you how much this means to me."

"You're very welcome." I give my seat neighbor a quick hug before she steps into the aisle and makes her way off the plane.

The first thing she'd said to me when she'd sat down was, "I hate it when people tell me to smile. What makes them think it's a good idea to say something as stupid as that?" Except she'd said it loud enough for the man in front of her to hear it as he continued down the aisle toward his seat.

Maybe he'll take her advice and keep his comments to himself the next time he comes across a twenty-two-year-old whose heart has been put through the wringer. Sure, I'm excited about Italy, but I'm also nervous, scared, and preemptively homesick. And to top it all off, I can't stop thinking or dreaming about Court. So sue me for not smiling, 24A.

"I don't know why either, but I hate it too," I'd replied to the woman.

To my surprise, she'd lifted her fist and bumped it against mine. "That's how you kids do it, right?"

I'd laughed, and rather than pulling out the book I'd brought and curling up against the window, I sat back and started up one of the best conversations I've ever had with a stranger. Eloise was returning from visiting her four great-grandchildren in Knoxville, her first trip there since losing her husband of fifty-three years. I was struck by how much love radiated off her despite the grief she carried. I'd told her as much, and do you know what she said?

"The heart is like the vagina. It can take one hell of a pounding and come out the other side grateful to have had the experience."

After cackling so loudly that every head in a two-row radius whipped in my direction, I'd carefully ripped the blank page from the beginning of my book (I'm not normally a monster, but I didn't have a notebook, so it was literally the only paper I had) and I asked to see a picture of Donald. For the rest of the flight, I listened to stories of their life while doing my best to capture that love on paper.

As we made our final descent, I'd passed her phone back to her along with the sketch I'd drawn—her in the middle seat and Donald in the vacant aisle seat beaming at his amazing wife.

It's not until I reach the escalator to baggage claim that I realize two things: Eloise never asked why I was upset, and despite the emotional baggage I'd brought on the plane with me, I'd pretty much laughed and smiled all the way from Knoxville to Raleigh.

Also—where the heck are my parents?

I scan the nearby baggage carousels in case they're waiting at the wrong one, then check my messages and see that the last text I sent to my mom was delivered but not read. She said they were on the way when I called her before boarding, so I know they didn't forget to pick me up. Maybe they're in the black hole of cell phone reception, otherwise known as the parking garage. How can we control satellites millions of miles away, but we can't talk on the phone in an open-air concrete structure?

For now, I focus on hauling my two massive suitcases off the carousel and fighting my way through the crowd to an empty bench in view of the exit. After plopping down, I dial my mom. It rings four times and switches to an auto-mated greeting saying the person at this number is not available. I immediately hang up and try my dad's number but get the same result.

Okay. No big deal. They probably left their phones in the car, and they'll walk through the sliding doors any second.

Fifteen minutes later, I will myself to stay calm and think. When I talked to Mom before I boarded, they were halfway to the airport and expected to arrive about fifteen minutes before I landed. It's just under three hours from Oak Island to Raleigh, so halfway would be . . . crap. Did they go through Wilm-ington or Fayetteville?

At twenty minutes, I try their phones again.

And again.

And again.

Each unanswered call adds another brick of dread in my stomach, quashing my earlier relief about being home and knowing I'd finally have some respite from everything I've been through in the past month.

Half an hour later, the Court-induced ache in my heart shifts to make room for the realization that something is very, very wrong. Do I keep waiting? Try to get a rental car? Call my brother even though it's—I check my phone and calculate the time change—almost midnight there? At what point do my parents officially become missing people? The thought of their faces on a poster sparks a new wave of panic, turning my chest into a vise.

This isn't happening.

I try their numbers seven more times while trying to regulate my breathing so I don't pass out on the gross airport carpet. When I can trust myself to stand and walk, I head to the rental car area and stand in the shortest line.

"Hi, do you have a reservation?" the desk attendant asks five agonizing minutes later.

I clear my throat and say, "No, but I need to make one. Please."

She taps on her keyboard. "How many days do you need it?"

"Um, I don't know. Three maybe?" Tears prick my eyes and I attempt to blink them away.

"Will you be returning the rental to this location?"

"Probably not."

"What type of vehicle do you need? We have a special right now on—"

"I just need one that has wheels. And gas," I add, my voice cracking.

She studies me with suspicion, then concern. "Ma'am, are you okay?"

I think something awful has happened to my parents and I don't know what I'm supposed to do right now.

"Um, my . . . ride hasn't shown up. So whatever your cheapest car is, I'll take that."

Fifteen minutes and just as many pages of forms that I didn't read later, I'm behind the wheel of a glorified wind-up car. One suitcase is in the trunk and the other is wedged in the back seat, nearly blocking my view through the rearview mirror.

I'm navigating to the exit of the garage when it occurs to me that I don't know where to go. How many hospitals are between the halfway point and Raleigh? Should I make a list and start calling? Or would the police know—

The police.

I pull into another parking space and unlock my phone. With shaking hands, I bring up a browser window and type, "How do the police notify next of kin?" The top five search results all say, "in person," so I quit scrolling and switch over to my map to plug in my parents' address. That's probably where they'd attempt a notification, right?

With no other logical guesses, I tap Go and follow the exit signs out of the parking garage. When I pass under the first sign directing me to I-40 East, my phone rings with a call from a 919 area code. I swipe my finger across the screen and veer to the shoulder, not caring about the handful of cars I just cut off.

"Hello?"

"Hartley?"

"Mom!" A tsunami of relief washes over me, only to be replaced with more panic when she says,

"We were in an accident."

"What? Where? Are you okay?"

She pulls in a raspy breath and coughs. "My arm is broken and a few ribs are fractured."

I've never heard her sound so small or weak, like it's only the shell of her doing the talking. Everything inside me hurts for everything inside her.

"And Dad?" I manage to say before my voice breaks.

"His top half is okay. They're . . . not so sure about the bottom half." She coughs again, and then the phone is passed to another woman.

"Hi, this is Doctor Vann at Benson Memorial Hospital. Your parents came in about an hour ago."

She says more things: A semi-truck. Their car flipping. Surgery. Critical.

But they're alive.

They're alive.

They're alive.

A few things changed after the accident:

1. Mom lost thirty percent of her function in her right arm.
2. Dad lost all function in his legs.
3. I declined my internship to move back in with my parents and run my dad's painting business.

What hasn't changed is my dad's and my love of Xtreme Quest. We've been fans since the show debuted when I was in middle school. One of our favorite things to do over the years was add on to the dream itinerary we started making in season one. The last time I counted, there were twenty-eight locations on the list. After the accident, Dad stopped updating our itinerary because wheelchairs and physical challenges don't mesh well.

But I think it's time for a new itinerary with activities he *can* do. And after I get my share of the prize money, we're starting with a helicopter ride in Costa Rica.

———

After touching down, we follow our instructions from the death bridges and make our way to a local bakery. Court opts to complete the solo challenge of sourcing coffee beans, grinding them by hand, and brewing a cup of espresso in exchange for our next clue, which says:

Ox or Cart?

"No animals," I say immediately. "They're too unpredictable."

"For once, we agree on something." Court pulls the challenge card labeled Cart from our envelope.

Go to the Carlos Hernandez Ox Cart Factory and assemble an ox cart.
When it passes inspection, you will receive your next clue.

We flag down a passing bicyclist to ask for directions and learn the factory is only a kilometer away.

"We can jog it," Court says.

"We'd get there faster if we took a taxi."

"Absolutely not. My lap is still recovering from your hatchet ass during yesterday's taxi ride."

What I mean to reply with is, "I don't have a hatchet ass," but what comes out instead is, "You never complained about my ass before."

Jaw muscle ticking and nostrils flaring, he analyzes some distant object over my shoulder, perhaps another invisible bird. When he finally looks at me again, his expression has transformed into mild annoyance. "There's also the issue of Tico time."

Okay, that's a valid point. Eduardo mentioned Tico time this morning on the way to Arenal. It's an extension of Costa Rica's "Pura Vida" motto, where life is pure and no one is in a rush. I absolutely adore the concept, just not when we might be in last place in a race for a million dollars. As such, Eduardo cautioned us that although customer service would likely be stellar, punctuality was not guaranteed.

"Fine," I huff, snatching the clue and adding it to my fanny pack.

It takes less than ten minutes to get to the factory. Ignoring Court's stupid gloating smirk about the time we saved, I head to the assembly area across from the main entrance to the building and drop my backpack at the workspace next to Padma and Bobby, who are nearly done with their cart.

"Is it hard?"

"There are a couple of tricky parts, but it's not bad. You shouldn't have any problems," Padma says with a reassuring smile.

I open my mouth to tell her thanks, but the sound of clattering boards cuts me off. "What are you doing?" I direct at Court, who's going back for more wood from our pile of supplies.

"What does it look like I'm doing? I'm building an ox cart."

"How about we check out the example so we know how it's supposed to look."

"If you want to waste time, by all means." He gestures grandiosely at the finished example near the factory entrance, then fills his arms with more wood.

I lift my eyes heavenward and release an exasperated sigh. "I'm so glad I have a partner who's averse to common sense and directions."

"I'm not averse to either of those things when necessary. Right now, it's not."

Right now, I want to smash his big toe with our hammer. Instead, I march over to the finished cart to study the little details, like which direction the nuts and bolts are facing. You know, the stuff contestants don't realize they've screwed up until it's too late.

Padma's just called for a check, and I haven't seen Moe and Randall so either they're still in a helicopter or they took the "ox" version of the challenge, both of which mean we don't have time for preventable errors.

I'm turning to head back when I notice one more important detail: I'm standing about twenty-five feet away from the work area. That's the farthest I've been from Court since arriving in Dallas. Do I handle this like a mature adult? Of course not. Instead, I plant my feet, cross my arms, and fill my lungs with asshole-free air like the rulebreaker I am.

"I thought you were in a hurry," he calls.

"I highly doubt taking five seconds to enjoy a reprieve from your presence is going to make or break our current standings." I say this with a victorious smile because although it's petty, throwing his words back in his face feels so, *so* good. He just shakes his head and gathers the last of our supplies.

By the time I return, the Niles are donning their backpacks. Padma tosses an encouraging, "Good luck!" over her shoulder, and then it's just me, Court, and a haphazard pile of materials.

"We should start with these," he says, toeing a stack of one-by-two boards.

"Those are for the side walls."

"I know."

"We don't need them yet. We should build the base first." I shove a few boards off a metal axle and attempt to remove it from the pile. "Help me with this."

Court steps around me and collects the skinnier boards. "Or you could help me with these. Once the walls are built, we can do the frame and pop the walls on."

"*Orrr* we can build the base first so we have something to attach the walls to."

"No."

I clench my hands into fists while wishing I could do the same to Court's neck. "Why do you insist on being so stubborn?"

"I'm being *logical*," he says as though he's a frazzled parent explaining the basics of bedtime to a toddler. "If we assembly-line the walls now, we won't have to stop and build them once we get the frame done."

THE. AUDACITY.

"So let me get this straight—me having a different opinion on how to start this project automatically makes me illogical? God, I feel bad for your girlfriend."

He pauses his . . . whatever the hell he's doing with those damn boards and squints up at me. "My girlfriend?"

"Well, you're not wearing a ring." Not that I was looking per se, it's just more of an overall observation.

He holds my gaze for another few seconds, then goes back to . . . seriously, what the hell is he doing?

"Grab those boards," he says gruffly.

Glancing from him to the heaping mess of lumber he created, I wiggle my fingers around an invisible crystal ball and say, "Just a moment while I magically read your mind so I can get the specific pieces of wood you're requesting."

He rises while muttering something that sounds like, "For fuck's sake," and walks over to the pile to extract the boards in question. "Just do what I do with mine," he says, passing one to me.

"Oh good. We're at the mansplaining portion of today's adventure. I was wondering when we'd get to that."

"You are such a pain in my ass."

I smile sweetly instead of hitting him with my board. "The feeling is entirely mutual."

Somehow, we manage to tolerate each other's presence long enough to build the ox cart. The wheels alone come up to my hips and probably weigh around forty pounds each, so the whole thing was more labor-intensive than I'd expected.

I flag the factory chief to ask for a check and down half my water bottle as he saunters over. While he makes a slow circle around our cart, Court lifts the hem of his shirt to wipe his face before chugging his own water. I absolutely do not stare at the brief display of muscles or watch his Adam's apple bob with each gulp, and I especially don't savor the sight of him swiping the back of his hand over his mouth when he's done.

"It's good," the man says, holding up his thumb.

Praise the lord and the universe and the ancient peoples of Costa Rica.

After thanking him, we tear open the envelope and read the clue out loud.

Travel on foot to Jardín Else Kientzler and search for Paul. The last team to check in will be eliminated.

I hitch my backpack onto my shoulders but Court leaves his and jogs over to the factory chief. They exchange a quick series of nods and pointing gestures, and then he's back. "It's a garden about two kilometers away. He said we can cut through here and follow the main road all the way there."

He grabs his backpack and we take off running (again) making me grateful for every mile I logged before the race started. There was nothing I could do to train for this humidity though. We're basically swimming down the road, and if my hair wasn't secured with two hair ties, it would have its own ZIP code right now.

Court, of course, still looks annoyingly perfect. I'm sure his girlfriend does, too. I bet she has a face that doesn't need makeup and a figure that can tolerate a dozen cookies for breakfast. And knowing him, she's even more intelligent than she is beautiful—an impossible task for mere mortals, but not her. She has a master's degree, or possibly a PhD, and she still makes time to volunteer at the local shelter or assisted living facility. Hell, she probably works at one or both of those places.

She most certainly doesn't turn beet red when she runs, nor does her hair attempt to impersonate a clown wig when left to its own devices in the humidity. And when Court dishes out his shit to her? She totally puts him in his place. Guaranteed. I suppose I should retract my earlier statement about feeling bad for her.

He hasn't mentioned what he'd spend his half of the prize money on, at least not that I've heard, but it's an easy assumption to say he'd put it toward their wedding and honeymoon. Then again, she could dream of an elopement or destination wedding, in which case him doing reconnaissance via Xtreme Quest is brilliant.

I've dated here and there, but I've learned there's not much of a market for twenty-eight-year-old women who live at home and work at a job they're good at but hate. While Court's getting married with his earnings, all I want to do is rent a studio so I can finally have a place to work on my art. Maybe then I'll start feeling like I can breathe again.

But all of that is irrelevant if we don't make it to the checkpoint before Moe and Randall. Hopefully they got an unruly ox and they're stuck in a field somewhere.

This thought gives me one final push as we Michael Phelps our way to the garden. If this was a triathlon, we'd have the run and swim covered already. How do Costa Rican athletes handle this humidity?

"Look." Court points to a display of handwoven bags as we run past a store front. "Maybe we should stop and get you one. You could use it to carry your grudge against me."

"Or I could use the strap to strangle you. Seems like a much better use."

"So what I'm hearing you say is you want to tie me up?"

My eyes narrow to slits. "Shut up and run."

Several sweaty minutes later, we arrive at the entrance to the garden.

"This isn't helpful," he says of the map.

He's not wrong. Dotted lines, solid lines, other lines that might be a road, and a handful of location markers are scattered around, and none of it gives any indication about where Paul would be.

I take that back. The small labyrinth of hedges would make for a great backdrop, but it's positioned at the bottom of a small hill so I can already see he's not there . . . which is probably why they didn't make that the checkpoint.

"There's a couple of lookout points he could be at." Court gestures to the lower corner of the map.

"I think that's too close to the entrance. They wouldn't make it that easy. What about the event zone?"

Miracle of all miracles, he doesn't argue. We take the trail that skirts the lake since that seems to be the most direct path, but we never make it to the event zone. We don't even make it past the lake. Or, more specifically, past the gazebo tucked into a nook beside the lake.

Where Paul is standing.

Talking to Randall and Moe.

My legs (along with my adrenaline rush, my dreams of seeing the world, and my plans for a studio) come screeching to a painful, hopeless, going-home-to-Oak-Island-North-Carolina halt.

Don't cry.

Do. Not. Cry.

I risk a glance at Court, whose face is oddly void of emotion. It's reminiscent of the day he broke up with me, adding another punch to my freshly bruised gut.

Neither of us say a word as we continue on our path, which has morphed into a funeral procession for the death of our chance at a million dollars. Maybe I can ask the producers to overlay somber music so viewers get the full experience.

And look—I know the chances of us actually winning were slim, but I never expected to be the first team to be eliminated. Even after I learned Court was my partner, I figured we were physically strong enough to hang on for a few legs at least.

As we approach the gazebo, Moe and Randall shift over to the railing to make room for me and Court.

"Team Hartbreak," Paul says with a conciliatory smile.

Yep, that's us.

"I'm sorry to say you are the eleventh team to arrive at the checkpoint."

I nod, not trusting my voice just yet.

"Court, it seemed like you two struggled with communication today. Was being teammates harder than you expected?"

He sets his jaw to the side and rubs his chin. "You could say that. She certainly didn't make it easy to work with her."

My eyes bulge, then narrow, because seriously, *what the hell*?

Paul must sense Court's imminent peril because he turns to me and says, "Hartley, what would you have done differently if you could go back to the starting line?"

I'm not worried about crying anymore. Now I'm just focused on not maiming Court in front of the camera. "I would've been the one in the ball pit, for starters."

"For starters?" Court challenges.

I laser a glare at him. "Your inability to find a football is the reason we got so far behind the pack, so yeah, *for starters.*"

"What else would you have done?" Paul continues.

"Left him in Dallas, locked him out of the hotel room, and/or duct taped his mouth shut."

This draws a laugh from Paul and the crew.

The silver lining in this whole mess is that at least I won't be held to the twenty-foot-radius rule anymore. Eliminated contestants are sent to another destination—usually tropical, from what I've gathered online—for the duration of taping to avoid giving any spoilers before the season airs. I can handle nineteen days on Elimination Island if I'm not in a forced proximity situation with the human equivalent of a rain cloud.

"Court, do you have any regrets from your experience?" Paul asks.

"Not auditioning with a friend from college ranks up there."

I agree with him, not that I'd admit it out loud right now. Or ever.

"Hartley, what do you think it would take for you and Court to learn how to communicate better?"

"A personality transplant couldn't hurt."

"She's right about that one." Court says, crossing his arms over his chest. "It would've been nice to have a teammate who isn't so"—his eyes move up in thought—"difficult."

"I'm not *difficult.* And I was referring to *you* getting a new personality so I could work with an actual team player instead of a caveman who makes all the decisions."

Paul brings his palms up in a placating manner, then clasps his hands together. "It sounds like you both have some strong opinions on that. Hopefully you'll make some progress by the next checkpoint."

Wait.

What?

I glance at Court and see that his expression mirrors mine: brows bunched into a V, mouth slightly agape, and head canted to the side. I can already picture the memes once this clip airs. (*When you remember song lyrics from high school but not why you walked into the room. When you order Diet Coke and they ask if Diet Pepsi is okay.*)

"What do you mean 'next checkpoint'?" Court asks.

"While it's true that you and Hartley were the last team to *arrive* at tonight's checkpoint, you are the tenth team to actually check in. Moe and Randall took a taxi here instead of traveling by foot and incurred a time penalty."

One glimpse of Team Rockville's matching frowns confirms what Paul is saying, but just in case, I add, "We aren't eliminated?"

Paul shakes his head, which means . . .

We.

Are.

Still.

In.

The.

Race!

I move to hug Court, then remember it's *Court* so I switch to a double high five . . . but it's still *Court,* whose arms are still crossed, and my arms are still moving and now I look like a weirdo who just walked into a spiderweb.

On (what will eventually be) national television.

So there's that.

But yay! We're still in the race!

Paul drops me a lifeline in the form of a question, allowing me to corral my hands and focus on something other than the second meme I just created. (*When you're auditioning to be an octopus. When it's your first time at a rave. When you watch tai chi on fast forward.*)

"Hartley, if Team Hartbreak wins the race, what do you plan to do with five hundred thousand dollars?"

Court unfolds his arms and extends an interrupting finger. "You mean four hundred ninety-nine thousand, nine hundred seventy-two dollars and eighty-eight cents."

"What are you talking about?" I ask.

"Your prize money. If we come in first place, you'll get four hundred ninety-nine thousand, nine hundred seventy-two dollars and eighty-eight cents."

"Why do you keep repeating a random, yet oddly specific number?"

"It's not a random, oddly specific number. It's your half of our prize, minus the money you stole from me. I want my twenty-seven dollars and twelve cents back."

CHAPTER 8
COURT

Day 3—Brazil

Despite Paul's hopes, Hartley and I did not make progress in our communication by the time we arrived at the checkpoint for leg two —a cathedral in São Paulo, Brazil. In fact, we barely made it there in time. Again.

And she blamed it on me. Again.

And now we're stuck in a hotel together.

Again.

But at least we get to have dinner with a few other teams before we're confined to our room for the night. Mitchell and Kennedy, also known as the A Team, are the current topic of discussion. Not their second first-place win or our strategies on how to knock them out of the race—we aren't allowed to talk about the competition itself when the cameras aren't rolling—but about Mitchell's abnormally white teeth.

"Just imagine the chemicals he's using. What's the point of having glow-sticks in your mouth if you're poisoning your body?" Treva says while loading her fork with salad.

"Yeah, but I bet those whitening strips take up less space in his backpack than a headlamp," Oscar says (loudly, as usual). "All he's gotta do at night is smile, and bam!" He mimics a tiny explosion with his hands. "Let there be light!"

Rather than contribute to trash talking that can bite me in the ass later, I use the opportunity to put out more feelers for future alliances. For example: Treva's family owns a health and wellness store in Colorado. When she's not selling locally grown, sustainably sourced products, she participates in ultra-marathons. Earlier this year, she completed a one-hundred-kilometer run through the Rockies.

For *fun*.

That kind of perseverance and strength is a goldmine when it comes to partnerships.

"It's a shame we're not allowed to have our phones with us, Treva. I'd love to show you the project I did at a high school back home."

Her face lights up. "You have kids too?"

Hartley, who's sitting across the table and a few seats down, stiffens and pauses her conversation with Kadeeja mid-sentence.

"No, none of my own, but I'm a substitute teacher."

Okay, is it me or did Hartley just let out a breath? Why would she care if I have kids or not? She's probably married to some art professor and owns her own gallery somewhere.

"What type of project was it?" Treva asks.

"The company I manage sponsored a garden at our local library. I brought seeds to all the ninth-grade classrooms as part of a module on the life cycle of plants. The students planted them in class and took a field trip at the end of the year to plant the seedlings in the library garden."

"I've always said that getting kids into nature is the best way to grow their minds and keep them out of trouble."

I don't have a strong opinion on the merits of good child rearing, but I figure there's no harm in playing along in the name of camaraderie and alliances. "I couldn't agree more," I say with a congenial smile.

"So . . ." Gianna sets her elbows on the table and rests her chin on the tops of her laced fingers. "If you don't have kids, does that mean you're single?"

Hartley's fork clatters to the floor. After mumbling an apology at her water glass, she bends to retrieve it, then fixes her gaze on the table of crew members sitting next to us. Yesterday in Costa Rica, she assumed I have a girlfriend based on my lack of a wedding ring. Although she hasn't said anything else about it since then, it's obvious she's interested in my answer.

But like I said—the only thing I'm interested in tonight is gathering intel for alliances.

"As a matter of fact, I am. How about you?"

———

I pull out my notebook and flip to a new page to jot down yesterday's standings from leg two in Brazil.

1. A Team (Mitchell and Kennedy)
2. Alaska Girls (Marcail and Stephanie)
3. Kick Asspen (Treva and Boyd)
4. Niles (Padma and Bobby)
5. Old Bay (Haylee and Kadeeja)
6. Bombshells (Alexis and Gianna)
7. Loudmouths (Oscar and Janessa)
8. Wise Guys (DeAngelo and Big Mike)
9. Us
~~High Tech (Ji-ho and Homer)~~

The Wise Guys—who forgot to tell their taxi driver to wait during the last challenge—kept their twenty-minute lead by pseudo-stealing Team High Tech's taxi instead of waiting for a new one. I say "pseudo-stealing" because Xtreme Quest is clear about penalties for removing another team's backpacks from their mode of transportation, but there aren't any rules against using their leg money to bribe the driver to remove their gear for you.

Unsurprisingly, Big Mike used that loophole to his benefit.

Very surprisingly, High Tech's new taxi got a flat tire a few miles up the road. I felt bad as we drove past them, but that delay kept Hartley and me in the race.

Our instructions this morning told us to search the grounds of San Ignacio Miní, a mission tucked into the northeast corner of Argentina, for our next clue. After confirming that our taxi driver will wait for us, we get out and jog down a dirt path toward the ruins.

"This is incredible," Hartley whispers as we approach.

It really is.

Two crumbling walls, each bearing two columns, mark the main entrance to the mission, which is made of massive red stones. It's about four hundred years old according to the plaque out front, putting the kapok tree at Arenal in the same chunk of history as the Jesuits who built San Ignacio Miní. Who knew history could be so cool?

"The clue could be anywhere," Hartley says, scanning the clusters of smaller buildings surrounding the behemoth rectangular structure at the center of the grounds.

I point to Team Niles, who are running across the far end of the main building. "True, but it's not in there, otherwise they would've already found it."

"Court!"

I spin to my left and find the Bombshells waving us over to a group of buildings.

"What do they want?" Hartley asks.

Immediately, I reply with, "Maybe they missed me," because getting under her skin is the best part of my day.

She rolls her eyes but follows me as we jog across the open field.

"What's up?" I ask when we're in speaking distance.

Alexis points to the end of the building behind them. "The clue box is in the back left corner."

I blink as my gaze bounces between Hartley, the building, and the Bombshells. "Oh wow. Um . . . thanks." I give them an appreciative smile, and to my surprise, so does Hartley.

"We're hoping to get to know you better, so you can't get eliminated yet," Gianna says.

Hartley isn't smiling anymore.

Whatever.

She can be mad tomorrow when we're still in the race.

"Guess this means we have an official alliance?" I crank up my smile at the Bombshells.

Alexis pops a brow and . . . did she just look me up and down?

"Only if we get a secret handshake," she teases.

"Excellent idea," Gianna adds. "We can make one after the next checkpoint. See you later." She squeezes my arm as they head out.

"We'll see you later," Hartley parrots in a high-pitched voice as soon as the girls are out of earshot.

"Don't be jealous because I'm making friends and you're not."

"Padma and Bobby are my friends and I'm not propositioning them."

"Alexis and Gianna weren't propositioning me either."

"Okay," she says sarcastically.

"And furthermore, why do you care who propositions me?"

"I don't. I just want you to stay focused on the race, not whose pants you're getting in." She turns in a huff and stomps in the direction of the clue box.

Not to be outdone, I stride past her.

So she runs.

And then I run.

By the time we reach the clue box, we're sprinting. At the last second, Hartley shoves my shoulder, which, combined with my momentum, sends me flying a dozen feet to the right of the clue box.

"Ha! I win!" She does a ridiculous dance as she pulls out a blue-and-orange envelope.

"Only because you cheated," I say, backtracking to her.

"Don't be a sore loser."

Taking my place behind her, I whisper, "Trust me. I don't lose."

———

Our clue from San Ignacio Miní took us to a kiosk in Plaza San Martín in the heart of a city called Posadas. A sweet older woman selling churros gives us our next envelope.

"It's a solo challenge," Hartley says.

WHO CAN WE COUNT ON?

"I'm better at numbers. I'll do it."

"Surprise, surprise," she mutters as I take the challenge card from her.

"What does that mean?

"You're hogging the solos."

"No, I'm not."

Her hands fly wildly through the air before landing on her hips. "I'm sorry, it must've been my *other* teammate who made espresso in Sarchí and worked at a fish market in São Paulo."

"You don't even like espresso, and I seriously doubt you wanted to be up to your elbows in fish guts."

She opens her mouth to say something but apparently changes her mind and settles on, "Whatever. Have fun counting."

"Thank you. I will." I unseal the card, which says:

Go to the Museo de Arte—

"What? Unbelievable." Hartley's arms are back in the air again, but this time she's pacing in front of the kiosk. "The auto chop shop guy gets to see an international art museum while I get to sit outside, and we can't switch without taking a three-hour time penalty. This is great. Just. Freaking. Great."

I hold my palms up. "It said *counting*! How was I supposed to know the challenge would be at an art museum?"

"Ugh!" She completes another paced circle, then stops and aims a finger at me. "The next solo challenge is mine, Courtney. So help me god."

"Fine."

Neither of us says anything on the half-mile walk to the museum. According to the directions, I'm supposed to count the number of tiles on five mosaics, then go back to Plaza San Martín to find a kiosk selling replicas of the mosaics and give them my answers.

Numbers and memorization. I can do that.

Except . . .

It's hard.

Really fucking hard.

We're not allowed to write anything down, and the first mosaic alone has two hundred forty-six tiles. And that's the smallest one in the group. Oh, did I mention Oscar is here too? Counting so loud that Janessa can probably hear him outside? I resort to plugging my ears so I can hear myself think, but that doesn't help either.

By the time we find the right kiosk, I've forgotten the last two totals. I'm not surprised when the woman shakes her head after scanning what I've written below each mosaic.

"Which one is wrong?" I ask.

She doesn't say anything, because of course she doesn't. Why would the producers make this show easy?

Frustrated (and a little embarrassed, if I'm being honest), I turn and start the jog back to the museum. Along the way, Hartley offers words of encouragement like, "Nice job, Mister 'I'm Better at Numbers,'" and "I was hoping to get more cardio in."

But I get the last laugh when we reach the museum and see Alexis waiting outside.

"Hey!" she says.

"Did you guys just get here?"

"No, this is Gianna's second try."

"Same. We must've missed each other on the way to the plaza."

She wrinkles her nose. "Did you get lost too?"

I laugh and shake my head. "I owe you guys, though. Maybe Gianna and I can work together and knock this out quicker so we can all get out of here."

"Excellent idea."

She lifts her hand for a high five and sends me off with a parting, "Good luck!" while Hartley plops down on the curb and frowns at her knees.

———

It turns out it's Kadeeja's twenty-ninth birthday, so a bunch of us are celebrating at a restaurant along the waterfront in Posadas. A live band started playing about a half hour ago, and Hartley, Haylee, Padma, and the Alaska Girls (who I haven't had much of a chance to talk to but seem nice) are dancing with the birthday girl.

Once we correctly counted the mosaic tiles, we were given a challenge of "In the Street" (delivering fifty hardback books on foot to six locations across the city) or "Fancy Feet" (learning a two-minute electrotango routine). Hartley and I originally chose Fancy Feet like everyone else but switched after discovering we'd have to touch each other all evening. How she's still upright and mobile after running five miles with twenty-five pounds of books is anyone's guess, but I overheard her tell Padma that she'll rest her feet on the plane tomorrow.

As for the checkpoint, would you believe we beat the Niles *and* we were a whole forty-five minutes ahead of the Loudmouths? It's a new record for us, and it's largely in part to our alliance with the Bombshells, who are a lot quieter and a hell of a lot nicer to look at than Oscar. They've opted to stay at the table with me instead of dancing with the other girls, while a few members of the security team sit nearby as chaperones.

So far, I've learned Alexis and Gianna are professional makeup artists from California and they dream of opening a boutique on the beach. Also, they really like my eyes. I appreciate the ego boost, because I haven't been on a date in a couple of years. Living in a small town where you already know everyone has that effect.

The band moves into another song that I recognize instantly thanks to my younger sister, Ella. The makeshift dance floor is only about fifteen feet away, so it's not difficult to hear Hartley belting the lyrics to "We Are Never Ever Getting Back Together" by Taylor Swift.

"Is it true you broke up with her so she'd go to Europe?" Gianna asks. When I lift a brow, she chuckles and shrugs with her palms raised. "Good gossip travels fast."

Can't say I miss that part of college. "It seemed like a good idea at the time."

"I think it's sweet. Like a real-life case of, 'If you love someone, let them go,'" Alexis adds.

"I'm pretty sure 'sweet' wasn't one of the 's' words she used when she found out."

Gianna gives my hand a reassuring pat. "She went six years thinking one thing and learned the truth right before an international race. She just needs some time to process it."

I find Hartley on the dance floor again. I haven't seen her this carefree since before I left for Wade's bachelor party, and I hate knowing that one look at me is all it'll take to ruin it.

"I promise you, the only processing she wants to do involves my body and a meat grinder."

They think I'm joking, but they haven't—

Hold on.

I give my full attention to the scene unfolding on the dance floor. Hartley's dancing with Kadeeja and Haylee, but the guy behind her keeps putting his hands on her waist. She turns and maneuvers to the other side of the girls.

That works for about five seconds.

Then the guy wedges himself into their triangle, wraps his arms around her from behind, and grinds into her ass.

I don't remember shooting out of my chair or making it to the dance floor in four strides, nor do I remember what I say to Hartley, but I vividly recall what I say to the asshole who groped her as I lift him by his shirt and haul him to the staircase leading to the sidewalk.

"Keep. Your. Fucking. Hands. Off. Her."

He holds his arms up, feigning innocence. "Hey man, she was the one shaking her ass at me."

White-hot rage burns through my veins as I lift him another inch off the ground and press his body further into the railing. "She was fucking *dancing*. That wasn't an invitation to touch her."

"Then maybe she shouldn't have—"

My fist connects with his jaw before he finishes his sentence, and it takes every ounce of self-control not to kick him in his face when he collapses on the concrete.

Through the rush of blood in my ears, I hear a male voice call my name from somewhere at my left. I turn and see our security team . . . along with everyone else in our group, two waiters, and a police officer.

Shit.

If I get kicked out of the competition for being arrested, Hartley's gonna be *pissed*.

The officer exchanges a few hushed words with the waiters, then approaches me slowly.

"He punched me!" The asshole pushes himself up and rises on two wobbly feet. "I want to press charges." I take great satisfaction in watching him swipe at the blood dripping from his nose and his bottom lip.

The officer removes a set of handcuffs from a pouch on his belt and eyes me. "You hit him." It's not a question, but his stony face and ensuing silence tell me he expects an answer.

What are the rules for international arrests? How do I get a lawyer when Hartley and I only have two hundred American dollars in leg money? Do Argentine jails allow collect phone calls?

As I consider my options, I spot her over the officer's shoulder. Five minutes ago, she was belting a breakup anthem and having the time of her life. Now, she's standing with one arm wrapped around her waist and her other hand pressed to her mouth. Burning hatred or not, I'd do it all over again without hesitation.

"Yes. I hit him."

The officer's gaze bounces between me, the asshole, and my bloodied knuckles. When his eyes meet mine again, he nods once and says, "Good."

I blink.

"Good?"

He extends his hand and grips mine in a firm shake. "Good." Then he turns to the asshole and says, "*Te jodiste.*"

The man pulls a face. "What the hell does that mean?"

"You fucked up. You want to touch women? Okay. Maybe I know some people who want to touch you tonight." With that, the officer handcuffs the asshole and shoves him forward through the small crowd of onlookers.

———

Unsurprisingly, we all decided to return to the hotel. I don't know the protocol for what to do or say after stopping a narcissistic tourist from feeling up your ex-girlfriend, so I mostly tried to stay out of Hartley's way as we wound down for the night.

Before we got on to the elevator, Gianna made a quiet remark about Hartley no longer needing a meat grinder for me. Maybe there's some truth to that because once we're in bed with the lights out, she says,

"Court?"

"Yeah?"

"Thank you. That could've . . ." She releases a long breath. "Just, thank you."

Stunned, it takes several seconds to come back with, "You're welcome."

It's not until I'm almost asleep that I realize for the first time in six years, she didn't call me Courtney.

CHAPTER 9
HARTLEY

Standings after leg 3, Argentina

1. *Alaska Girls (Stephanie and Marcail)*
2. *A Team (Mitchell and Kennedy)*
3. *Wise Guys (DeAngelo and Big Mike)*
4. *Old Bay (Haylee and Kadeeja)*
5. *Kick Asspen (Treva and Boyd)*
6. *Bombshells (Gianna and Alexis)*
7. *Us*
8. *Niles (Padma and Bobby)*
9. ~~*Loudmouths (Oscar and Janessa)*~~

"**N**o way! Hartley, did you know that?"

I look up from my notebook and find a handful of wide-eyed faces staring back at me. It's the beginning of leg four and also the first equalizer, meaning no matter how many hours ahead the Alaska Girls were in Argentina, we all have the same itinerary to Queenstown, New Zealand. We're currently at a layover in Sydney and I've been drawing to pass the time while everyone else has apparently been gossiping.

"Know what?" I say to Kennedy.

"That your ex-boyfriend"—she points to Court, who's sitting a few chairs down from me—"is from the same town that Raquel Ezra and Sienna Diaz live in." Now she's pointing to the tarmac, but I'm pretty sure that's not the direction of Tennessee.

"Court never mentioned it when we were dating."

"No, this happened after you two broke up. I just figured you would've made the connection."

Suppressing a wry smile, I say, "I've pretty much spent the last six years actively not thinking about Court. And who are Raquel Ezra and Sienna Diaz?"

Jaw hanging open, Kennedy grips her skinny metal armrests and leans forward. "Are you kidding me? They're only two of the most successful, amazing, gorgeous actresses of our time."

Ah, that explains it. "I don't watch much television."

"They're *movie stars*, and I'm their biggest fan. I've literally seen every film they've been in at least fourteen times." To Court, she adds, "Do they hang out in town? Can we come visit you after the show airs?"

"Easy there, tiger." Mitchell gently eases her back into the uncomfortable airport chair. "Acting like a crazed fan isn't going to earn you any invitations to Green Valley."

They move on to a game of six degrees of separation while I go back to drawing in my notebook. I'm just glad they're not talking about what happened last night. Or maybe it was two nights ago now that we've crossed the international date line?

Anyway, when we got to the airport in Argentina, the Bombshells and the Alaska Girls were swooning over Court's display of muscular mayhem (their words, not mine) which invited a few questions from the teams that weren't out with us. I gave a six-second rundown of the events and assured them it wasn't worth any more of their time because I'd already moved on from it.

Except that was only partly true.

Once we were back at the hotel that night, I'd given myself an hour to sit with my anger and indignation because nothing about what that asshole did was okay. But since then, my thoughts keep drifting back to Court. Why did he feel the need to defend me? How far would he have gone if the security team hadn't intervened? Would he have done the same thing if it'd been Kadeeja or Haylee or the Alaska Girls? Thirty-six hours of traveling later, I'm still no closer to an answer.

"That's *really* good."

This time when I look up from my notebook, I get an eyeful of Gianna's midriff. The Bombshells made a big announcement about taking a "sink bath" in the restroom and apparently that involves perfume, fresh makeup, and thirty percent less clothing. But in their defense, they do look and smell amazing.

"Court said you were an artist, but I didn't realize how talented you are," she continues.

"For real." Alexis comes around to my left for a better look at my close-up sketch of Court's fists gripping the asshole's shirt. "The details are absolutely incredible."

What's happening right now? This is the most they've spoken to me in . . . *ohhh*. Of course. If I'd been drawing anything else, they would've walked right past me. Still, I don't want to be rude, so I smile and say, "Thank you."

"For what it's worth, he couldn't take his eyes off you that night," Alexis says.

"He reminded me of a sad puppy. You know, the cute ones you find on the side of the road and end up taking home?" Gianna adds.

And just like that, thirty-six hours of confusion transform into clarity.

"You're more than welcome to take him home. I don't think he'd mind."

They exchange a glance and then Alexis says, "We got the vibe that he's not over you."

Now I snort laugh. "He was over me the night he paraded his new girl-friend in front of me, and he recently told Paul I need a personality transplant, so . . ." I let my sentence die off as I rip the drawing from my notebook and hold it out to Alexis. "Thanks for the conversation though. It's been enlightening."

"How so?"

"I've had a few things on my mind and you've both really helped with that."

Specifically, how Court coming to my defense was all an act. I mean, how else is he supposed to look like an emotionally wounded knight in shining armor in front of the Bombshells if there's no dragon to slay?

"Oh. Well in that case, you're welcome."

They give me a quick wave and go back to their seats (you guessed it, right next to Court). He smiles when they flank him and then I hear Kennedy ask whether they know Sienna Diaz and Raquel Ezra.

As they launch into a lively discussion about visiting Green Valley, I flip to a fresh page in my notebook and start sketching a knight sitting in an airport chair surrounded by heart-eyed fair maidens.

———

Meeting an Olympic gold medalist in speed skating? Ten out of ten, would absolutely recommend. Going against her Olympic-gold-medal-winning time in a five-hundred-meter race? That's a different story.

After landing in Queenstown, we went to the Basket of Dreams for our first clue and the Below Zero Ice Bar for our second. From there, we chose "Speed" over "Spice" and got our asses handed to us at the ice rink. The only upside was watching the A Team struggle too. They've dominated much of the race so far, so seeing them lose to the Alaska Girls was extremely satisfying. So was watching Court eat it when we first got on the ice, but I digress.

A gust of cold air greets us when we head back outside. We open our clue and find a solo challenge.

WHO CAN HACKETT AT THE PLAYGROUND?

"Hackett," Court says. "Is that what people in New Zealand call an ax or a hack saw? Maybe we're building playground equipment?"

"*We're* not doing anything. I already told you in Argentina that the next solo was mine." I unseal the card, which says:

GO TO THE AJ HACKETT BUNGY CENTER AND BOARD A BUS TO NEVIS PLAYGROUND,
WHERE YOU WILL COMPLETE A 134-METER BUNGY JUMP TO RECEIVE YOUR NEXT CLUE.

Oh no.

No, no, no, no.

I read the clue again, but this time my brain translates it to:

GO TO THE AJ HACKETT BUNGY CENTER AND BOARD A BUS TO NEVIS PLAYGROUND,

WHERE YOU WILL HURL YOURSELF OFF A STATIONARY OBJECT AND PLUNGE
HEAD-FIRST TO THE GROUND. IF YOUR TINY RUBBER BAND DOESN'T BREAK AND
YOU SURVIVE, YOU WILL RECEIVE YOUR NEXT CLUE.

An invisible vise squeezes my chest, making it almost impossible to breathe or think or remain upright. To avoid footage of me passing out on the sidewalk, I zombie-walk to a nearby bench and collapse onto it.

Sighing, Court follows and crosses his arms. "What are you doing?"

"Trying not to have a heart attack."

"What are you talking about?"

"I can't do this."

"Weren't you the one who made a big deal about doing the next solo challenge?"

"Yeah, but I didn't think there'd be any bungee jumping this season since they did it last season in Africa. I don't even know how much life insurance I have. And how do they get bodies back to the US? Would they embalm me first or send me in one of those refrigerated boxes? And why does New Zealand spell bungee differently?"

Court wholly ignores my panic in favor of checking his watch and counting on his fingers. "We started with an equalizer, and we only know for sure that we're ahead of the Niles and Old Bay. We can't afford a three-hour penalty if we switch, nor can we afford to waste more time while you relax on a bench."

"Clearly, I'm not relaxing," I say, sweeping a sweaty hand over my borderline-hyperventilating body.

"But you *are* wasting time. You can fall apart in a taxi on the way there." He hoists me up by my backpack strap and practically drags me to the curb.

"Your compassion and ability to encourage others are astounding. If your career at the chop shop doesn't pan out, you should get into motivational speaking."

In case you think I'm acting like a baby, allow me to present the following:

1. The personal information card they give you at check-in is called a "customer toe tag."

2. The bus driver played a song called "We're All Going to Die" on our drive up to the platform.
3. Said platform (you know, the one in which I'll jump to my death) is an enclosed metal-and-glass pod that has been SUSPENDED BETWEEN TWO MOUNTAINS in the Southern Alps. As in, I'll be dangling over the Nevis River while I'm connected to something that's also dangling over the river.

Oh! And the only way out to the platform is via a cable car, which means . . .

So.

Much.

Dangling.

AND.

They don't even give you a helmet. Probably because literally nothing will save me, so why waste money on extraneous equipment?

"Hartley!" Kennedy shouts as her cable car approaches the last piece of solid ground I'll ever stand on. A staff member unlocks the gate and unclips their carabiners from the safety cable so Kennedy, Mitchell, and their crew can exit.

"That was *amazing*! I wish I had time to do it again."

Her cheeks are pink and her bright white smile takes up the entire lower half of her face, but knowing she didn't die is little comfort.

"Are you so excited?"

I laugh (a little maniacally if I'm being honest) while Court nudges me forward, where I learn that instead of standing on a solid floor, I get to ride out to the jump pod on a metal grate with guardrails.

Who is AJ Hackett and why is he this cruel?

Kennedy gives me a thumbs up and a far-too enthusiastic, "You're going to have a blast!" as the cable car starts its return to New Zealand's highest bungee jump, AKA: the world's third-highest bungee jump, AKA: *what in the actual hell am I doing right now?* A fresh wave of terror rolls through me, forcing my hands to white-knuckle the frigid guardrail while I focus on not puking.

"Damn, this is a beautiful view," Court says.

I wouldn't know because I closed my eyes as soon as we started moving.

"Hey." He pokes my side. "You're missing out."

"I'll see it plenty enough on the way down, I'm sure."

Did I mention I'll freefall for eight-point-five seconds? SO MUCH FUN.

"On the bright side, we're officially ahead of three teams. The Bombshells just got to the cable car platform."

"I'm about to jump to my death, Courtney. There is no bright side." Especially considering they'll feel bad he doesn't have a teammate, so he'll join their team and they'll win the race, become a throuple, and live happily ever after.

Or maybe that's the bright side he's referring to, in which case I'll haunt his ass out of sheer spite.

"Are you really that scared?"

My eyes pop open so I can glare at him because seriously? "You're *just now* figuring that out?"

He lifts one shoulder and lets it drop. "I kind of thought you were being dramatic."

Un-freaking-believable. "Contrary to what your idiotic pea brain thinks, not everything I do is about you. This"—I make a trembly circle around my head and chest—"is about *me* and how *I* feel. Which, in case you haven't figured it out yet, is *really fucking terrified.*"

My tirade is just gaining steam when we reach the jump pod. An employee opens the gate and unclips us, but Court holds me in place.

"If you want to take the time penalty and go back, I'll respect your decision. But I also know you can do this."

Hot tears prick my eyes as I shake my head. "I don't think I can," I whisper.

He lifts my chin and cups my face in his hands. The gesture is oddly calming, and I feel myself pull in a deep breath.

"I know you, Hartley. You don't half-ass anything. Even if we took the penalty and still ended up winning the race, you'd kick yourself for the rest of your life for backing out of this jump. Nod if I'm right."

I let out a watery laugh when he moves my head up and down for me.

"How about this. When you get back on the platform after you're done, I'll let you kick me in the balls."

I wait for the "just joking," but it never comes.

"You're serious? I can kick you in the balls?"

"Yep."

I turn to our crew. "Did you get that on video?"

Our camera guy nods while subconsciously covering his groin.

"I accept your offer, but we need to make this official. Raise your right hand and repeat after me."

His lips hint at a bemused smile, but he does as he's told.

"I, Court Mueller

Do solemnly swear

To let Hartley Billings

Kick me in the balls after she bungee jumps.

So help me New Zealand."

The fact that I'm genuinely smiling by the end of our makeshift oath gives me hope I can do other impossible things like surviving a one-hundred-thirty-four-meter freefall into a canyon or even just another two and a half weeks on Xtreme Quest with Court.

Before I lose my nerve, I lead the way into the jump pod. Court and our camera crew stand behind a railing along the back wall while I'm guided to a chair in the front that resembles something I'd see in a dentist's office. A chair, mind you, that's all of three feet from the edge. If I lean to my right, I'd fall over and roll right out of this damn pod.

Why do people think this is fun?

An employee who looks like he's barely out of high school kneels at the base of the chair to fasten padded straps around my ankles. "What's your name, champ?"

"Hartley."

"Nice to meet you, Hartley. I'm Oliver and I promise you're in good hands, so don't worry. Is this your first time jumping?"

I will absolutely worry because I'm in the hands of a child. "Yes, this will be my first and last jump."

"Then I guess we'd better make it worthwhile." His lips curve into a flirtatious smirk that's about ten years too late and one hundred thirty-four meters too high.

"As long as you make it to where I'll survive, I'll be happy."

"What are you talking about? This is going to be the best sixty seconds of your life."

Not even anxiety can keep me from looking at Court and saying, "This isn't the first time I've heard that."

"Excuse me?" One brow rises slowly, and his jaw kicks out to the side. "You were supposed to wait until *after* you jump to kick me in the balls."

I shrug while maintaining my death grip on the sides of the chair. "We'll count this one as a practice kick."

"Only if you admit that you owe me twenty-seven dollars and twelve cents. Otherwise, I rescind my previous offer."

"You can't rescind your offer. You already took the Oath of Ball Kicking."

"And you broke the terms of our agreement by kicking early. I think the real question now is whether your one opportunity to inflict pain on my most prized physical possession is worth twenty-seven dollars and twelve cents." He leans forward on the railing. "How badly do you want to hurt me?"

"Very," I say before my brain even registers the question. "Extremely. It will be my honor and pleasure."

"I accept payment through most money-transferring apps. Also, your platform awaits." He lifts a hand and gestures to the ledge beside me.

"I still need to get hooked—oh." I glance at the umbilical cord of elastic connected to my harness and GoPro camera attached to my wrist. When did that happen?

"You ready, Hartley?" Oliver asks.

I wiggle my feet. "Are you sure everything's attached properly? It's not too loose?"

"It's perfect. Up you go." He extends a hand to help me off the chair before shuffling me to the platform. "See that strap at your ankle?"

I nod.

"On your second bounce up, I want you to pull it. This will release your legs—"

"*Release my legs*? Isn't that the opposite of what I need to happen?"

"Relax. You're still connected at your harness." He reaches around to my front and pats the system of cords and clips. "Releasing your ankle strap allows you to sit upright on the way back to the platform."

"So I won't die if I pull it?"

"No."

"What if I don't pull it? Will I die then?"

"Your blood will rush to your head, but you won't die."

"How can someone so young sound so sure about the fate of someone else's life?"

He laughs. "I'm twenty-four, and I've been jumping since I was sixteen."

Oh.

"What I want you to do now is find a target way out there in the distance and keep your eyes on that. I'll count you down. When I get to one, you'll take a big jump out toward that target."

"Don't push me."

"I won't."

"Because if you do, I'll kick you in the balls too."

He laughs again. "You have my word. Okay, arms out like you're getting ready to fly . . . three, two, one."

My feet don't move because my lungs aren't working properly and now

I'm going to pass out on the platform and fall over the edge and I won't be able to pull the strap—

"No worries, champ. Let's try that again. Arms up high and . . . three, two, one."

"I'm going to die. I'll fall out of this harness and my body will splatter into tiny pieces in the river. They won't find all of my parts, so my parents will get a refrigerated box that's only half full, which is way worse than getting a box that's completely full. I can't . . . I can't do this."

I can't, I can't, I—

"Hartley," Court says, except this time his voice is coming from right behind me. I carefully turn my head and see Oliver standing off to the side. When did they switch places?

"If you're here to push me over, I'm going to kick you in the balls twice."

"I'm going to touch you, but I promise I won't push you." Before I can protest, he brings his hands to my neck and kneads a path from the base of my head down to my shoulders and back up again.

I don't mean to sigh like a woman who hasn't been touched in six years, it's just that my lungs and I aren't on the same page right now, okay? But regardless of how good this feels, it doesn't change the truth.

"There's no way I can do this. We're gonna have to take the penalty."

"Forget about jumping for a minute."

"Kind of impossible given my current view."

"Then close your eyes."

"Fine. Now what?"

"Do you remember the night you described how your muse works?"

My bedroom door opens and a pair of upside-down, denim-clad legs come into view.

"Let's go grab some din—uh, what are you doing? Is this a new technique?"

"It started out as a way to get a different perspective. Now it's just a state of surrender."

"I see." Court joins me on the mattress and mirrors my position, resting his feet at the head of the bed and dangling his head over the bottom edge. "And how long have you been lying like this?"

"Long enough to know there's no hope for my future. I'll be the only person with an art degree who can't actually create art." I wave my hand dramatically at the blank canvas on my easel. It's supposed to be a painting of

me and my muse, except that bitch took a permanent vacation and didn't bother telling me. "Maybe I'll submit this and call it Washed Up.*"*

"I don't think it's time to throw in the towel just yet."

"I appreciate the vote of confidence, but I've been staring at this damn thing for two weeks and it's due tomorrow."

"Okay. First things first. The rest of your body needs blood." He flips over to pull me up from the foot of the bed and I blink against the subsequent wave of lightheadedness. "Secondly—and don't shoot the messenger here," he adds, holding a finger up, "I maintain my stance from our discussion last week: you're overthinking it and you need to turn your brain off."

"My brain is all I have left, and even that's failing me because I haven't thought of a single way to get my muse back. Is halfway through your senior year too late to change majors? Am I gonna have to repay my scholarship?"

"I don't know, Ella."

My jaw drops in mock offense because Court's sister is crazy talented on stage. "Is that your polite way of telling me I'm being dramatic?"

"All I'm saying is that she'd be proud."

"Good. Maybe she can get me an acting job instead."

"You don't need an acting job; you just have to figure out what your muse looks like."

"Which is exactly what I've been doing for literally fourteen days, but it's not working."

"Why not?"

I flop backward onto my mattress and splay out my arms like a helpless starfish. "Because she isn't a figure, she's a feeling."

". . . So, your muse is an emotion?"

"Not exactly. It's more of a bubble or a spark or a percolation that lives right here." I pinch my fingers together and touch the base of my sternum. "A lot of artists say they get inspiration from their muse. The two other people in my group are like that. KeriAnn did an ethereal-looking fairy that's whispering in her ear, and Pranesh did one with the top of his head open like a box and his muse popping out. But mine gives me a feeling that creates the idea for the art. It's the energy behind the inspiration if that makes sense."

"And you can't do this project because you don't have that spark of energy to inspire the idea?"

I nod. "I know I could assign random characteristics to my muse and paint that, but it wouldn't be an accurate representation. As dumb as it sounds, I'd rather turn in nothing than turn in something that's fake or wrong."

"Wanting to stay true to your heart is authentic and admirable, not dumb."

Gah! If I wasn't already lying on my bed, his sincerity and validation would've sent me swooning to the floor. I'm about to tell him this when he ruins the moment by saying,

"Also, you're kind of an idiot."

"Excuse me?" My jaw drops for the second time as I yank the pillow from behind my head and playfully whack him with it. "And here I was thinking you were being so sweet."

He laughs and tosses the pillow aside, then pulls me up and presses a kiss to my forehead. "You're incredible and talented and brilliant and adorable."

"This is better. Feel free to keep going."

"But you're kind of an idiot because you've already solved your problem and you don't even realize it."

I squint up at him. "Is this a psych major mind trick? I'm pretty sure all I did was explain *my problem."*

"Allow me to summarize our conversation." He extends his thumb and says, "Your assignment is to paint you with your muse, but you can't find her and that's giving you artist's block." He adds a finger. "Your muse is a feeling that lives in your chest and feeds your inspiration." Another finger. "You don't want to personify her because she's not a figure that directly communicates with you."

Well, I can't say he wasn't listening to me. But still. "I'm not seeing the solution in there," I say, pointing to his hand.

His beachy eyes sparkle with amusement when he ticks off his thumb and index finger. "Your assignment is to paint you with your muse, which is a feeling that lives in your chest and feeds your inspiration. Hartley, this doesn't have to be a self-portrait. That's where you're overthinking it. Don't limit yourself to what the people in your group did. All you need to do is paint this feeling coming out of you."

"Yes, I remember that night, but I'm not sure what it has to do with bungee jumping," I say.

"You were ready to completely give up because you were overthinking it, and instead, you ended up creating a piece that your professor said was what?"

Despite the fear coursing through me, my lips relax enough to form a small smile. "He said it was among the best he'd seen in his tenure at Central Tennessee State." How has Court remembered something I'd completely forgotten about?

"And that's how it relates to bungee jumping. You've proven you're capable of doing incredible things when you turn your brain off. I have no doubt this will be another one of those things. You got this." Court squeezes my shoulders one last time and swaps places with Oliver.

"Okay, Hartley. You ready?"

I shake my head with an emphatic, "Absolutely not," but somehow manage to shuffle forward anyway.

"Remember, don't think, just do. Now let's give you one more countdown."

Don't think, just do.

Don't think, just do.

"Three . . ."

Don't think, just—

Ignoring Oliver, I push off the platform and swan dive down, down, down into the canyon, icy air whipping through my hair, heart slamming against my ribs, blood rushing to my head, throat running dry from screaming, still falling . . . but now I'm laughing and crying and embracing the unexpected peace that comes with this kind of freedom.

All too soon, the bungee tightens around my feet and waist, bringing me to one perfect second of stillness before slingshotting me back into the air like I'm on an upside-down roller coaster that's gone off its track. Oliver was right—I didn't die, and this is the best sixty seconds of my life.

It takes me a few tries to yank the ankle strap after the second bounce, but I finally manage and flip right-side up so I can enjoy the view while my circulation returns to normal.

I did it.

I fucking did it!

And to my surprise, I already want to do it again.

After my fourth bounce, my harness locks into a connector cable and I start the journey up.

Court double fist-pumps the air the second I'm back in the pod. "That's what I'm talking about! You were awesome, Hart."

"Thanks," I say while trying to make sense of the weird fluttering in my chest. It's not the surge of adrenaline I've been riding on—that's still going strong—and it's not the fear I felt earlier. This is more of a warm buzzing that's oddly comforting. I don't have much time to figure it out though, because Oliver makes quick work of unhooking me and then I'm on the receiving end of high fives from everyone in the pod.

Well, almost everyone.

In place of a high five, Court spreads his arms and legs and says, "I'm nothing if not a man of my word. Go ahead."

I hear a few, "Oh shits," and an under-the-breath, "You're crazy," from the cameraman, but Court doesn't flinch.

In fact, he smiles. And it's not a reverse psychology smile to make me feel bad so I don't go through with it. This is his I'm-so-damn-proud-of-you smile, AKA: the one he gave me after I finished my muse painting. The warm buzzing grows extra warm and extra buzzy.

"I can't believe I'm about to do this, but . . ." I step forward, snake my arms around Court's waist, and lay my head on his chest. "Thank you."

He remains frozen for several seconds, then clears his throat and returns my hug. "You're welcome."

"And you were right. I'm really glad I did it."

He breathes out a soft laugh. "I'm glad you listened to me for once."

I lean back and smile up at him. "Don't go getting cocky. I don't plan on making it a habit."

"Duly noted. Now"—he briefly scans the jump pod—"can we get the hell out of here?"

"Yeah, that's a good idea if we want to maintain our . . . wait." I tilt my head and study his face—the slight pinch of his brows, the tension on the corners of his lips now that he's not smiling. "Are you scared of heights?"

"No, but as you're aware, we're in a tiny box that's suspended about six hundred feet off the ground and that, I've learned, is terrifying."

"So you've been pretending to be okay this whole time?" I'm flabbergasted. Bewildered. Astonished. You could knock me over with a literal feather right now.

He lifts a shoulder like it's no big deal. "One of us had to believe in you. And besides, there's no way you would've jumped if you knew I was scared too."

Again, he's right, but also . . . *the whole time?*

"I . . . I don't even know what to say. That's . . ."

Any chance I had at finishing my sentence dies when Court's gaze drops to my lips. It's brief, a second at most, but effective given the influx of tingles climbing up my neck.

"We should probably head back," he says.

I nod but weirdly make no effort to move.

Even weirder? Neither does he.

It's not until Oliver unlocks the gate to the cable car that I come back to my senses and discover Court and I are still hugging.

Why are we still hugging?

And why am I suddenly reluctant to let go?

And most importantly, what the hell am I supposed to do now?

The only solution, I decide, is to downplay it by hugging everyone else.

That's right—Oliver; the other two employees I didn't actually speak to; our crew (which is a logistical nightmare on account of the equipment they're holding)—they all get a hug because I'm an idiot who apparently can't keep her hands to herself.

"Let's get a quick confessional," the sound guy says on the way back to solid ground.

The last thing I need is for all of America to hear a voiceover of my thoughts on what just happened, so I wave my hand nonchalantly at Court and say, "Go right ahead."

"Nice try," the sound guy says with a knowing smile that has me wondering what kind of footage is on his camera. "We'll do an easy one, though. How do you feel now that the scary part of this challenge is over?"

I can't help the dry laugh that escapes me, because jumping a hundred and thirty-four meters has nothing on the growing realization that I don't think I hate Court anymore.

And I don't think he hates me either.

CHAPTER 10
COURT

Day 9—On the way to China

Standings after leg 4, New Zealand

1. Kick Asspen (Treva and Boyd)
2. Alaska Girls (Stephanie and Marcail)
3. Old Bay (Haylee and Kadeeja)
4. A Team (Mitchell and Kennedy)
5. Us
6. Bombshells (Gianna and Alexis)
7. Wise Guys (DeAngelo and Big Mike)
8. Niles (Padma and Bobby)

*Non-elimination leg

The opposite of jet lag must be jet fuel because I'm wide awake while everyone else is zonked on the plane. I blame it on restless legs and incessant thoughts about those last few minutes in the jump pod when I'd braced myself to be nailed in the balls and instead had taken a hit square in the chest.

It's worth mentioning that I've touched Hartley since the race began—it's impossible not to given our proximity and requirement to participate in challenges—but those were static-charged micro-zaps compared to the full-blown, fork-in-an-outlet, high-voltage hug she gave me.

I'm assuming the extra layers I wore muffled my pounding heart because she didn't give any indication she heard or felt it. I certainly did. Still do. Without thinking, I press the heel of my hand to my chest and rub, something I've apparently done so much today that Treva asked if I injured myself and whipped out her travel pack of essential oils. I politely declined because there's no cure for this. Only more aching that, from personal experience, should go away in a few years.

No big deal.

With a heavy sigh, I close my eyes and try to get comfortable. New Zealand was a non-elimination leg so instead of checking in and having a twelve-hour break, Paul gave us our next clue and told us to keep racing. Now we're on a half-empty flight to Japan, which means Hartley and I got to spread out—she took the window seat and I took the aisle. I guess having full access to both armrests and some much-needed distance from her are a decent tradeoff for feeling like an oversized sardine.

A quiet but firm, "We need to talk," from Gianna interrupts my thoughts.

"Pretty sure the only thing I *need* is twelve more inches of legroom. Also, I'm sleeping."

"What a coincidence, that's exactly what I came to talk to you about."

"The tragic lack of legroom on airplanes?" I ask, eyes still closed.

Fabric brushes my arm and then I hear the click of a seat belt. "No, you sleeping. More specifically, with whom."

So much for attempting to relax.

I roll my head to the right and find Gianna in the previously vacant seat across the aisle, elbow on the armrest and chin cupped in her hand. The dark cabin keeps her expression hidden, and her tone doesn't give any clues as to why she's asking, so I'm not sure if this is the beginning of a proposition or an inquisition.

Not that it changes my answer either way.

"I'm not sleeping with anyone."

"I didn't mean currently, but that's good to know. I'm talking about six years ago."

Okaaay, this took an unexpected turn. "You want to know about my sex life when I was in college?"

"Before the last leg started, Hartley said you cheated on her and rubbed your new girlfriend in her face. You don't strike me as that kind of guy, though, so I wanted to hear your version while the cameras aren't rolling."

Every interaction I've had with the Bombshells has been genuine . . . also flirty, but genuine, nonetheless. Gianna asking about this off-camera is further proof I made the right decision when choosing who to form an alliance with.

I release a long breath and run my palms over my thighs. Hartley's still curled up asleep against the window and I literally have nothing else to do, so why not?

"She's talking about her art showcase right before her graduation. I didn't cheat and she was never even supposed to see me that night."

A loud bang jolts me awake and I whack my shin on the coffee table.

"Motherfucker," I mutter, rubbing my leg with one hand and fumbling around for my phone with the other. I find it sandwiched between the couch cushion and armrest, a blurry 2:49 p.m. staring back at me. That makes what . . . four hours of sleep?

Fuck.

I'm debating whether to take a piss or close my eyes again when someone knocks on the door. Pounds, actually. With a heavy sigh, I push off the couch and trudge across the living room.

"It's about time," a lady says when I open the door.

I wince against the blazing daylight and attempt to focus on the person.

"Are you going to invite me in or just stand there like a doofus?"

Wait. "Ella?" I blink several times. When I saw her during Christmas break, her dark blond hair was to her waist. The person on my doormat has jet black hair that stops in a sharp angle at her chin. But damn if she doesn't sound just like my younger sister. I blink again.

"I was going to surprise the family next week when the official announcement comes out, but then you went and had a personal crisis." She pushes large sunglasses to the top of her head and grins. "You're looking at the lead role for Bargain Assassin. *A wig would be nearly impossible, so I embraced my inner Simone and went to the salon."*

It takes my sluggish brain a few seconds to process what she just said. "You got the part? El, that's awesome." I step back so she can come inside, then wrap her in a hug. "What are you doing here?"

She pats the bag hanging at her hip. "I came to support you in your time of need."

In retrospect, implying that Hartley was the one who ended our relation-

ship may not have been the best idea when Ella called last night, but it was easier than explaining why I was distraught over a decision I'd voluntarily made. How was I supposed to know she'd drive two hours to support me in my "time of need"?

"Do you want some coffee?" I ask on the way to the kitchen.

She drops her bag on the couch and follows me. "You realize it's almost three in the afternoon, right?"

"I just woke up and I need caffeine." I retrieve a mug from the cabinet and drop a pod in the Keurig.

"I know it's tempting to sleep all day but messing with your circadian rhythm won't help your mental health."

I let out a sardonic laugh. "More like the opposite. I was awake until ten-thirty this morning."

"Ouch. What about melatonin? Have you tried that?"

"No." Mostly because I deserve sleepless nights after the way I treated Hartley.

"Okay. We're going to the store this afternoon to get some. And fair warning—this is the only cup I'm letting you have today," she says as I toss the spent coffee pod in the trash.

I don't have the energy to argue, so I just nod and take my mug to the couch.

Ella slides her bag to the coffee table and sits beside me. "What would you rather do, watch an action movie, go for a walk, or play darts with Hartley's picture on the dartboard? Oh! Or this." She reaches into a side pocket and holds up a booklet that says, "53 Ways to Fold a Paper Airplane."

My lips form a faint smile. "I didn't know there were fifty-three ways to fold a paper airplane."

"Me neither."

"Also, you really packed a dartboard?"

She opens the main compartment of her bag and removes a travel-sized bullseye (complete with the aforementioned picture of Hartley) and two sets of magnetic darts. "I know the real kind would've been more enjoyable, but I didn't want to risk damaging your apartment."

"You're so weird," I say over the rim of my mug, "but I appreciate your efforts to cheer me up." I swallow a heaping dose of guilt along with my coffee because Ella should be at Hartley's apartment with my face on that dartboard.

"You just sounded so sad last night, and I didn't want you to be by yourself all weekend."

My roommate surprised his girlfriend with tickets to some country concert in Knoxville for their six-month anniversary. It's nice to have the apartment to myself for a few days. There's only so much saccharine a guy can tolerate when he's had a breakup-induced stomachache for the past three weeks. I appreciate Ella's effort, though.

"So, which one do you want to do?"

I weigh my options as I stare into my coffee. I've already watched every action movie on my streaming subscription thanks to insomnia, and the dartboard is out for obvious reasons. Origami and physical activity don't sound enticing either.

"Truthfully? I just want to see Hartley one last time," I confess. "I know it's crazy, but . . ." I need to make sure she's okay, or at the very least, functioning better than I am. Maybe then I'll be able to get more than a couple hours of fitful sleep. Except I can't say any of that to Ella, so instead I settle on, "I miss her."

"Court, you loved this girl. You thought you had a future with her. There's nothing wrong with wanting closure after what she did to you."

My sister's well-intended words spear me in the chest. I am such an asshole. But before I can tell her we're staying here and making paper airplanes—which is the most random breakup pick-me-up ever, I might add— she stands and removes the mug from my hands.

"Do you have any idea of where we can find her?"

"The art gallery. Her showcase is tonight."

"What time does it start?"

"Six, I think, but I don't want her to see me."

"We'll go at six-thirty and watch the crowd. When there's enough people in the gallery, we can go in and see her without her knowing."

Maybe it's the sleep deprivation, but I actually consider Ella's plan and whether we can pull it off. The crowd should provide enough cover, right? But if it doesn't work, I risk traumatizing Hartley all over again on the one night she's worked all year for. "I don't know, El. It seems pretty risky to me."

"Is it a private event?"

"No."

"Okay, then." She pulls me off the couch and pushes me toward my bedroom. "You're taking a shower, we're going out for some melatonin and something nice for me to wear, and we're going to the gallery."

"I think it's safe," Ella says.

*The knots in my stomach pull tighter. This is a terrible, terrible idea.
"Maybe we should—"*

*"Get out of the car? I agree." She exits the driver's side and starts toward
the gallery with the same level of confidence that undoubtedly landed her the
role in* Bargain Assassin.

"Dammit," I mutter, catching up to her lead.

*She grabs ahold of my arm and we shuffle in behind a small group of atten-
dees. "Do you know where she's set up?" she whispers.*

*I shake my head, a familiar vibration coursing through my veins as I scan
the crowded room. Even though I don't see Hartley yet, I swear I can feel her. I
pull in a slow breath and then my feet are moving of their own accord,
weaving us around clusters of bodies and other capstone displays until we
reach the back corner of the gallery.*

*I hear her first—a quiet laugh that ignites a fresh ache in my heart—
before a patron steps aside, giving me a clear view of the woman I forced out
of my life. My lungs seize in a weird paradox of not being able to breathe
while simultaneously feeling like I can breathe for the first time since our
breakup.*

"I hate that she looks so beautiful," Ella whispers.

And she is.

So. Damn. Beautiful.

*Her floor-length dress is what she calls "van Gogh blue," and her wavy
brown hair has been clipped to one side to cascade over her shoulder. She
looks like a Hollywood starlet rather than a woman whose boyfriend ripped
out her heart three weeks ago.*

*Her only outward sign of nerves is the way her fingers twist together, but I
don't think anyone will notice that. They'll only see exactly what Ella sees—a
gorgeous, phenomenally talented artist on the brink of an incredible career. I
want to pull her into my arms and tell her how proud of her I am, but it's not
worth the damage to my balls and/or windpipe.*

*I'm about to tell Ella we need to leave when Hartley's gaze collides with
mine. Her luminous smile vanishes, and her face becomes a kaleidoscope of
emotions: shock, confusion, hurt . . . and then rage.*

"Oh hell no," Ella says quietly. "This is a public event. She does not *get to
break up with you and then get mad when you show up here."*

*It's on the tip of my tongue to defend Hartley, but I can't do that without
coming clean about the lies I told my sister yesterday . . . and the lies I told
Hartley when I ended things. I go for a partial truth instead. "I don't think she
recognizes you and assumes I've brought a date."*

Ella's eyes sparkle with mischief. "Now that's something we can work with."

"Meaning . . . ?"

She tosses her head back with a slightly too-loud giggle. Several heads around us turn in our direction, but Ella ignores the attention.

"What are you doing?" I whisper-shout.

"Exacting some revenge." Her hands fiddle with my tie while she beams up at me. "No one treats my big brother like crap and gets away with it."

My stomach lurches as I glance back at Hartley, whose glare reads, Fuck off all the way to Satan's tea party in the seventh circle of hell. *I'm debating whether to set the record straight when she cocks a fist and sends it through the blank canvas beside her. The gallery falls into stunned silence, but she just smiles like it was all planned.*

"Thank you for attending tonight's performance of The Evolution of a Lie. *Good night." Without missing a beat, she gives her audience a quick bow and beelines toward the back exit.*

"Wow, dramatic much?" Ella mutters.

Or at least I think that's what she says. It's hard to hear over the echo of Hartley's announcement reverberating through my head. Abandoning my sister, I maneuver around the crowd to read the sign introducing her capstone.

"Central Tennessee State College presents, The Evolution of a Lie, *by Hartley Billings."*

The first canvas is titled Pancakes a la Gordon.

Then, Falling Stars.

Then, Rubber Ducks.

Wait . . . is this . . . ? No fucking way.

Knots of dread settle heavy in my stomach as I register what I'm looking at —Hartley's capstone is a journal of our relationship, one piece of art for each month we were together. I skip the rest of the canvases and walk straight to the blank one at the end.

A Coward's Escape.

"Whoa," Gianna says.

"Yep."

"Have you told her any of this?"

I shake my head. "I wanted her to look at Italy as a place to escape to after her heart was broken, not the reason I broke her heart in the first place. The less she knew the truth and the more she believed I cheated, the better."

"But why not tell her now?"

I can't fault Gianna's hopeful smile. Once upon a time, I believed in pipe dreams too.

"It wouldn't do any good. That was six years ago, and I guarantee she'll still think I'm lying."

"That's—"

"And because talking about it upsets her and I've done enough of that already."

"Yes, but—"

"And because the race ends in twelve days, so . . .." I let my resigned shrug say the rest: Hartley will go back to her life, I'll go back to mine, and we'll never see each other again.

I knew this was coming. Hell, at the starting line, I was already planning my own personal party to celebrate not having to be around her anymore. But that was before I remembered how well she fits against me. Before she blasted me with light I haven't felt since the day I walked away from her.

Fuck.

How am I supposed to just *go home* after this?

———

"I got it," Big Mike announces, showcasing his McDonald's bag like it's a prized possession. When no one acknowledges his presence, he continues with, "It wasn't that hard to get there, either. You just gotta go outside and take the shuttle to terminal one."

Boyd shoots a sardonic look at the Wise Guys. "I still can't believe that we've had access to authentic cuisine for nine days and you go out of your way to get the most Americanized food you can find."

"This is the *samurai mac burger*," Mike says, pulling a wrapped object from the bag. "You can't get this in America, just like you can't get a McFiesta or a Hongos Deluxe or a Serious Angus."

"That's not what—never mind." Boyd waves a dismissive hand. "Enjoy your whatever the hell that is."

"Oh, I will. This thing smells amazing."

"It smells like a cheeseburger," Hartley mutters to me. Although we haven't agreed on much during the race, we're united in our dislike for Big Mike. We all are, for that matter.

"Do you guys mind if we cop a squat in the corner?" Mike asks.

First of all, who the hell says "cop a squat"? And second, yes, we do mind.

"Uh, I'm not sure there's a whole lot of extra room," I say as diplomatically as possible. One of the best parts about our layover at Haneda Airport in Tokyo is that it's literally the cleanest airport in the world. After we ate (sushi and ramen, for the record), a bunch of us sprawled out on the floor because being horizontal is a luxury when you're traveling.

And now Big Mike and his big dumb cheeseburger are ruining it.

"What are you talking about? There's plenty of room." He kicks my backpack to the side to clear a space for DeAngelo. "Also, we should bet on what we're gonna see in China."

"With what money?" Boyd asks.

"Don't you have leftover leg money?"

"Considering they only give us a little bit and taxis and food aren't free, not really."

"You should budget better. Me and D have a hundred and four dollars in our spare pot." He holds his fist out for DeAngelo to bump.

"I don't even want to know how you've managed that."

My guess is cheating, but I keep that to myself.

"Anyway, I bet twenty bucks that we're gonna see that giant wall," he says, waving his palm through the air to apparently demonstrate the Great Wall of China. "Oh! Or a dragon. A couple of them, probably. Don't Chinese people love dragons?"

Hartley catches my eye with a look that says, *Does it hurt to be this idiotic?*

My discreet smile says, *Apparently not.*

———

Arriving at a new destination usually goes something like this: The pilot rolls up to the gate, we get off the plane, and we get outside to the taxi queue as fast as possible. If anyone asks about the cameras along the way, we give the standard, "We're filming a travel documentary."

This is not what happens when we land in Kunming, China, because this time, Big Mike has the great idea of saying, "We're famous musicians from America," when a teenage tourist notices the cameras following us.

Chaos ensues.

We're talking pictures and autographs and requests to sing our nonexistent songs from at least two hundred travelers. That leaves us with choosing between wasting valuable time to perpetuate a lie or looking like asshole Americans and blowing everyone off while we literally run away from them.

Thankfully, Hartley comes through with a third option.

"Follow my lead." She clamps a hand over her mouth and holds her stomach, then takes off. I'm two steps behind her when it clicks that she's doing the universal signal for *I'm about to puke*, also known as the perfect antidote for crowds. Suddenly, the people closest to us are shuffling back in horror, creating a clear path out of the concourse. She drops her hands as soon as we escape the crowd, but we continue our sprint through the airport.

When we reach the ground transportation area outside, she pulls the clue from her fanny pack and shows it to the first taxi driver we see. "Do you know where this is?"

He studies the close-up picture of colorful writing for five long seconds, then nods. "The stone staircase at Yuantong Temple."

"Can you take us there?"

He nods again and pops the trunk.

We waste no time offloading our packs and sliding into our assigned positions. We've done this so many times now that Hartley knows to lean forward a little while I turn my upper body slightly to the right to maximize the available space and avoid her sitting in my lap.

Along the way, our driver tells us Yuantong is a Buddhist temple that's about twelve hundred years old.

"Interesting," I say.

"What is?" Hartley asks.

"It was built around the time the Vikings discovered Iceland. It's just cool to see how history overlaps."

Her lips quirk up in an amused smile. "Are you trying out for Jeopardy after the race is over?"

"More like grading projects for a friend's history class a couple of months ago. It was pretty awesome because the kids had to make a longboat out of a paper towel roll and turn in diary entries as if they were on the boat the day they landed in Iceland."

She quietly studies me, then says, "The teaching thing suits you. Maybe it's time you considered making it permanent."

"I'm only helping out because the district is short staffed."

"You just don't want to admit I was right that night I kidnapped you from the library."

Ah, yes. Behavioral Neuroscience and Dr. Crespo, the asshole professor who taught it. From day one of my junior year, he made it clear that I was in his crosshairs. It's not my fault his daughter couldn't take "No thank you, I'm not interested" for an answer when we were sophomores, or that he couldn't separate her personal life from his academic career. I swear that guy had an entirely separate grading scale for my assignments.

By the time first semester finals rolled around, my GPA was dangerously close to dropping below the minimum for my scholarship. On my fourth straight night of holing up in the library to study, Hartley dragged me out under the threat of burning my backpack, then confiscated my vending machine snacks and cooked a real meal for me. While we ate, we played a game of backup plan, where we came up with alternate careers if I needed to switch majors to save my scholarship. After I tossed out a bunch of nonsense jobs, Hartley said it was time to suck it up and face the fact that I'd make an excellent teacher.

"I guess teaching *is* better than being a rectal thermometer tester . . . although some days it feels the same."

Her head falls back with laughter I haven't heard in years. It hits me like a full blast from the sun, but it's the sight of her exposed throat that sets my skin on fire. Rather than look away, I relish the burn and allow my eyes to linger on that little space just below her ear that always made her moan when I kissed it.

Would she still make the same sound now?

Is someone else the cause of that sound now?

The intruding thought reminds me once again that I know nothing about Hartley's life today. We still haven't talked much aside from our short conversation in the jump pod and she certainly hasn't shared any details with the other competitors.

Steering the discussion into safer territory, I say, "Thanks for taking the lead at the airport. That was a great idea."

Her jaw hinges open as she blinks back at me. "I'm sorry, did you just admit my amazing decision-making skills are the sole reason we're in first place?"

I swallow a laugh. "Not in so many words, but sure."

"Well in that case, you're welcome."

CHAPTER 11
HARTLEY

Day 9—China

I knew going into Xtreme Quest that I'd live in a weird state of isolation for three weeks, where I'd have the world at my fingertips but no contact with anyone back home. To be honest, I'd been looking forward to every second of my time away from North Carolina, my well-meaning parents, and a business I said I loved but secretly resented.

Mom was the only one who teared up when they dropped me off at the airport. I tried to summon a few of my own for her sake but couldn't stop smiling long enough to make it happen.

And now I'm crying over a boat.

Let me explain.

Since the existence of my dad's and my personal Xtreme Quest itinerary, China has been my dad's number one country on our list. He'd take a ton of notes any time the show came here and even talked about learning some Mandarin to make our trip easier.

Naturally, when I saw we were stopping here for leg five, I felt a one-two punch of excitement and guilt for experiencing it without him. But rather than marinating in the negative, I focused on my continuing plan of revising our itinerary with wheelchair-friendly options. (Side note: Did you know there's an accessible bungee jump location not too far from where I jumped in Queenstown? How cool is that?)

Anyway, our clue at Yuantong Temple sent us to Green Lake Park in search of marked boats. This is where the tears kicked in because these boats? They're pedal-operated. And my body? Utterly exhausted, slightly dehydrated, and likely in need of some fresh vegetables. In other words, primed for a momentary breakdown over the unfairness of my dad losing all function of his legs at the age of forty-six because a careless driver fell asleep at the wheel.

I manage to hide my first few sniffles and eye swipes as we set off, but Court quickly catches on and stops peddling in favor of assessing my physical state.

"You okay? Did you hurt yourself?" He cranes his neck in front of and behind my seat, then runs his hand along the guardrail at my side for good measure.

"I'm fine. Just overly emotional and feeling a little homesick. It's dumb, really," I add, embarrassment warming my damp cheeks.

Two days ago, I would've expected laughter or a snide retort. Instead, he waits until I give him my eyes to say, "Being homesick isn't dumb."

His earnest words and reassuring smile catch me off guard and damned if that doesn't take another little chunk out of the wall around my heart. What's even more alarming is that this has happened three other times since we left New Zealand.

The first was on the flight to Japan when I'd woken up to find a bottle of water and airplane snacks arranged on the middle seat-back tray. Court was asleep, but he'd written *For you* on the napkin tucked under the water bottle. Given that no one was sitting in the middle seat, the process of elimination was easy. The second time was during our layover in Haneda Airport when we'd sprawled out on the floor and he'd loaned me his balled-up fleece jacket to use as a pillow. The third was when he complimented me in the taxi for coming up with our escape plan from the airport in Kunming.

Now the wall around my heart is filled with dents and fissures and I don't know whether I should repair the damage or sweep away the debris and see what happens.

What I *do* know is that I don't have the time or proper headspace to think about it right now, so I blot my face dry and turn my attention to more productive things like double-checking our last clue.

TRAVEL ON FOOT TO GREEN LAKE PARK. WHEN YOU ARRIVE,

USE A MARKED BOAT TO SEARCH FOR YOUR NEXT CLUE.

"It doesn't say where to look. It has to be in the water or along the shore though."

Court scratches his chin as he scans the lake. "Americans tend to travel counterclockwise, so most of the teams would probably go left. If I was a field producer, I'd put the clue that way"—he points off to the right—"because it would take people longer to find it. What do you think?"

"I think you've been paying attention to Xtreme Quest strategy, and I agree."

Despite our difference in height, it doesn't take long to figure out how to steer the boat and then we're pedaling past willow trees and water lilies and countless other plants. The whole place reminds me of Central Park with the way it's tucked neatly in the middle of downtown Kunming.

"Feeling better?" Court asks a few minutes later. The sincerity in his voice is obvious and I bet if I looked at him, I'd see two little lines of concern resting between his brows.

Maybe that's why I surprise us both by saying, "Yeah, I just didn't expect to miss my dad this much."

It's only one sentence, hardly a blip out of the thousands that will appear in the closed captioning for this episode, but the editors should put a disclaimer on the screen anyway: *Warning: Hartley Billings is about to volunteer personal information, which may result in an actual conversation and/or serious regret. Do not try this at home.*

After a brief pause in Court's pedaling, he extends an olive branch of his own. "How is he?"

"Doing good. Still a huge fan of the show, so he can't wait to tell everyone I'm on it."

Chuckling, he says, "Knowing him, he'll probably cover himself in blue-and-orange body paint for his next marathon, and then when they interview him, the text on the bottom of the TV screen will say, 'Ryan Billings, whose daughter was on Xtreme Quest.'"

The mental image draws a bittersweet smile because that's exactly something he'd do if it wasn't for the accident.

"You're on the right track, but it's more like decking out his wheelchair for the adaptive 5K race."

Court's head rears back. "He's in a wheelchair? What happened?"

"Car accident a few years ago. A semi-truck driver veered into their lane."

"*Their* lane? Your mom was in the car too?"

I nod. "The car rolled off an embankment. She lost some function in her right arm, but she's okay otherwise. Dad was paralyzed from the waist down though."

"Damn," he says, mostly to himself. "That's . . ." He blinks and shakes his head. "I'm sorry to hear that."

"It was rough for a while, but it could've been a lot worse. And thanks to their otherworldly stubbornness, they both made more of a recovery than doctors expected."

His lips twitch like he's fighting a smile.

"What?"

"Hartley O. Billings, always looking on the bright side."

Once again, how has he remembered something I'd totally forgotten about?

"It's Ophelia," I say, playing into the running joke we shared a million years ago.

"It's Optimist. They just didn't know how to spell it."

I roll my eyes but we're smiling now, and it's . . . pleasant. Easy. Familiar. The last day or so has given me a glimpse into what it might've been like if we'd auditioned for the show when we were in college.

Traveling together.

Completing challenges together.

Sightseeing together.

Sleeping together—in hotels, I mean. (Although we probably would've done the other kind of sleeping together too.)

The point is, we would've had a blast on the show back then, and I'm starting to get the sense that we can have just as much fun now. Minus the non-sleeping sleeping together, of course.

Not that I've thought about that.

Okay, I did a few times.

Several times.

Fine, a whole damn lot but can you blame me? Court was insanely gorgeous in college, and the last six years have only served to improve upon his body. His heart, too, for that matter. Even if he was trying to impress the Bombshells when he punched that guy in Argentina, there wasn't anyone else from the race with us in the jump pod so he didn't need to be sweet and encouraging unless he'd wanted to.

Unless he's playing the long game to impress someone back home.

The errant thought from the scorned side of my brain takes root before I can brush it away. It's a basic fact that women across America will fall in love with Court when the show airs. If he's trying to win someone over in Green Valley, playing the role of the nice guy hero is a guaranteed way to make that happen.

But what about the airplane snacks? And lending me his jacket? And—

Duh—didn't you already say he's a nice guy? That's why you fell in love with him in the first place.

I don't appreciate the tone of voice from the logical side of my brain, but it's not wrong. Court literally took the phrase "If you love someone, let them go" and broke his own heart so I'd get a shot at a once-in-a-lifetime opportunity.

Then explain the infidelity, smartypants, my Scorned Brain says while illuminating a neon sign that says Cheater! *Who was the woman he brought to Gallery Night? Is she the same one he hooked up with during that bachelor party weekend? Did he—*

Ugh! Enough! I silently shout to both sides of my brain. *I already said I'm not dealing with this until I've slept, hydrated, and eaten a vegetable, so unless either of you has a cot, a water bottle, and some broccoli, I don't want to hear another peep out of you.*

Silence.

That's what I thought.

———

The universe really wants me to think about Court.

I know this because of the two-hour nap I took on the drive to our next location, the bottle of sour plum drink we chugged to get our next clue, and the bamboo basket full of fruit waiting for us at our "What a Teas" challenge. It's like the universe heard my inner monologue at Green Lake Park and said, "Ask and ye shall receive."

Well, mostly receive.

I'm not fully hydrated yet and tangerines aren't a vegetable, but the cosmic nudge gets a solid two and a half out of three. Even so, analyzing how I feel is still going to have to wait until tonight, because right now I'm dividing my attention between what the Bombshells are whispering to each other and how Court has managed to turn the act of rinsing tangerines in a shallow barrel into the kind of forearm porn people pay money to watch.

Focus. You can think about that one later, too.

Fixing my attention on the Bombshells, I lean toward Court and say, "Don't look now, but are Gianna and Alexis acting weird?"

His head immediately pivots in their direction, earning him a playful whack on the arm from me. "I literally said, 'Don't look now.'"

"How was I supposed to tell if they're acting weird if I can't look at them?"

"I meant that you should've waited a few seconds so it didn't seem like we were talking about them."

"Duly noted."

"Well?" I motion for him to continue talking.

"Well, what?"

"Are they acting weird?"

"I'm not sure, since I was only able to look at them for point-two seconds before you smacked me and drenched my shirt." With a ghost of a smile on his lips, he glances at the wet splotch on his sleeve while he continues swirling his hands among the bright orange fruit.

Today's challenge brought us to a small village northwest of Kunming, where we're tasked with making a hundred and fifty pu-erh tea pods out of tangerine husks. Basically, we cut and gut each tangerine like we would a pumpkin, stuff it with tea leaves, and put it on a drying rack. When we're done with that, we'll individually wrap a hundred and fifty previously dried tea pods. Once the tea maker approves our paper-wrapping technique, we'll get our next clue.

But first, we need to finish rinsing the tangerines.

"I hardly drenched your shirt," I say, mimicking Court's movements in the barrel of water.

He surveys his sleeve again. "I dunno, seems pretty wet to me."

"Then maybe you need a refresher on what 'wet' actually means."

Okay, in my defense, that didn't sound dirty in my head.

Without missing a beat, his gaze rakes over my body in a blatant display of heated appreciation. When he's taken his fill, he arches a brow and leans in. "Care to jog my memory?"

I open my mouth to tell him there isn't a snowball's chance in hell, but what comes out instead is, "I would care so hard."

Those damn lips of his settle into a smirk that begs me to come closer. "And how do you plan on doing that?"

"Wouldn't you like to know, Mr. Mueller."

Wait. Why am I flirting with Court? And why am I enjoying it so much?

"Actually, I would." His smirk slowly transforms into a sexy, smoldering thing that cranks up the temperature in ways that have nothing to do with the balmy afternoon sun.

He's flirting back.

And I'm enjoying that too.

And now I want to touch him.

Don't you dare, my Scorned Brain says as it gesticulates wildly at the Cheater! sign. *You're supposed to end this race with half a million dollars, not another broken heart.*

It's a valid point, but then my Logical Brain pipes in with, *Do you not see the opportunity for a compromise right in front of your face?*

Huh?

On cue, my fingers flex in the water and then I'm fighting a grin because *yes*. It's the perfect solution.

"How about I show you right now?"

Court swallows thickly as I remove one hand from the barrel and slowly draw it toward my chest. As expected, he tracks the movement, giving me the perfect opportunity to scoop out a handful of water and smear it across his face.

"Now you're wet." I finally unleash my grin.

He blinks back at me for several stunned seconds before lifting the bottom of his shirt to dry off. I'm pretty sure the camera guy gets high-definition footage of me ogling his abs, but it seems like a fair trade for a close-up view of this caliber. I should buy a large-screen TV and beg for a copy of the footage.

Reluctantly, I return my gaze to his face as he lowers his shirt.

His expression is equal parts mirth and mischief when he says, "Well done, Miss Billings, but you're forgetting one very important thing."

"What's that?"

"Two can play at that game." Half a second later, he locks one arm around my shoulders and douses me with a giant man-paw full of water that I would've seen coming if I hadn't been ensnared by the wicked gleam in his eyes. I sputter against the onslaught of liquid as he says, "Now we're even."

Our proximity means I can't use my shirt to dry my face, so I snake my arm up between our bodies to clear the water from my lashes. "We are hardly even. If anything, you deserve another round because I'm twice as wet as you."

There are a million other things I should be focusing on right now (like how we're technically wasting time and I still don't know whether the Bombshells are acting weird) but all that takes a back seat when Court murmurs, "What I'm hearing you say is I made you extra wet?"

"You did," someone says. Me, maybe? The sudden rush of warm buzzing makes it impossible to think. Actually, no. I can think just fine—specifically about how beautiful Court's lips are and how they'd feel on mine after all these years because *my god I want to kiss him.*

And he's so close. All I'd have to do is—

"Yoooo! Who's ready for a tea party?"

I startle at Big Mike's obnoxious greeting, taking one step back like I've just been caught with my hand in a cookie jar (or more accurately, splayed across Court's chest). The upside is I can finally dry my face, which I do while Mike and DeAngelo high-five the group of tea makers and officially announce that "the Wise Guys are in the house."

"Jackasses is more like it," Court says, pressing his lips tight. His expression gives no indication he'd been caught up in the moment like I was, and that's probably an upside too. Getting through the next two weeks will be challenging enough without adding fresh hormones to the mix.

Refocusing on the logistics of the race, I say, "We should talk to the other teams about working together to eliminate Mike and DeAngelo. I don't know how much more of them I can take."

———

There are twenty-three lounge chairs on the deck of the heated indoor pool at our hotel in Kunming, and each chair has seven slats. That's what . . . a hundred and fifty-ish slats? From there, I move on to counting foam chairs on the pool's Baja shelf (five), lights in the ceiling (sixteen), and artificial topiaries (twelve) to keep from staring at Court's eight-pack and the generous contents of his swim trunks while he and the other guys from the race play basketball in the deep end with a few tourist families.

I use "deep end" loosely—the pool is only four feet deep, causing Court's trunks to cling to his groin every time he jumps for the ball . . . which he's done at least two dozen times in the last five minutes.

I'm relaxing on the Baja shelf with the other Xtreme Quest women and unfortunately, I can't turn my foam water chair around without being obvious. Instead, I scan the pool deck for more things to count until it's time to head upstairs. Tonight is the first time since the race started that the teams are in separate rooms, and I'm kind of looking forward to—

"Watch out!" Boyd hollers seconds before the basketball smacks my forehead.

Court is out of the water in an instant, rushing to my chair to inspect my face for damage. "Are you okay? Does anything hurt?"

"I'm okay." Well, aside from the torture of having his dripping-wet pecs inches from my face.

He lets out a relieved sigh but that doesn't stop him from gently rubbing where the ball hit me. Although unnecessary, his concern is sweet. I start to say as much, but every word on my tongue evaporates the moment I gaze up at the blue-green irises I can still draw from memory. For a millisecond, I indulge in the fantasy of sinking my fingers into his hair and pulling his lips to mine. There's no doubt he'd taste just as good, if not better, than he did all those years ago, but one, we're surrounded by people, and two, indulging in said fantasy would have disastrous consequences.

Holding on to what's left of my senses, I gently remove his hands from my cheeks and scooch over, putting several necessary inches between us. "I'm good. You can stop worrying."

"Sorry, Hartley," Boyd calls from the pool deck, the errant ball now tucked under his arm.

"Sorry yourself. It's gonna take more than a kid's toy to knock me out of the race," I fire back playfully.

With a mischievous grin aimed my way, he says, "Challenge accepted," and jumps feet first into the water to continue the game.

Court, on the other hand, stays rooted in place, so I nudge him back and push myself out of my chair before he can start assessing me all over again.

"Where are you going?" he asks, immediately rising beside me.

"To the restroom."

"Come on, Mueller, we need you!" Mitchell says.

"Be right there." He follows me as I walk to the lounge chair and secure my towel around my waist. "You sure you're okay?"

"That thing is basically a rubberized beach ball. I promise I'm good."

I glance back at Court when I reach the restroom and find Gianna locking elbows with him so they can jump into the deep end together. It's fine. I mean, who cares if we exchanged in some flirty banter earlier today? He's flirted with the Bombshells since day one, and he and Gianna are two consenting, single adults. If they want to . . . whatever, that's fine by me.

Totally, completely fine.

I yank open the door and head to the first stall, hanging my towel from the hook so I can pee.

A few minutes later, I'm at the sink when Alexis breezes into the restroom with Nikki, one of the female crew members, in tow. The twenty-foot proximity requirement is relaxed after checkpoints, but we're still chaperoned in isolated places when we aren't wearing mics to ensure we don't discuss Xtreme Quest matters with other teams.

"It looks like things between you and Court have been going better in the last couple of days," Alexis says, leaning against an adjacent sink.

Unsure of where the conversation is going, I answer cautiously, "I haven't wanted to strangle him, so I'd say that's an improvement."

"Has he talked to you about anything important recently?"

Wait, does she mean the Wise Guys elimination plan? Because in case she forgot, Nikki is standing right here, and the producers have made it very clear that they have a zero-tolerance policy for cheating.

"Nothing that comes to mind." I turn on the faucet and work a pump of soap into a lather.

"So he hasn't mentioned anything about your breakup?"

Surprise has me snapping my eyes to hers in the mirror. "What? No."

"Stupid boys," she mutters to herself. "Hartley, Court never cheated on you."

"That's impossible. I literally saw it with my own eyes."

Her expression twists into an odd combination of sympathy and hope. "I think it's time for you to ask him who he brought to the gallery that night."

CHAPTER 12
COURT

Day 10—China

1. A Team (Mitchell and Kennedy)
2. Old Bay (Haylee and Kadeeja)
3. Alaska Girls (Stephanie and Marcail)
4. Bombshells (Gianna and Alexis)
5. Us
6. Wise Guys (DeAngelo and Big Mike)
7. Kick Asspen (Treva and Boyd)
8. ~~Nites (Padma and Bobby)~~

Hartley enters the hotel lobby a few minutes after I arrive looking about as rested as I feel, which is to say: not very. I thought having a room to myself for a change (more specifically, not being subjected to the intoxicating aroma of her fresh out of the shower) would allow me to relax easier and sleep better.

Turns out, all it did was make me toss and turn while my brain treated me to a slideshow of her wearing that damn bikini. I tried everything—and I mean *everything*— to fall asleep and failed miserably.

"How was your night?" I ask her around a yawn.

"I got an hour of sleep if I'm lucky."

"Same." We have about twenty minutes before it's time to meet the crew, so I hook a thumb toward the breakfast area. "Caffeine?"

"Absolutely."

As we enter the dining room, I spot an open table near the wall. "You want to grab that one while I get the coffee?"

She starts for the table, then hesitates. "I can take your backpack. It'll make it easier with all the people walking around."

A week ago, I'd have been worried that she was planting a bomb or throwing away my toiletries. But lately, things have been . . . nice. Enjoyable. I'd even go so far as to classify yesterday as fun.

"Thanks." I unsling my bag and hand it over. "Two sugars and drenched in cream, right?"

Her brows rise. "How do you remember that?"

"It's not a complicated order." More like she's impossible to forget, but I keep that to myself.

A few minutes later, I deposit our mugs on the table. "Your coffee, madam, and"—I retrieve two bananas from my pocket—"the goldilocks of fruit because oranges are too hard to peel and apples are too hard to chew."

Hartley breaths out a soft laugh. "The hangover breakfast of champions. I haven't needed to use that trick in years."

"Figured if it worked for a hangover, it would help with exhaustion too."

We drink our coffee and eat our hangover bananas in comfortable silence, except that I can practically hear Hartley thinking. She confirms this a few minutes later when she wraps her hands around her mug and takes a breath.

"There's something I want to talk to you about before we get mic'ed up."

"Okay, what's—"

"Hey guys!" Padma approaches the table carrying Bobby's bag while he trails behind on crutches. They've been at the back of the pack since he injured his knee in New Zealand, and yesterday's pedal boating only added to it. No one was surprised when they came in last place at the checkpoint.

The women exchange a hug while I offer a handshake and conciliatory smile to Bobby.

"What's the word on your knee?"

"They're thinking an ACL tear. I'll meet up with a doctor once we get to our hotel to figure out the plan, but it looks like I won't need surgery."

"That's great news," Hartley says. "Have they told you where Elimination Island is?"

"Not yet, but they promised sunshine."

"And a pool," Padma adds.

Ever the optimist, Hartley says, "There could be worse places to relax and recuperate. We'll miss you though."

"Don't you two get any ideas about joining us," Bobby says, pointing a finger at Hartley and me in mock sternness. "The only place we want to see you is when you come in first at the finish line."

"We'll try our best," she says, smiling.

"Anyway, we'll let you get back to your breakfast. Good luck, guys!" Padma says.

After another round of hugs and handshakes, they head for an open table in the center of the dining room.

"So . . . the thing I want to talk to you about."

"Right."

"I had a lot of time—"

"Wait." I lift my palm, then gesture to a table about ten feet away. "Do you see what I see?"

Hartley cranes her neck. "People eating breakfast?"

"Also that. But more specifically the Wise Guys at the table next to the group of tourists."

"Okay."

"Look what DeAngelo is holding."

Her eyes squint, then bulge. "That's a cell phone. How does he have a cell phone?"

"No idea." I scan the room for anyone from the crew but come up empty. I'm just about to go find someone when DeAngelo passes the phone to a woman at the tourist table, who drops it into her purse. "Damn. False alarm."

Hartley sighs because while Xtreme Quest contestants are prohibited from bringing smart technology of any kind, we're allowed to borrow phones or computers from people we meet during the race.

"We'll just have to keep an eye on them," she says. "And we definitely need to talk to the other teams about the alliance today."

"Agreed. But back to what you wanted to tell me. What's up?"

Before she can respond, the alarms on our digital watches go off, signaling that we need to meet up with the crew.

"Really?" she huffs, mashing the off button. "The one time I actually want to have a conversation with you and I get interrupted three times."

I can't resist the obvious pun. "Talk about shitty timing."

She attempts a glower but quickly loses the battle and succumbs to a half smile as we gather our trash and mugs. "It's a good thing you're—"

"Intelligent? Witty? Incredibly handsome?"

Her half smile ratchets into a full grin. "I was going to say, 'My one hope of winning a million dollars or I'd leave your butt here.'"

"You'd miss my butt too much to leave it here."

"Maybe I'll keep your butt and leave the rest of you here." She hooks her backpack on her shoulder and heads for the exit. I follow while slinging mine on.

"Is that so you can officially say your teammate is a total ass?"

"Pretty sure I already said that a few times at the beginning of the race."

"And now?" I untwist her strap as I fall into step beside her.

"Eh, I guess you're tolerable."

"So what I'm hearing you say is that I don't need to worry about you murdering me in my sleep anymore?"

Her eyes are bright with mischief when she glances up at me. "Murdering, no. Maiming is still on the table though."

I snort a laugh. "Good to know."

Today's crew is waiting for us outside the main entrance of the hotel. We usually meet about ten minutes before our start time to get everything situated before reading our clue, except I'm not quite ready to go out there yet. I snag Hartley by the arm and pull her off to the side.

"What you wanted to talk about—are you okay? Is it urgent? Because if it is, we can start a couple of minutes late."

She tips her head to the right as she studies me, the amusement on her face transforming into an expression of pleasant surprise. "I'm fine, and no, it's nothing that can't wait until tonight."

"You sure?"

"I'm having flashbacks from the pool last night," she quips. "It's a personal thing, but it's not urgent."

I hold her gaze for a moment, then nod. Personal is good. Maybe she wants to share more about her family or what she's been up to for the last six years. I need to as well, starting with the truth about my "chop shop" job. Just because it's not where I saw my life going doesn't mean I need to lie by omission. And if that discussion goes well, maybe it'll pave the way to staying in contact after the race is over.

"Thanks for checking, though." After a brief pause, she continues with, "If I didn't know any better, I'd think you were starting to care about me." Her tone is playful and sarcastic, but her death grip on her backpack straps says otherwise.

Does she *want* me to care about her? I mean, I could. It's not like it would be hard to do. I might even care a little bit already.

"As we recently established, you're my only chance at winning this race," I say, tapping her on the nose. "I'm just making sure my teammate won't be distracted all day."

"Did you—did you just boop me?"

I lean in, crowding her space and enjoying the hell out of the way her breath catches. "You know the rules, Miss Billings. A gentleman never boops and tells."

———

The one thing you can't prepare for in this race is the waiting.

Case in point: Our start time was 7:42 this morning, but our flight to Nepal doesn't take off until 12:30 in the afternoon. Hartley and I went from exhausted to energized after reading our first clue to tired all over again while we sat at the airport.

To keep from falling asleep, we decided to lay the groundwork for Operation: Elimination. The Bombshells were our first stop—obviously—and were in before Hartley could finish the first sentence of her pitch. They suggested a divide-and-conquer strategy to keep from being obvious that we're hatching a plan. They'd talk to the A Team and the Alaska Girls, who should land in Kathmandu about an hour before we do, and we'd talk to Old Bay and Kick Asspen.

According to Hartley, the universe fully supports our plan because of what our clue said this morning.

Fly to Kathmandu, Nepal. When you arrive, make your way to Swayambhunath Stupa to receive your next clue.

This leg features two new elements: a Shortcut and a Repeat.

THE SHORTCUT ALLOWS ONE TEAM TO BYPASS ALL CHALLENGES AND PROCEED DIRECTLY TO THE CHECKPOINT.
THE REPEAT REQUIRES ONE TEAM TO COMPLETE A CHALLENGE TWICE BEFORE RECEIVING THEIR NEXT CLUE.

"So whoever gets to the Repeat board first will put the Wise Guys up there," I say to Treva and Boyd.

"But what if they get to the board before any of us do?" Boyd asks.

Hartley gives him a reassuring smile. "That's not going to happen."

"You don't know that for sure," he says, crossing his arms over his chest.

I don't mean to chuckle out loud, but there's one thing Boyd doesn't know. "Hartley's a master manifester. I still haven't figured out how she does it, but if she says one of us will get to the board first, you can take that to the bank."

"Works for me," Treva says. "The sooner those disrespectful assholes are gone, the better." As one of the more even-keeled contestants, her rare use of a curse word only emphasizes the group's disdain for DeAngelo and Big Mike.

"It'd be nice not to hear them whine about the lack of McDonald's," Boyd adds.

I nod. "That's an excellent point. Also, be careful if you discuss the plan with the other teams so the Wise Guys don't overhear it."

"What plan? There's no plan," Treva says innocently. "We're all just chatting about how Boyd isn't a disgrace to his family."

"Huh?" My gaze darts between the two of them as I attempt to process the abrupt shift in conversation.

"I told you to let it go," he grumbles to Treva.

"Why would you be a disgrace to your family?" Hartley asks.

He sighs. "It's what they've told me since I graduated college."

"Is it because—" Hartley looks to me for . . . I don't know, moral support maybe? I offer an encouraging smile and she turns her attention back to Boyd. "—you're gay?" She winces when she says it, like that will soften the sting of her words.

"What? No. They couldn't care less about that. They're pissed because I refused to follow in my dad's oxford-covered footsteps like everyone else in the family. I haven't talked to them in almost a year."

"Oh thank god." Her whole body deflates with relief. "Because I'm not above mailing anonymous glitter bombs when we get back to the real world."

For the first time since we sat down with Kick Asspen, Boyd's lips curve upward at the corners. "I appreciate your creativity and support."

"I never became an official psychologist, but one thing I know is there's nothing wrong with cutting toxic people out of your life, even if they're family. Actually, *especially* if they're family because that just exacerbates the toxicity. A family's love should be unconditional, not transactional."

Three sets of eyes land on me, but it's Hartley's look of pride and awe that catches me off guard. Setting boundaries isn't revolutionary, and it's obvious that Boyd made the right decision in doing so. All I did was remind him of that.

Still, it feels damn good to be on the receiving end of that look.

"Court's right," Treva says. "And besides, you've got us in your corner now."

"An Xtreme family beats the hell out of a nepotism orgy any day," Hartley adds.

"Thanks, guys." Boyd sits up a little taller and relaxes his shoulders, then looks at me. "You're not bad for an unofficial psychologist."

"You should add that to your resume," Hartley teases. "Court Mueller, illegal chop shop manager, substitute teacher, and unofficial psychologist."

"Illegal chop shop manager?" Treva asks, brows climbing her forehead.

Playfully rolling my eyes at my would-be tattletale, I shake my head and decide to set the record straight. "When we were doing our team interviews back in Dallas, I mentioned that one of my jobs was a COO of a startup in the automotive industry."

"See?" Hartley grins with amusement as she lifts her palms upward. "That reeks of mafia chop shop."

"I mean . . . she's not wrong," Boyd says to me.

"Except she is, considering I'm not Italian and don't have a criminal record."

Hartley shrugs. "Non-Italians can be in the mafia, and maybe you just haven't been caught yet."

I breathe out a laugh as my jaw moves to the side. "It should disturb me that you've put this much thought into it."

"Are you some sort of venture capitalist?" Treva asks.

I flip back to my thoughts this morning about sharing personal information with Hartley. I didn't expect to include Kick Asspen as well, but I guess now's as good of a time as any.

"More like the opposite. Being a COO of a startup in the automotive industry is just the pretentious way of saying I manage the car wash my best friend owns. It's a long way from the career I planned on having, but life doesn't always work out the way we want it to."

There.

I said it.

And although it wasn't technically a lie to begin with, I feel better about coming clean. Slightly embarrassed, but better nonetheless. To my surprise, no one bats an eye. In fact, Hartley looks . . . excited?

"I used to *love* going to the car wash when I was a kid! I always felt like our car was the canvas and the soap was paint that the giant brushes could spread around."

Huh. "I never thought of it that way, but I can see that."

"The car wash was the only thing that calmed my youngest when she was a baby," Treva says. "For about eight months, I was on a first-name basis with the entire staff and had the cleanest car in town."

"Now that you mention it, a handful of our regulars are moms with little kids."

"Umm . . . while we're on the subject of jobs and curveballs from life, I wasn't entirely truthful either," Hartley says, wrinkling her nose. "I'm a painter, but for houses instead of canvases."

"As in murals?" I ask.

She shakes her head. "As in, I took over my dad's house-painting business after his accident because it turns out that being in a wheelchair makes it diffi-cult to climb a ladder."

"That's actually really sweet," Treva says.

"It's definitely not *my* thing, but I promised I'd stay and help."

"So why didn't you say that in the interview? I mean, I know why I wasn't forthcoming, but running your dad's business isn't anything to be embarrassed about."

She stares at her hands while she considers my question, finally responding with, "Self-preservation, basically. I figured the less you knew about me, the less ammunition you had during the race."

I almost laugh at the irony. She thinks I was the one looking for ammuni-tion, but she's the one who's had the power to destroy me this whole time.

CHAPTER 13
HARTLEY

Day 11—Nepal

The Shortcut is still in the clue box when we make it to the shrine called Swayambhunath Stupa, which tells us that the A Team and the Alaska Girls didn't use it. After reading the task, it's easy to see why.

"Does every country have a mathematical society, or is this a Nepal thing?" Alexis asks.

"Don't ask me, I'm allergic to numbers," Haylee replies, retrieving a challenge envelope from the box.

Court reaches around me and grabs an envelope for our team. "I can handle subbing for high school calculus in a small town, but there's no way I can hang with the Nepal Mathematical Society."

The Bombshells take a clue of their own and we spread out enough to get the required shot of each team reading it.

FORGE: CREATE A KUKRI KNIFE BLADE.
FORAGE: SEARCH A BAZAAR FOR INGREDIENTS AND COOK A FULL-COURSE
NEPALESE MEAL.

"So basically, do we want to rely on ourselves, or do we want to work with other people?" Court asks.

I've seen so many challenges go wrong when contestants get lost inside markets or can't find items. Add that to the unpredictability of cooking something we've never even seen before, and it becomes a recipe for disaster (no pun intended).

"I vote for relying on ourselves."

"Agreed."

I'm stuffing the clue in my fanny pack when Old Bay approaches. "What did you decide?" Kadeeja asks.

"We're forging.'"

"We're going to forage."

"That's because she's hungry," Haylee adds.

"How about you two?" Court says to the Bombshells.

They exchange a look before Gianna says, "We're not sure yet."

"Well, good luck, whatever you decide. We're gonna head out," Kadeeja says, hooking a thumb over her shoulder.

After waving them off, we join Gianna and Alexis, whose clue envelope is still sealed.

"Those work better when you open them," Court jokes.

"About that . . . ," Alexis says. "We're going to try the Shortcut."

His brows inch upward. "You're doing the math test?"

A smile slowly blooms on my face as I think back to my initial impression of them in Dallas and how over-the-top they've acted since then. "I freaking *knew it*!"

"Knew what?" Court asks.

"That the stereotypical bombshell thing was an act. Which you pulled off quite well, I might add."

Gianna shrugs. "It's pretty easy to show people what they expect to see."

Damn.

"That's a heavy statement, and one worth unpacking in a later discussion, but right now I want to know how you plan on passing this test."

She smiles and extends her hand. "Hi, I'm Gianna, PhD in biochemical engineering, adjunct professor, member of the Society of Cosmetic Chemists, two patents pending."

While I stand there gaping like a fish, Alexis points to Gianna and says, "Same as her."

Well.

Okay then.

———

"I'd like to go on record and say this is the last time I forge anything," I say two hours later. Court and I are drenched in sweat, I have a blister on my thumb, and we're only halfway finished with this damn knife blade.

"I'm trying to remind myself that we're not even making the whole thing but it's not helping much," he says.

During our demo, the team of bladesmiths showed us how to chisel the basic shape of the kukri blade from a piece of flat steel and then pound it with a six-pound hammer, all while making regular trips to the charcoal oven that's approximately a bajillion degrees to keep the steel hot. Once we're done with that, we'll hand it over to the bladesmiths so they can finish the knife-making process and they'll give us our next clue.

There's just one problem.

"What does it mean when you can't feel your arms?" It's my turn to wield the hammer while Court mans the metal tongs, except I've missed the last three times I've aimed for the blade.

"It means it's time for a break."

"Fabulous." The hammer falls to the packed dirt floor with a soft thud and I plop down beside it.

Court makes a quick detour to our backpacks to retrieve our water, then joins me, uncapping my bottle. "Can you hold this?"

"I think so." It takes a few seconds to get my fingers to cooperate, but I'm eventually able to down about half of the bottle while Court drains the rest of his.

"It's a good thing we didn't come to Nepal first," he says, swiping the back of his hand across his mouth in a move that's entirely too sexy given our current circumstances.

"Why's that?"

He draws his legs up and rests his arms on his knees. "Because this place is filled with knives, fires, and sledgehammers. You could've killed me three different ways in a matter of minutes."

"Damn," I say, fighting a smile. "Such a missed opportunity."

"You'll have to file a complaint with the production team when we get home."

Despite his lighthearted tone, his comment takes me back to day one and the scathing email I planned on sending to the casting team after the race ended. How was that only ten days ago? And if what Alexis said is true, why did Court let me think the worst of him this whole time? It's almost as if . . .

"You did the same thing as the Bombshells."

"I what?" Court asks, brows pushed together.

Shit. Do I ignore the fact that we're wearing mics and talk to him now or wait for tonight? Except there's no guarantee we'll be in a hotel room tonight, let alone in the same room, and maybe the rest of America will want to hear this too.

I take a fortifying breath and shift to face him.

"You let me use my assumption as the truth. The Bombshells did it as part of their strategy for the race, but I haven't figured out why you'd want to do the same thing."

His brows remain in place. "I'm not quite following you."

"Last night in the pool bathroom, Alexis said you didn't cheat on me and told me to ask you who the woman was at the gallery."

"Damn traitors," Court mutters to himself, though his small smile tells me there's no heat behind his words. "And I'm guessing this is what you wanted to talk about this morning?"

I nod. "That's why I couldn't sleep last night." Well, one of the reasons, but America doesn't need to know about my fantasy about Court in his swim trunks. "At first, I struggled with whether to believe her because they constantly flirted with you. It doesn't make sense that they'd want us to smooth things over if they were trying to get in your pants."

"So what made you believe her?"

"When I was drawing in my notebook at the Sydney airport, they mentioned the idea of you not being over me. When I look back, I realized that's around the time they stopped flirting. I guess it felt like they respected the possibility of us calling a truce and being friends and didn't want to get in the way of that."

It's Court's turn to nod. "Gianna talked to me about the breakup on the flight to Japan while you were sleeping. She said I should tell you the full story about Gallery Night."

"So why haven't you yet?" Of all the questions that have run through my head, this is the one I can't figure out. At any point, he could've set the record straight instead of allowing the first week and a half of the race to be unnecessarily miserable.

Court stares at the ground for several moments before checking his watch. "We should get back to work. Do you think you can hold the tongs?"

I flex my fingers and find them functioning better now that we've had a short break. "Yeah."

"Good." He rises and extends a hand to pull me onto my feet, then passes the tongs to me. "If we're going to stay ahead of the Wise Guys, we need to work while we talk."

———

We're drenched and a little muddy when we roll into our hotel room at almost two in the morning. My mind is still reeling from the day's events. Or is it the night's events? In any case, here's a recap:

1. Court brought his sister, Ella, to the art gallery.
2. I kind of yelled at him for continuing to make decisions for me (more on that in a moment).
3. Operation: Elimination backfired because the Alaska Girls' taxi driver took off with their backpacks, leaving Marcail and Stephanie without passports. In related news, Court agreed to stop teasing me about my fanny pack.

Anyway, the only plan that actually worked today was the Bombshells winning the Shortcut. Paul gave us the news on their behalf when we checked in, but Court, Gianna, Alexis, and I have decided to keep that under wraps. Everyone else thinks they came in first after catching a lucky break on the forage challenge.

And as far as me yelling at Court goes, it was more like me using his full name and refuting every stupid conclusion he's jumped to on my behalf. For example, he doesn't get to decide that I wouldn't believe him if he told me the truth about Ella, or that he's a failure because of something as ridiculous as his current profession, or that I wouldn't want to be friends with him for any other dumb reason his brain concocted.

Last I checked, I'm a grown woman who's completely capable of determining who I want to have in my life. I cemented my point by telling him I fully expect us to stay in contact with each other once the race is over whether he likes it or not.

"Since I got the first shower last time, it's your turn tonight," he says, kicking the door shut and toeing off his shoes.

After setting my shoes by his, I snag two hangers from the closet and pass one to him so we can hang our waterproof backpack covers to dry. Apparently, July is Kathmandu's rainiest month, a fact I wasn't upset about when Court and I finally finished that damn knife blade and got a chance to cool off courtesy of Mother Nature. The downside is that the rain continued all evening and we rolled into tonight's checkpoint looking like drowned rats.

Well, I did anyway. Court looked like he stepped off a photo shoot for an aquatic wear campaign.

"Do you need the bathroom before I shower?" I ask.

"Nah, I'm good." He peels off his wet shirt and drapes it over the back of the wooden chair next to the desk.

To keep from ogling him, I focus on chores. "I can do a load of sink laundry while I'm showering. Want me to add your shirt?"

"Sure," he says before glancing at his shorts. "Might as well save soap and give you this stuff too."

He grabs his shirt, makes his way to the bathroom, and emerges a few seconds later with a towel cinched around his waist. "I left everything in the sink, and I can do the next load so we're even."

At least that's what I think he said. It's hard to concentrate when every cell in my body is on fire. To be safe, I settle on a generic, "Mm-hmm," as he passes me on the way to his backpack. The view from behind is just as glorious as his front, especially when he bends down to retrieve his notebook and a pen.

Unfortunately, he stands up and turns around before I can avert my focus. Any hope of feigning casual nonchalance is dashed when his lips curve into a smirk that says, *I caught you red-handed.*

Payback is the only option now.

With my eyes locked on his, I reach for the hem of my tank top and wrestle it over my head. I'm wearing a black sports bra so it's not exactly a striptease, but Court immediately loses our staring contest when his gaze slinks down to my chest, my stomach, my legs. His throat moves in a thick swallow, and if it weren't for my thong, I'd up the ante and take my shorts off too.

I don't bother hiding my satisfied smile when his eyes finally meet mine again. Whether we both lost the game or won is up for debate, but regardless, I'm feeling victorious as I gather my toiletries and a change of clothes and head for the bathroom.

After dropping my shirt in the sink and starting the water for the shower, I allow the mental image of Court to keep me company while I undo my pigtail French braids and comb through my waves. The last time I saw him in a towel, he was a twenty-one-year-old college kid. Now he's a full-blown man with a smattering of hair on his pecs and a happy trail I'd surrender my last protein bar to touch.

How in the hell am I supposed to sleep six feet away from him tonight? With my luck, we'll co-star in the kind of sex dream that comes with real-life, full-body movements and I'll be forced to leave the race and stay in Nepal out of sheer mortification.

Then again, I could save my pride (and my shot at a million dollars) by taking matters into my own hands in the shower.

But first, laundry.

Court's already plugged the sink, so I flip the faucet handle, add the rest of my clothes to the pile, and reach for the packet of soap.

That isn't on the counter.

Or in my toiletry bag.

Or anywhere else in the bathroom.

Which means if the dirty laundry walk of shame isn't already a thing, it's about to be.

———

The plan was simple: wrap myself in a towel (yes, I'm aware of the irony) and make a mad dash to my backpack for the soap.

Except.

EXCEPT.

I get two steps into the room and discover my sex dream has started without me. More specifically, I find Court on his bed, eyes closed and towel undone, working himself in long, steady strokes.

None of my Xtreme Quest research covered what to do when you walk in on your ex-boyfriend jerking off. Logic says I should leave. Turn around and announce myself. Anything other than standing here like a horny voyeur, but instead I remain transfixed on the glorious sight in front of me. It's like the universe heard my thoughts in the bathroom and decided I could have my protein bar and eat it too.

Court grips the base of his shaft with his right hand while his left slides up to the head, twisting and squeezing in a way I can somehow feel between my thighs even though I'm still across the room.

As he increases the pace, his breathing becomes louder and more pronounced. I can feel that too, just below my ear where my skin prickles with a lethal combination of memory and need.

"Yes, baby. Just like that," he whispers.

His hand moves faster, and his hips thrust upward, triggering a fiery ache in my center that begs for release.

"Fuck, Hartley."

That is a fantastic idea.

Also, *he said my name*. Does that technically count as an invitation? Because I will RSVP to him so hard. And he is so. Very. Hard. I press my legs together and imagine it's my hand wrapped around him, coaxing the low, raspy growl from his lips. That it's my mouth causing the muscles in his thighs to flex and quake. That it's my body seated on top of him, bringing us closer and closer to the edge.

I'm so lost in my fantasy that it takes a few seconds to realize Court's staring at me. Rather than cover up or tell me to get the hell out of the room, he holds my gaze and resumes touching himself.

"I, uh . . . forgot . . . the thing." I wave a finger in the direction of my backpack. "The soap. For our clothes. I didn't mean to . . ." I stop there, because we both know whatever I say next would be a lie. I absolutely meant to, and I enjoyed every long, thick second of it.

His fist moves from base to tip and back down again, and I feel myself take a step in his direction. Then another. And another.

"Don't do something you're going to regret." His words are a warning, but his voice is all gravel and desire, and right now the only thing I'll regret is not taking off my towel and climbing on top of him.

So I do.

His gaze burns with arousal as I lower myself onto his upper thighs, achingly close to his cock. His hand stills, as if any movement while we're this close will destroy the final vestiges of his restraint.

"Last chance," he grits out, proving my point.

I lean forward, rocking against him, and splay my hands on his chest. "I need you to listen to me very carefully."

He nods.

"I admire and appreciate your respect for my consent, but if you don't fuck me in the next ten seconds, I'm going to die and you'll have to finish this race alone."

He shifts beneath me, an inch, maybe two, but the friction is enough to ignite the ache of desire between my legs. "We can't have that, can we?"

I shake my head, relishing the feral smile blooming beneath me. "It would violate at least five contractual agreements."

"And the producers would be pissed." He trades the grip on his cock for greedy handfuls of flesh on my hips, my ass, my thighs, each kneading touch a confirmation that he wants this as much as I do.

Emboldened by this discovery, I take over for him and press the base of his shaft against the wetness pooling between my legs. He rewards me with an ungodly sexy moan that causes my hips to grind against him while I jerk him off. "I'm glad you understand the severity of the situation."

"I am extremely understanding." His expert hands travel up my sides and around the front to massage my breasts and pinch my nipples in a way only he has ever mastered.

Arching into his touch, I return my palms to his chest and rock my hips faster and faster as I surrender to the slick friction we've created. How it can feel this good when he's not even inside me yet is anyone's guess. I should probably fix that, but then I'd have to stop what I'm . . . I'm . . .

"That's it, Hartley. Come for me."

High-pitched cries echo across the room as my body explodes from the inside out. I feel Court's arm wrap around my waist, increasing the friction, and my hips buck wildly against each surge of white-hot electricity. It's been years since an orgasm has rocked me like this—six, to be exact—but the confident look on Court's face tells me I won't be waiting long for the next one.

"Lift up."

Still floating somewhere between earth and oblivion, I happily obey and he rewards me again, this time by teasing my entrance, then sliding up to trace torturous circles around my clit. It's too much and not enough, which should be impossible, but so was the thought of sex with Court not even two weeks ago. Now we're naked on a bed in Nepal and I'm halfway to my second orgasm in as many minutes.

The only problem? He's still not inside me, so I take matters into my own hands—literally—and guide him there myself.

"Fuck," he says through clenched teeth as I sink down, inch by exquisitely hard inch.

He remains still once I'm fully seated on top of him and uses the pad of his thumb to resume his circles on my clit. If I were with anyone other than Court, I'd be embarrassed by the groans of pleasure he's coaxing out of me. Then again, if I were with anyone other than Court, I wouldn't be making these sounds in the first place because no one has ever been able to work my body like him.

I try to savor the moment. To remember the line of contrast where smooth abs meet that sexy-as-hell happy trail. To catalogue the sound of his throaty growls and grunts as he fights the urge to thrust his hips, but his thumb is moving too fast and my breaths are coming too fast and I'm coming again and *ohmygod, OHMYGOD.*

He anchors his hands around my waist and drives into me from below. By the feel of it, I'll have ten souvenir bruises tomorrow morning, if I even survive until then, because I'm *still* coming thanks to the pace and angle of Court's magical dick. My headstone will say HERE LIES HARTLEY. SHE ORGASMED TO DEATH.

Seconds later, his thrusts become erratic and he tumbles over the edge with a series of deep, guttural grunts. Boneless and wholly spent, I collapse on top of him and focus on regaining control of my lungs while his hands roam lazily up and down my back.

After I learned Court never cheated on me, my Scorned Brain took its neon cheater sign and went home. My Logical Brain, however, is currently pinching the bridge of its nose and sighing. Whatever. It can sit there waving its giant ball of attachment string and tapping its foot all night if it wants to. Just because I had sex with Court doesn't mean it has to be a *thing*, right?

Right.

I should clarify one small detail, though. Especially if we're going to have a repeat of tonight's lifesaving performance.

"There's no good segue for this, but I'm on the pill so you don't have to worry about the no condom situation."

"I know."

"You do?" I push up to look at him.

Hazy eyes and a sated smile greet me when he says, "You've left your toiletry bag open a few times."

Oh. That makes sense. "And all the tests we did for the race mean we're negative for everything."

"It does."

"Yep." I stupidly nod at my own response and then continue with more verbal diarrhea. "Also, I really was just coming to get the laundry soap. I had no idea you'd be . . . you know." I make a circle with my finger in the direction of his dick . . . which is still inside me. God, why is this so awkward? It's sex. Something we've done hundreds of times before. Who cares if my exceedingly long dry spell means I'm a little out of practice? Court obviously had no complaints. Or maybe he did and he's just being nice. In that case—

"Hey."

"Hmm?" I say to the pillow.

"Please look at me."

I reluctantly slide my gaze to the right, but only because he asked nicely.

"I can hear you thinking."

"What? I'm not—"

"Hartley," he says, squeezing my upper thighs.

The gesture is as sexy as it is comforting, which makes it a little easier to give him my eyes again.

"I know you didn't purposely barge in on me, and in case you couldn't tell, I enjoyed the hell out of that."

"Thank god, because it's been a few years for me and I was afraid—"

This time he cuts me off by bringing his finger to my lips. "Here's what we're gonna do. We're going to get off this bed, take care of the laundry, and get in the shower."

I swallow. "Together?"

"Together. I'm not done with you yet."

CHAPTER 14
COURT

Day 12—On the way to Egypt

Standings after leg 6, Nepal

1. Bombshells (Gianna and Alexis) Shortcut*

2. A Team (Mitchell and Kennedy)

3. Old Bay (Haylee and Kadeeja)

4. Kick Asspen (Treva and Boyd)

5. Us

6. Wise Guys (DeAngelo and Big Mike) Repeat*

7. ~~Alaska Girls (Stephanie and Marcail)~~

"**A**ct natural," I whisper to Hartley as we near our gate.

"I am acting natural."

"You have a shit-eating grin on your face for no reason."

Her smile grows impossibly wider. "I assure you it is *not* for no reason."

Okay, that's fair, but still. "They're going to figure us out. If you can't stop grinning, we at least have to walk farther apart."

"You're being ridiculous."

"I'm being cautious. There's a difference."

She rolls her eyes but adds a few feet between us.

We finally sacked out around eight this morning and managed to get about four hours of sleep before we had to meet the crew downstairs. As Hartley says, we can always sleep on the plane.

The same can't be said for anything else we did before the sun rose.

I actually thought I was hallucinating when I first saw her watching me last night. After a grueling day, I was dehydrated, exhausted, and ready to crash for the night.

Until our game of strip laundry, that is.

In my defense, getting out of my dirty clothes and into a towel was purely about logistics because it made no sense to put clean clothes on when I hadn't showered yet. I didn't expect her to look at me like I was her next meal, and I damn sure didn't expect her to throw gasoline on the fire.

Should I have waited to jack off until it was my turn in the bathroom? Yes, except I was powerless against the defiant little smirk she unleashed as she took off her shirt. Then I started thinking about whether *she* was in the bathroom touching herself, and jacking off became a need rather than a want.

I was halfway to my release when she came back into the bedroom, but there was no point in trying to cover up since we both knew what I was doing. In fact, mutual masturbation used to be one of our favorite methods of foreplay.

And then she climbed on my bed and came on my cock and I spent the rest of the night worshipping her body in all the ways I've fantasized about since the race started. Not being able to touch her for the next who knows how many hours is going to be hell.

"Hey guys," Hartley says to Treva, Boyd, Haylee, and Kadeeja, who are sitting in a row of chairs near the window. We sit across from them, and I put a chair between me and Hartley for good measure.

The girls greet us with smiles and hellos, but Boyd's is more of a flat grunt than an actual word.

Hartley looks to Treva, who waves a dismissive hand at her teammate. "Don't mind him. He's grumpy because he didn't sleep well."

"I'm not grumpy because I didn't sleep well," he interjects with a pointed finger before recrossing his arms. "I'm grumpy because of why I didn't sleep well."

"What happened?" Hartley asks.

Fighting to keep a straight face, Treva says, "Our neighbors kept him awake."

"Were they fighting?"

Kadeeja clamps her lips between her teeth and shakes her head while Haylee gives him a conciliatory pat on the knee.

"Apparently, poor Boyd couldn't sleep because the people in the room next to him were up all night getting it on."

I know for a fact that Hartley and I didn't see anyone from the race in the lobby, elevator, or hallway when we were going to and from our room so there's no possible chance that Boyd knows it was us. Or maybe it wasn't, and two couples were having an all-night sex fest?

"Four times. *Four times*!" he says, hands flailing out and falling to his lap with a loud slap. "They'll probably have to pay for the headboard."

Okay, it could've been us. If so, it was technically five times—once was in the shower—and the headboard was intact when we left.

"And that wasn't even the worst part," he continues. "I think they were into some dom-sub stuff because I kept hearing her yell, 'Lord.' It was so annoying."

Yeah, that was definitely us, except that Hartley was screaming *Court*, not *Lord*. I steal a quick glance to gauge her reaction and relax when I see she's listening with amusement rather than embarrassment.

"Well *I* slept like a log, but someone here"—Treva pokes Boyd in the shoulder, eliciting another grunt from her teammate—"was too stubborn to take melatonin and use my essential oils. Maybe next time he'll listen."

"I think it's romantic," Kadeeja says wistfully. "I mean, spending the whole night with someone who has moves and stamina like that? We should all be so lucky." She fans herself with her hand for effect.

"For real. Maybe they were on their honeymoon," Haylee adds, waggling her brows.

Still scowling, Boyd crosses his arms again. "Well whoever they were, they should tone it down or pass out some earplugs."

"I'm sorry you didn't get any sleep, Boyd, but I have to admit I'm with Kadeeja on this one," Hartley says. "That sounds like an amazing way to spend the night."

I hide my laugh behind a cough while they exchange high fives because only Hartley could fess up without actually fessing up.

"Also, you're forgetting the very best part about today," she continues.

"You mean besides not having to listen to Mr. and Mrs. Headboard anymore?"

"Yes, besides that," she playfully huffs. "Where are we going?"

Hartley's question cues Boyd's first smile of the day. He loosens his arms and sits up a little. "Egypt."

"Cairo freakin' Egypt," she says, tapping his knee to emphasize each word. "And you can borrow my eye mask and sleep on the plane."

———

I grew up believing I'd been cursed by Isaac Newton.

I realize this sounds ridiculous but stay with me.

My mom was a science teacher and loved showing us that science is everywhere. The grocery store. The bathtub. The airport. Great Smoky Mountains National Park. While other kids were listening to superhero stories before bed, Mom was reading Magic School Bus books. I could tell you who Marie Curie was before I knew how to tie my shoes.

In elementary school, she started talking about this guy named Isaac Newton who saw an apple fall from a tree and used that to basically change the world. When I got older, she told me all about his laws of motion and how they applied to everyday life. She was big on that stuff—connecting lessons to things we did on a daily basis so we'd remember them—and it worked.

It was also annoying.

I mean, sometimes a kid just wants to play baseball without hearing about inertia and acceleration and all the other things some dead guy wrote about three hundred years ago. Especially when there were more important things to discuss with his teammates, like whether Eliza Van Allen was wearing a real bra and who had the newest cheat codes to *Intergalactic Apocalypse Three*.

You know . . . real baseball talk.

So when it was Mom's turn to work the Gatorade table at practice and she started up on every action having an equal and opposite reaction and that's how baseballs are hit and blah blah blah, I said, out loud and straight from the diaphragm, "No one gives a shit about Isaac Newton."

I was thirteen.

And grounded.

And officially in the crosshairs of the Father of Physics himself.

Among the mounds of empirical data I've collected over the years, I present the following:

Bobby Gallagher moved away and I finally became the starting pitcher . . . and then I broke my arm and was out for the rest of the season.

I saved money for almost two years to buy a car . . . and a week later the transmission died.

I planned a picnic date with my high school girlfriend . . . and had to ditch everything and drive her to the emergency room when she got stung by a bee and nearly stopped breathing. (She was fine after a dose of epinephrine and some fluids.)

Then there was the time I cooked dinner for a different girlfriend . . . and we both got food poisoning.

So there you go. Concrete proof of my "every action has an equal and opposite reaction" curse. To be honest, I thought it'd struck again in Dallas because why else would my once-in-a-lifetime chance to win a million dollars rest in the hands of the woman who hated me most? But then things started going well between us, and the possibility of coming in first place didn't seem so far-fetched anymore.

Which is exactly why I should have seen Isaac Newton coming.

————

We arrive in the City of a Thousand Minarets just after 10 p.m. Boyd, fresh off a half-dozen hours of sleep, is in a much better mood. Giddy, even, if it's possible to describe a twenty-nine-year-old man as such.

I can't say I blame him though.

Cairo is mind-boggling.

There are people everywhere doing all matter of people things—shopping, dining, running errands—even though we're approaching midnight. Hartley described it as "bustling," but that's like calling a tornado "breezy."

Now we're looking for a clue box in Khan el-Khalili. Technically, it's a market in the heart of Cairo, but in reality, it's more like a sprawling labyrinth of narrow corridors stuffed with cafés, shops, and—you guessed it—more people.

Also, there's a decent chance we're already lost.

"Didn't we just pass this shop?" Treva asks.

Boyd hooks a thumb over his shoulder. "I think that was the other lantern vendor back there."

"It still feels like we're going in circles though."

"I wish we had a map," Hartley says, craning her neck over the crowd.

"The producers are probably counting on the fact that we don't." We've only been here for twenty minutes so it's not time to panic yet, but it is becoming obvious that we're essentially searching for a needle in a haystack. For all we know, we walked right by the clue box and didn't see it because the corridors are so packed. "What does our clue say again?"

Hartley unzips her fanny pack and removes the blue-and-orange envelope.

. . .

FLY TO THE CITY OF A THOUSAND MINARETS. WHEN YOU ARRIVE, MAKE YOUR WAY TO KHAN EL-KHALILI TO FIND YOUR NEXT CLUE.

"Damn. I was hoping they would've given us a hint."

"Where's the fun in that?" she says with a wry smile. "But on a positive note, we haven't seen the Bombshells or the A Team and they got here an hour before we did. Maybe that means it won't be that hard to find after all."

"Or it could mean they're on the other side of this maze just as lost as we are," Treva says. "Wait, where's Boyd?"

"He was just right here." I point to the now-vacant space at my left.

Hartley peeks into the adjacent shop.

"He couldn't have gone far." I look down both directions of the corridor and come up empty.

Hartley turns to the crew. "Did either of you see where he went?"

They shake their heads.

"Boyd?" Treva shouts into the din of the market.

"Don't worry, we'll find him," I say, still scanning our surroundings.

Hartley cups her hands around her mouth, but before she can call his name, he pops up on my left, grinning like an idiot as he holds up a clear plastic bag. "Look what I got!"

"Where the hell were you?" Treva says in her mom voice.

"Over there." Oblivious to the panic he created, he points to a wall of lanterns about ten feet behind me. "There's a food cart on the other side of that shop. I got enough for all of us and it was only a *dollar*!" He waves the bag again, and this time I get a better look at what's inside.

"Is that . . . a pita?"

"Aish baladi. I guess you could think of it as the pita's Egyptian, whole-wheat cousin. I've been dying to try it. Plus, I figured we could use a snack since it looks like we're going to be up for a while." He delves into the bag and passes one to each of us, including the crew, before biting into his with a hearty moan. "Ohmagoh. Ih amahing."

Hartley, Treva, and I have a silent conversation to the effect of:

Bread? Seriously?

He's worse than a two-year-old.

Do we say thank you or wring his neck?

It is pretty good, though. I'll give him that.

Treva tells Boyd to lead the way when we set out again, probably so he stays within eyesight, and we continue working our way through the market. A few minutes in, we hear an American voice shouting, "Make a hole!" behind us. A second later Big Mike and DeAngelo run past us, shoving me into a rack of clothing. I narrowly avoid knocking it over but roll my left ankle in the process.

"Court! Are you okay?" Hartley's arms are around me in an instant, steadying me as I regain my footing.

"Yeah."

"Are you sure?"

I wiggle my foot and ignore the pain firing through my ankle. "I'm fine. But more importantly, they're either running toward a McDonald's or someone told them where the clue box is. I vote we follow them."

Boyd shrugs. "We don't have any other leads."

Treva and Hartley nod their agreement, so we pick up a jog and do our best to dodge oncoming pedestrians while keeping the Wise Asses in our sights.

Well, *they're* doing their best. I'm just trying to keep up because fuck, this hurts.

"Why don't we slow down a little," Hartley says, eyeing me.

"We don't have time to slow down," I say.

We can assume the Bombshells and the A Team are already onto the next clue, but we haven't seen Old Bay since we left the airport. If they beat us to the box, that means we're in the back of the pack with the Wise Guys and Kick Asspen.

Not a great place to be, especially with an injury.

"We also don't have time to make your ankle worse," she continues. "Maybe we should have the medic look at you."

"You're annoyingly persistent."

"You're annoyingly stubborn."

I smile, despite the throbbing in my ankle. "Pretty sure those are synonyms."

"Pretty sure—"

"There's the box." Boyd points to where the Wise Asses have stopped long enough to toss something on the ground, snag a clue, and take off again.

Treva frowns when she picks up a wad of paper a few seconds later. "I guess not littering in a foreign country is too much to ask."

"Assholes," Hartley mutters. "What is it?"

Treva unfurls the paper, revealing a crudely drawn clue box and something written in Arabic at the top. "They must've been asking locals if they'd seen it."

"I hate having to admit that's not a bad idea," Boyd says.

"All that matters is it worked in our favor." I open the clue box and exhale my relief when I see three envelopes inside. Boyd and I each take one and we move off to the side to read them.

Travel on foot to Bab al-Futuh to find your next clue.

Shit. I guess Ol' Isaac isn't quite done with my ankle yet.

CHAPTER 15
HARTLEY

Day 13—Egypt

There is an eighty-four percent chance I'm going to murder the Wise Asses before we leave Egypt.

It's one thing for me to talk about maiming Court. I earned that right as part of the Standard Exit Clause that comes with a breakup. (It's in section 2.A., after *The Breakup-er hereby sacrifices any belongings in the Breakup-ee's possession at the time of the breakup*.)

But after barreling into us and injuring Court, the only right the Wise Asses have earned is to sit on a cactus. A huge one with spiny ribs and thorns and cute little flowers on the tips. I'd even volunteer my hairbrush at this point.

Needless to say, Operation: Elimination is still in full swing.

Also, Court never asked for a medic.

Shocking, I know.

Our clue at Bab al-Futuh instructed us to take an overnight train to Luxor. We still had one team behind us when we got to the station, but waiting for a medic would've meant missing the next departing train and Court didn't want to lose our buffer. It was hard to argue with that logic, especially considering he'd be off his foot for the next nine hours.

Oddly, our room in the sleeper car is taller than it is wide. Two beds are anchored to the left wall and there's a tiny sink and vanity on the right. The last thing we need is Court on a bunk ladder, so I sling my backpack onto the upper bunk and say, "You get bottom."

With a smile as quick as it is mischievous, he drops his bag somewhere behind him and tugs me to his chest. "You like it when I'm on bottom." One hand goes around my neck and the other on my jaw. "And on top." He swipes his thumb across my lower lip. "And from behind, if I remember correctly."

Sweet mother of Pablo Picasso.

"You have an excellent memory."

I sound entirely too breathy for someone who had all of her faculties a few seconds ago, but that was before Court was tilting my chin up and brushing his lips against mine, so it's obviously not my fault.

"Do you know how hard it was not to touch you all day?" he murmurs.

I reach between us and run my hand over the thickening bulge in his shorts. "I have a pretty good idea."

The low rumble in his chest becomes a sharp hiss when the train lurches forward, shifting my body weight into Court.

"Shit, I'm sorry. Are you okay?"

"Yeah. Just caught me off guard."

Way to go, Hartley. How about you just stomp on his ankle next time? I step back to avoid another mishap when he pulls me to him again and says,

"Stop beating yourself up."

"I wasn't."

"You were." To prove his point, he touches my furrowed brow and the corners of my downturned lips.

"I just feel bad for hurting you. I planned on making you sit down and prop your foot up as soon as we got in here, but then I got distracted by all your"—I circle my finger in front of his body—"and forgot."

"All my what?"

I fight to maintain my pout because I really do feel bad for hurting him, but it's impossible when I'm in point-blank range of his adorable, amused smile. "All your sexiness. It scrambles the brain."

"I see. And, if it makes you feel any better, you were right."

"About what?"

He lowers himself to his bunk and pulls me onto his lap. "I should be sitting."

Now here's the thing about wardrobes for Xtreme Quest: It's all decided by how well it packs and how well it layers with other items. Generally speaking, the rule is, the thinner and more breathable, the better. So when my hips instinctively rock forward, I quickly learn there isn't much difference between now and last night because I can feel *everything* underneath Court's athletic shorts.

He captures my moan in his mouth, then twists his fingers in my hair and deepens our kiss while I silently thank whoever invented synthetic fabric.

"I have wanted you all damn day," he says when we finally break apart.

"Same." I spread my knees, sinking further down, and revel in the appreciative groan he gives me.

"I can already feel how wet you are."

"So much for moisture-wicking thongs, right?"

"I don't think they included this type of testing in the product development stage."

"At least the material is nice and silky. Makes for great grindability."

"Is that even a word?"

"You tell me," I say, swirling my hips over the impossibly hard bulge in his shorts.

"It's definitely a word."

We're both smiling when our lips come together again. I've always loved that about sexy time with Court. Just because we're in the throes of passion doesn't mean we can't have fun.

Also . . .

"I'm already close."

"Yeah?"

I nod as an exquisite ache builds between my legs. "I told you, it's the grindability. And that flexing thing you're doing."

"This?" He raises his hips an inch each time I rock back.

"Yep. It maximizes the dick-to-clit friction ratio. Very effective."

"What if we added another element to your ratio?"

"Like what?"

Grinning wickedly, he slips a hand into my shorts and glides his finger along the crack of my ass.

"Ohhhkay," I moan. "Yes, I see the value of analyzing this new element for mathematic and scientific purposes."

"Anything for research."

"Exactly."

Desperate for more of whatever he's doing, I arch my back to give him better access.

"The subject seems to like this ratio," he says in a researcher voice.

"The subject loves this ratio," I reply in a pre-orgasmic, scrabbling-for-breath, non-researcher voice.

He gently presses a finger against the tight muscle, and I let out a squeal of pleasure when the tip slides in.

"Early testing of this element shows promise for future experiments."

"So. Much. Promise." I anchor my arms around his neck and writhe against his cock, feeling him below me and behind me and everywhere else too.

"That's it, baby. Ride me until you come." His researcher voice is now a sexy, gravelly, lust-filled voice an inch from my ear, and I explode on a silent scream. While my body takes orbit in a mathematical nirvana, Court whispers things like,

"Good girl."

And,

"You're so fucking sexy."

And,

"I love watching you come."

All while doing that hip-flex thing and gently massaging my ass though the aftershocks.

I am now literal putty in his hands.

"We're gonna need to take a water break," I say to the hollow of his neck a minute later.

"Oh yeah?"

"Mm-hmm. Any good researcher knows you have to complete the experiment multiple times."

———

Rested is hardly the word I'd use to describe ourselves when we roll into Luxor, but we did spend a few hours horizontal without having sex, so at least there's that. Also, I managed to get two doses of ibuprofen into Court and his ankle looks more like an apple than a grapefruit. As long as we can keep his activity to a minimum today, I think he'll be back to normal in another day or two.

Our first stop is Luxor Temple. We're still racing with Boyd and Treva, who shared an essential oil blend earlier this morning that she swears helped her through a sprained ankle at mile forty-two of an ultramarathon. Court mentioned something about defeating Isaac Newton and said he'd take all the help he could get. This also includes manifesting, which means no one is allowed to mention his injury because according to him, his ankle is "just fine."

Anyway, Luxor Temple is about ninety-four percent less crowded than Khan el-Khalili and doesn't sell food, so we're far less worried about losing

Boyd, who is, dare I say . . . *delighted*. Seriously. I've never seen him smile as much as I have in the last ten minutes. The man has talked in exclamation points since we got here, and you know what? I can't blame him at all.

Luxor Temple is truly something to behold.

As we move through the ruins, we get what Boyd calls the "ten-cent tour," which is more like a rundown of facts he's learned from years of doing school projects on Egypt. Court's even able to add a few courtesy of his time as a substitute. The best I could do was reciting a few of my favorite lines from *The Mummy*, and Treva just kept reminding us to stay on task and look for the clue box.

We eventually find it nestled in the Sanctuary. Boyd's disappointment at having to leave the temple is short-lived when he sees where we're going next.

TAKE A WATER TAXI TO THE WEST BANK, THEN MAKE YOUR WAY TO QV66.

"Holy shit," Boyd whispers when we reconvene after reading the clue for the cameras.

"What's QV66?" I ask.

He glances at the clue again, and this is when I notice his hands are literally shaking. "The tomb of Queen Nefertari. Remember the statues of Ramses II at the entrance to the temple?"

I nod.

"This is his wife. Her tomb is known as the Sistine Chapel of Ancient Egypt."

"Holy shit," I whisper.

———

The Valley of the Queens is incredibly, astonishingly . . . *beige*. Fifty shades of it, as if antiquity knew to save all of Egypt's colors for what lies below the surface.

I'm buzzing by the time we jog up the dirt path toward Queen Nefertari's tomb, partly because of what I'm about to see, but mostly from the circles Court traced on the back of my neck with his thumb on the drive out here.

It reminded me of our ride to the airport in Dallas on day one—how wonderful and awful it'd felt being crammed in the back seat together. How

I'd analyzed every touch, wondering whether it was intentional. How difficult it'd been to maintain a façade of imperviousness.

For the record, that last one is still a challenge because now those touches *are* intentional and I'm freshly and acutely aware of how skilled his hands are. I spent the final minutes of this morning's drive staring at the sea of beige outside and trying not to look like I was praying we'd have a hotel room tonight.

Which I totally was.

"Is this it?" Court asks when we reach the tomb.

"Boyd said it wouldn't look like much."

"I wonder if they beat us here."

"Guess we're about to find out."

The small, dome-shaped entrance is as underwhelming as everything else in the valley, and the plain metal door at the bottom of the staircase looks more like an entrance to an underground club in New York City than an ancient burial site.

But the threshold is where the similarities end.

Actually, threshold isn't even the right word. This is a portal into Egypt more than three thousand years ago.

I gasp when I reach the bottom step and get my first glimpse of the floor-to-ceiling artwork celebrating Nefertari's life and her journey to the world beyond.

"How is this even real?" I whisper.

Court's hands come around my hips, ushering me the rest of the way into the chamber to make room for the crew. "I'm wondering the same thing."

Together we move into the adjacent room, where we find two-dimensional depictions of gods and goddesses and offerings and livestock, each with a table of food. I curl my fingers into my palms to keep from reaching out and touching the walls. It's no wonder Boyd practically wept earlier, or that people dedicate their lives to the study of ancient Egypt.

"I think this is a good time for one of your five-second appreciation breaks," I say.

Court breathes out a laugh as he marvels at our surroundings. "We're gonna need a lot longer than that."

Everything in the tomb—each image, each color, each design—is steeped in symbolism and has been carefully placed by skilled artists to create a storybook on stone. The Sistine Chapel comparison makes sense now. Even the ceiling—*ohmygod the ceiling*. I pause halfway down the next staircase to take in the sea of tiny yellow stars painted on a backdrop of deep blue.

"Reminds me of your bedroom," Court says behind me. "Except that we can't make any wishes on these."

I smile at the memory of sticking glow-in-the-dark stars on my ceiling on our first date. For some reason his kept coming down, which turned into a joke about wishing on falling stars. We must've made two dozen wishes that night.

"That's because they know how to use sticky tack."

He laughs to himself as we continue down the stairs and into the next room. "So do I."

"Says the guy whose stars kept coming down."

"Says the guy"—he steps forward, just shy of invading my space but close enough for me to feel his intensity—"who wanted an excuse to make more wishes."

I watch him swallow and then do the same. "And did they come true?"

His eyes lose focus over my shoulder and he's quiet for a good five seconds. I'm about to tell him never mind when he sighs and says, "There's no 'they.'"

"What do you mean?"

"It was the same wish every time." Then, quieter, he adds, "I'm not sure that it'll ever come true."

Something in my heart twists at the somberness in his voice. Without thinking, I reach for his hand and squeeze. "Well, whatever it is sounds important, so I hope it does one day."

He returns his gaze to me, eyes sweeping across my face like he's searching for an answer to a question neither of us has asked. "I do too."

CHAPTER 16
COURT

Day 13—Egypt

I t helps to have friends in high places.

Specifically, it helps to have an alliance with actual geniuses who are currently in first place.

Today's team challenge had us choose between "Dictate" (memorizing a five-minute script and giving a museum tour) and "Translate" (decoding text from the Book of the Dead). We opted for the latter because sometimes a guy (who doesn't have an injury) feels like sitting down.

We got to the university as the Bombshells were leaving. It's the first time we've seen them since Nepal, and after taking one look at us, they had a silent conversation involving eyebrow raises and head nods and pulled us to the side to give us the answer. For context, it took them an hour and a half to translate the hieroglyphs, so this was a Very Big Deal.

The only catch? We had to do a little acting first.

And . . . scene:

I flip through our packet of hieroglyphs and decoding charts and sigh dramatically. "This is stupid."

"Just keep trying. We've almost got the first word." Hartley points to the paper we've written nothing on.

"But look how many words are left. At this rate, we're gonna be here all day."

Mitchell and Kennedy peek at us from their table across the room. The Bombshells said they got here about forty-five minutes ago and have struggled to make progress. Our goal is to get them to leave this challenge and go to the other one, thus wasting more time and increasing their odds of coming in last.

And if you're thinking this sounds a little Operation: Elimination-ish, you'd be right—but that's because the Bombshells learned the A Team has an alliance with the Wise Asses.

A lot, apparently, has happened since yesterday. Gianna and Alexis promised to give us the full scoop as soon as we catch up with them.

"It's been ten minutes," Hartley whispers.

"We're getting nowhere. Can we please go to the other challenge?"

She frowns at the packet. "I guess memorizing English words would be a lot easier than translating Egyptian symbols."

"That's what I tried telling you before." I lift my hands and let them fall to the table with a loud slap.

"Okay, okay, will you stop being Mr. Grumpypants now?"

Kennedy coughs to cover up a laugh and I bite down on the inside of my cheek to do the same. That was *not* part of the script.

"If you get me the hell out of this room, then yes. No more Mr. Grumpypants."

We stand up and Hartley shuffles our papers, bringing the one with the answer to the top. "Let's give this back to the instructor and tell him we're leaving."

As I hook my backpack onto my shoulder, Mitchell and Kennedy huddle together and start whispering.

I think it's working, I mouth to Hartley.

This is confirmed a few minutes later when the A Team comes barreling out of the building.

"Don't let that taxi follow us," Hartley says to our driver as we leave the parking lot.

"No problem."

When we reach the road, she checks the clue again.

ASK MARSAM'S EMPLOYEES FOR THE WATER BUFFALO TO RECEIVE YOUR NEXT CLUE.

. . .

"And you're sure it's a hotel?"

The driver shrugs. "It's the only Marsam I know."

Hartley turns to me with bunched brows. "Why would a hotel have a water buffalo?"

———

It turns out Marsam really is a hotel, and water buffalo milk ice cream is a thing.

It's actually pretty good, although Egypt's summertime temperatures may have something to do with how much we enjoyed it. Now we're heading to the solo challenge. The envelope from Marsam asked, "Who wants to rest in piece?" so I volunteered thinking I'd be doing some sort of puzzle while sitting down. An easy task for someone whose ankle doesn't hurt, right?

Wrong.

Because of course this isn't a regular puzzle.

GO TO THE LOTUS ALABASTER WORKSHOP. WHEN YOU COMPLETE A FIVE-BY-TEN-FOOT PUZZLE, YOU WILL RECEIVE YOUR NEXT CLUE.

When we arrive, Hartley and I drop our backpacks on the ground and peer out at the literal chunks of stone that have been cut into puzzle pieces. I'm already not excited.

"Did it work?" Alexis asks.

Hartley grins. "It did, and Court and I are now nominated for best actor and actress." As the Bombshells exchange a high five, she turns to me. "Is your foot going to hold up to this? Your right one I mean, since we've established that your left one feels great."

"What's wrong with your foot?" Gianna asks.

"Big Mike plowed into him at the market last night and he rolled his ankle."

I wave a hand through the air. "It'll be fine. It's not even swollen anymore."

Well, as long as you have bad lighting and don't get too close.

"And now Court's manifesting his healing. According to him, he's the picture of health."

Gianna glances at my foot and eyes me skeptically. "How about we manifest this puzzle instead?"

I follow her over to our workspaces, which are spread out in a dirt field in two rows of three. What we have includes a wooden frame in the dimension of the finished product, a massive pile of alabaster blocks, and gloves.

What we don't have? Any idea of what we're supposed to be making, because of course we didn't get a picture to work from. My best guess is a desert scene based on the overwhelming amount of khaki on the face of each piece. After a brief discussion, we decide to finish unstacking Gianna's pieces and sorting the edges. After that, we'll do the same for mine and start building our respective puzzles.

"So how'd you find out about the A Team's alliance?" I ask.

"Remember how we won the Shortcut in Nepal?"

"Yeah."

"They upgraded our room and gave us certificates for a free massage. We were heading down to the spa when Mitchell and Kennedy checked into the hotel and we overheard them. I might've had a really hard time tying my shoe long enough to learn the Wise Guys approached them in New Zealand."

I pause my unstacking to look at her. "But they agreed to help eliminate them at the airport in China."

"Exactly. And now the Wise Guys know about the plan."

Shit.

"That's probably why that asshole ran me over."

"Wouldn't surprise me. The good news is, Old Bay has doubled down on Operation: Elimination, and Kick Asspen probably will too as soon as we can talk to them. The plan is to help each other as much as possible in the next leg or two to make it harder for the A Team and the Wise Guys to stay in the race."

"Hey, thanks again for helping us earlier. Hartley was worried about being farther back in the pack after last night's hit-and-run, so this is a huge help."

"Speaking of Hartley . . ."

I glance over and find her laughing at something Alexis is saying. It's nice to see her relaxed and enjoying herself compared to the day Gianna and I worked on the mosaic challenge together—which, now that I think about it, feels like a month ago rather than last week.

It's strange how time flies when you let go of old grudges and have a few orgasms.

As I turn my attention back to the stack of rocks, I catch Gianna staring at me with an amused smile.

"What?" I ask.

"You know exactly *what*," she teases as we cross paths.

"I'm just sorting the world's most annoying puzzle pieces."

"And making ga-ga eyes at your teammate."

Stifling a smile of my own, I return to the stack for another load. "I'm making regular eyes at everything but these damn rocks."

She points eastward and says, "Denial is right over there if you want to go for a quick swim."

"With this heat, I actually wouldn't mind that if it weren't for the crocodiles."

"Good point. Hartley wouldn't be happy if you lost any dangly bits."

I cough out a strangled laugh and nearly drop the puzzle piece I'm carrying. "Did you just refer to my manhood as 'dangly bits'?"

"Did you just refer to your manhood as your 'manhood'?"

"I was trying to be polite, and you sound so much like my sister right now."

"I like her already."

"I can't believe I'm saying this, but I actually miss her."

"Do you see her often?"

"Yeah, she still lives in Green Valley, not far from my house. Well"—I shrug— "everything's not far in Green Valley but you get the point."

"Did you ever tell her the truth about your breakup?"

"No." I set the final stone on the ground and rise. "I guess I'm going to have to come clean to her and my parents so they don't find out in the first episode with the rest of America."

Not that I expect a lecture or anything. It's been so long that I doubt Mom and Dad would care much, and Ella's only complaint will probably be that I let a broke community college student spend forty bucks in gas to come nurture me in a crisis I created. Note to self: repay her when I break the news.

Despite her earlier teasing, Gianna's more cautious when she asks, "Do you think you and Hartley will stay in touch after the race is over?"

I let my eyes wander to where she's sitting as I recall our discussion at the bladesmith. My favorite part was when she said we were exchanging numbers when we got our phones back *or else*, and that if I stopped responding, she'd drive to Green Valley and paint my house pink. I considered doing it just to see if she'd come.

"She said she wants to be friends."

"Is that what you want too?"

My gaze swings back to Gianna. "To be friends?"

"To be *just* friends."

"Sure, why not?" I head over to my section and grab the top rock off the closest stack. If we keep up the pace we had before, we'll be manifesting this puzzle in about ten minutes.

"Maaaybe"—she aims a pointed look at me—"because being friends with someone you have feelings for is actually pretty hard."

"Who says I have feelings for her?"

"Now you're insulting my intelligence."

"You really do sound like my sister," I mutter, which makes her smile.

"All I'm saying is it's my literal job to understand the properties of bonds." She stops in front of me and rests her hands on her hips. "I also know what it's like to be afraid to take another chance on something that backfired. But when you revisit a formula and fix those things you missed the first time . . . or in my case, the first eighteen times," she adds with a laugh, "you can get some pretty incredible results."

———

Standings after leg 7, Egypt

1. Bombshells (Gianna and Alexis)
2. Us
3. Old Bay (Haylee and Kadeeja)
4. Kick Asspen (Treva and Boyd)
5. A Team (Mitchell and Kennedy)
6. Wise Guys (DeAngelo and Big Mike)

*Non-elimination leg

Yes, you read that right.

We came in second.

And the Wise Guys were last.

And it was a non-elimination leg and they're still here. Hartley compared them to cockroaches, but honestly, that's an insult to cockroaches.

The non-elimination leg also meant we kept racing, so for the second night in a row, we didn't have a hotel room. We didn't even have a bed. Instead, we slept on the airport floor with a foam sleeping pad and a sleeping bag courtesy of the production team.

Other highlights of our airport accommodations included:

- Washing up in the bathroom sink,
- Listening to Big Mike and DeAngelo whine about not getting the "real Egyptian experience" because we didn't ride a camel,
- Listening to them tell everyone about going to McDonald's in Cairo *and* Luxor, and
- Losing our lead because we were all on the same flight to Athens, Greece.

But in better news, my ankle is less purple today, and Hartley and I are getting an upgraded hotel room and a day off from racing . . . right after we throw ourselves out of a perfectly good airplane.

The Shortcut was waiting for us in the clue box tucked inside a rental car office in the Athens airport. As fate or luck or manifestation would have it, we snagged seats right behind first class on the flight from Luxor, putting us in prime position for getting off the plane and reaching the box first.

Our conversation went like this:

Take one of the six marked rental cars and drive to Skydive Athens. If your team completes a jump from 14,000 feet, you can proceed directly to the checkpoint. If you don't jump, you must return to this box to receive your next clue.

"After New Zealand, this is probably the last thing you want to do," I say, returning the Shortcut to the box.

"I mean, in theory it's the same as bungee jumping and I was ready to do that again."

Wait, is she serious?

"And this would guarantee a first-place finish, not to mention an upgraded hotel room," she continues.

I nod in thought. "The crew did say this break will be eighteen hours instead of twelve."

"Just think of all the sink laundry we could do in eighteen hours."

"Four or five loads, at least."

She matches my mischievous smirk with one of her own and grabs the Shortcut. "Who's driving?"

So that's how we ended up in a matchbox-sized airplane with a jovial pilot, two tandem instructors whose hands our lives are now in, and two cameramen from Skydive Athens standing by to capture it all.

Am I scared? A little, but adrenaline and thinking about all the "laundry" we're going to do after the checkpoint are helping. Thankfully, Hartley's in better spirits than the day she bungee jumped, and I'm hoping like hell it's not because of the Adonis she's strapped to.

Literally—her instructor's name is Adonis, and he looks every bit the part of a Greek god. My instructor is a mortal named Philip, but he smells nice at least. When we reach fourteen thousand feet, he runs through the basics one more time: keep our heads back and grip the front straps of our harnesses when we exit, then assume the standard freefall skydive position when they tap our right shoulders.

Hartley's cameraman wastes no time opening the door and positioning himself. She gives me one last thumbs up and lets out an excited squeal as she scootches toward the exit with Adonis. After ensuring her head is against his chest, he nods once to the cameraman and then they're gone.

That's it.

The whole thing happens in less than five seconds.

Just as quickly, we're out the door and I'm face-to-face with the purest, bluest sky I've ever seen. I didn't even know blue came in this shade. I certainly haven't seen it during any of our flights, but maybe it only works when there's no plexiglass in between.

Another surprising discovery? We're plummeting to the earth at terminal velocity, yet it doesn't feel like we're falling at all. Resting on air would be a better description. Weird, right?

Philip taps my shoulder, so I spread my arms and spend the next forty-five seconds in euphoria. We spin in circles. We make silly faces for the cameraman. I wave hello and mouth, *Hi, Mom!* just in case this footage makes it on air. I spot Hartley's canopy just before Philip deploys our parachute. As soon as it opens, the deafening rush of wind is replaced by a gentle breeze, punctuated with Hartley's exuberant, "Woo!"

After getting us situated, Philip maneuvers our canopy toward her.

"Can you believe that?" she shouts, her grin taking up most of her face. "We just jumped out of an airplane!"

I make the mind blown motion with my hands because it's the only way to encompass the wild rush of emotions coursing through my body. The ironic part is only half of those emotions are from skydiving. The other half is from skydiving with *her*.

Simply put, Hartley is an amplifier.

She makes the bad times bearable and the good times better. She emits light and spreads love without even realizing she's doing it. Even Boyd, who's chronically grumpy everywhere but Egypt, is drawn to her. But most of all, she's exactly the kind of person who deserves to be on this race and I already know I'll spend the rest of my life thanking the universe (and the Xtreme Quest casting department) for letting me be the one to experience it with her.

We land a few minutes later—her first, and me about thirty seconds after—and thankfully for everyone's ankles, it goes as smoothly as the rest of the jump. As soon as I'm unclipped, I jog over and scoop her into a celebratory hug, letting my momentum launch us into circles as we laugh at the awesomeness and absurdity of what we just did.

Once her feet return to the ground, I mean to step back. I really do. But then she looks up at me with those sparkling eyes and that big, beautiful grin and before I know it, my mouth is on hers.

It starts out as a slightly breathless, messy kiss on account of our laughter but quickly evolves into a slow dance of sweeping tongues and teasing nibbles that earn us a few cheers from the crew.

"Shit," I say against her lips.

"What?"

"I forgot about the cameras."

She pulls back and to my relief, she's still smiling. "You know they've been salivating for this anyway, so I suppose it's time we gave the people what they want."

CHAPTER 17
HARTLEY

Day 14—Greece

I t's a good thing I drove to the checkpoint, because Court plastered his face to the window as soon as the Acropolis came into view. It was actually pretty cute. I promised him we could be tourists once we got to the checkpoint and kept hold of his hand all the way up to the Parthenon to prevent him from wandering.

It wasn't a hardship, I promise.

"Court and Hartley," Paul says when we step on the mat. "It's been an interesting journey. Two weeks ago, you were the last to check in and only remained in the race due to Team Rockville's time penalty. Is it safe to say it's not as difficult to be teammates anymore?"

"Eh, she's growing on me," Court says.

"Hartley, what made it easier to get along with each other?"

There's no way I'm talking about how the Bombshells basically intervened on our behalf, so I go with, "A lot of things, but if I had to choose something specific, I'd say letting go of our assumptions."

Paul nods. "Obviously, it's working. Your communication has greatly improved, and it looks like you're even enjoying yourselves now."

If he only knew. "They do say anything's possible on Xtreme Quest."

"What about your relationship? Court, do you think there's chance of something beyond the race?"

Alexis asked the same thing yesterday while Gianna and Court worked on their puzzle. I wish I could've told her we'd ride off into the sunset together, but Court and I have two separate lives. We both run businesses we can't leave, and he has the added responsibility of being a substitute—a pretty damn good one, if my suspicions are correct. And even if I *could* pack up and move, he may not be looking for a relationship right now. So, in the meantime, I'll be grateful for the chance to rewrite the ending we had in college and make new, wonderful memories while we're at it.

Will it be enough to soften the blow of flying home next week? Absolutely not. I know my heart well enough to understand it's about to take another hit. But the good news is I survived it once before, and this time we can walk away as friends instead of me hating him.

I'm actually a little mad at myself for that one.

How could I have truly thought for six entire years that the man standing beside me was the villain instead of the hero? Why didn't I understand that he loved me enough to sacrifice himself in a fairytale he wrote solely because he believed I was worthy of a happy ending bigger than himself? And then I went and cheapened it by accusing him of making decisions for me, which isn't the case at all.

It's in this moment that I become acutely aware of three things:

1. I owe Court a genuine, face-to-face apology.
2. My heart is going to take a harder hit next week than I originally thought.
3. There is a hundred percent chance I'm in love with him again. Or maybe I always was.

I see Court rub his chin out of the corner of my eye. I don't dare look his way out of fear he'd be able to read my mind. Instead, I squeeze my backpack straps and brace for the answer we both know is coming.

Instead, he shocks me by saying, "That's an interesting question. Unfortunately, I didn't pack my crystal ball, but I guess it goes back to what Hartley said—anything's possible on Xtreme Quest."

———

When the front desk agent told us about the amenities in our deluxe corner suite (specifically, the rainfall shower, Jacuzzi on the wraparound balcony, and view of the Acropolis), we negotiated a deal with her to swap our complimentary spa service for laundry service. She looked at us like we were nuts, but that's because she doesn't understand that fabric softener is a far greater luxury than a massage.

Besides, the room itself is so gorgeous that there's no need to leave. I'm talking high-end wood flooring, wood accents on the walls, the sleekest bathroom I've ever seen, and fabrics that likely cost more than my car payment per yard. There's also one king-sized bed instead of two queens.

I suspect that was Wendell's doing, but I'm not complaining.

After taking full advantage of the shower (very spacious), deluxe toiletries (very bougie), and complimentary bathrobes (very plush), we send our clothes away with a nice young woman named Elena who says she'll have them back to us in about six hours.

I'm sitting at the foot of the bed flipping through TV channels when Court comes back from locking the door. "Anything good?"

"Lots of soccer, a cooking show, a newscast, and"—I study the screen, where a man and woman are having an impassioned discussion on a couch—"a Greek soap opera."

Clapping his hands in mock excitement, he says, "I've been *dying* to watch a Greek soap opera," and plops onto the mattress beside me. "What do we think this one is about?"

"Some sort of lovers' disagreement."

"Hmm." He watches for a moment, then says, "I'm leaning toward an inter-office affair. He's her boss and he's trying to break it off. She's begging him not to."

"I think you're right about begging, but that's a worried face. See?" I mimic the woman's position and shift to face Court, gripping the lapels of his robe. "Don't go, Acropolis! It's far too dangerous."

Without missing a beat, he clutches my wrists and holds me in place. "I have to, Tzatziki. It's the only way to break the curse and restore philosophy to the village."

"We'll learn to live without philosophy. It doesn't make sense anyway."

"Uncle Socrates says a life without philosophy is a life half-lived, and Tzatziki"—Court takes my face in his hands and peers into my eyes—"everyone in the village deserves to live a thousand full lives together."

I rise along with the woman on the TV and open the imaginary door. "Then go with Jason and the Argonauts and defeat the jackalpottamus so you can return to me."

He hops off the mattress and kisses me before stepping through the threshold. "My heart has always been yours, Tzatziki. There is no mountain I wouldn't cross, no fire I wouldn't forge to be with you again." He pauses in thought, then says, "Except for maybe the bladesmith in Nepal, but I'm sure you understand. Farewell, my little green olive."

"Goodbye, Acropolis. I will see you in seven to ten business days."

Court snort laughs as the show cuts to commercial. "Seven to ten business days?"

I tilt my head and shrug. "It seemed like a reasonable amount of time to defeat a jackalpottamus."

He's still laughing when he pulls me to his chest, but we fall silent soon after. I let myself get lost in the moment. To pretend Court's improvised words were meant for me. That we could be the ones living a thousand full lives together. We wouldn't even need that many.

I'd happily accept one full life with him, and I'd slay the jackalpottamus myself.

———

After taking a dip in the Jacuzzi, I hang our wet bathing suits in the shower and don my robe, then grab Court's off the hook and return to the bedroom.

"Here," I say, tossing it to him.

He catches it with one hand and sets his bottle of water on the nightstand. "What's this for?"

"I need to talk to you, but I can't think straight when you're naked."

The grin he blasts me with is a heady mix of cocky and adorable. In an effort to stay focused, I cover my eyes. "Put that thing away too."

"Okay, okay," he laughs.

A few seconds later, I remove my hand and find him standing there with his robe open, hands on his hips, still wearing that damn grin. It's an act of warfare, obviously, so I reach for the nearest weapon and launch my assault.

"If you don't cover up your man parts," I say, whacking his chest with a pillow, "I'll be forced to—"

Court catches the pillow and holds it over my head. "You were saying?"

It's tempting to lose myself in the devilish glint of his blue-green eyes. I very nearly do, in fact, leaving me with no choice but to break out the big guns.

I tickle him.

I reach right inside his open robe and attack his sides before he even knows what's coming.

Yelping, he drops the pillow and goes for my hands, returning fire with expert precision while shouting, "You'll never take me alive!" and something else I can't hear over the sound of my own laughter.

"Uncle!" I cry between breaths as we fall onto the bed in a tangle of arms and legs.

He lands half on top of me, which wouldn't be that big of a problem except that my robe came untied somewhere in the battle and now my naked parts and his naked parts are dangerously close to each other.

"You're making it really hard to apologize to you."

His head pops up, brows bunched together. "For what?"

The mood shifts from playful to serious, cueing a flood of nerves. "So much."

Still concerned, Court rolls to the side to fix his robe, then settles against the pillows.

I do the same but decide to stand because this is the kind of thing you say while standing, right? Like a respect thing? Or would that look like a power move because he's sitting while I'm standing? I don't want to look powerful, just sincere. In that case, maybe I should be on my knees?

"Hartley?"

"Hmm?" I say around my thumbnail.

"You've stood up and sat down twice. Is everything okay?"

Nodding, I drop my hand to my lap and gather a breath for courage. "I had a mini epiphany at the checkpoint today, and now so many things make sense and I'm kicking myself for not realizing it before."

I pause to sort through my thoughts, but they're swirling around like little tornados of clarity, each just as important as the others and all of them clamoring for which one goes next. I wish I could tell him everything exactly the way it came to me—full-force and all at once, like the universe revealed the answers in a completed painting, then whacked me in the face with it.

Not that I want to whack him in the face, but you know what I mean.

"Anyway, what I want to say is I'm so sorry for doubting you and calling you a coward and a liar and for spending the last six years, and most recently the last week and a half, hating you for things you never did.

"I'm sorry for forgetting that you've always been an incredible human being, and for accusing you of making decisions for me when all you were trying to do was put my life and my needs ahead of your own. I'm sorry you had to break your own heart in the process, and I'm sorry for all the nights you hurt more because of what I said or how I acted.

"But mostly, I'm sorry for thinking the worst of you when all you've ever wanted is the best for me."

Silence blankets the room as Court absorbs my long-overdue apology. Compassion and understanding wash over his face, drawing my throat tight. I don't realize I'm crying until he reaches over and wipes my cheeks.

"Sounds like quite the epiphany."

I let out a garbled laugh. "On camera, no less."

"Is it my turn now?"

"Yeah, I think I'm done."

"Okay. Remember when we learned the Bombshell thing was an act?"

"This is an interesting segue, but yes, I remember."

"What did Gianna say?"

"That it was easy because people see what they expect to see."

Court lifts his brows and holds my gaze. "Say that last part again."

"People see—*ah.*"

He nods when I make the connection. "It's not your fault. You saw what I wanted you to see. The one promise I made to myself on the drive home from that bachelor party was to lie to you as little as possible. The downside was that meant the excuse I gave you was shaky at best. When you brought up the cheating angle, I knew that was the only way to keep you off my doorstep while still keeping my promise, so I ran with it. It actually worked out well, though. I still got to tell the truth by denying it, and the fact that I was denying it made me look even guiltier."

"It definitely worked," I say dryly as I scoot up to the crook of his arm. Once I'm settled, Court presses a kiss to the top of my head and I pretend not to die from it. "What did you mean about keeping me off your doorstep?"

"You're the most stubborn optimist I've ever met. I was afraid you'd show up on my doorstep the next day with a bulleted list of options and counterarguments and tell me to pull my head out of my ass."

I breathe out a laugh. "I probably would have."

We're quiet for several moments and then he says, "For what it's worth, your showcase on Gallery Night was phenomenal. I don't think I've ever had a chance to tell you that."

Aaaand there goes my damn heart again.

But before I can respond, there's a knock at the door. Court dodges my gaze as he slips off the bed and tightens the sash on his robe. I hear him talking to a man, and then the door is shutting and he's coming back around the corner with a cart carrying a charcuterie board, a bottle of wine, two glasses, and a gift bag.

"Did the show order room service for us?"

Ignoring my question, he situates the cart beside the bed and reclaims his spot, only this time he faces me and links our fingers. After a few seconds, he finally meets my eyes. His Adam's apple bobs once before he says, "I also have something I want to talk to you about."

"Okay." I give his hand a reassuring squeeze.

"I couldn't tell you what the view looked like today once my instructor pulled our chute because I couldn't take my eyes off you. We could've been over land or sea or an opening to the center of the earth, except I know it had to be land because you talked about the ground being covered in a patchwork quilt of green and brown and yellow. And there was a flock of birds nearby, and you put your arms out to fly alongside them. I know there were clouds because you laughed at how amazing it was to be that close to them."

Tears prick my eyes. Out of everything we experienced, *these* are the things he chose to remember?

"I know that every time you got excited about something you saw, you did this little kick thing with your feet. And that I was so damn proud of you for overcoming a fear and embracing the experience we had today. I know your face was the first one I saw when I landed and I couldn't wait to get to you."

I lose the battle against my tears. Court wipes them away again, but this time I'm holding my breath while he does it.

"I know we'd have a lot of logistical things to figure out and it may not be easy at first, but I can't breathe when I think about walking away from you next week, so I was wondering"—he grabs the gift bag off the cart and removes what's inside—"if maybe you'd like to hang some stars with me?"

CHAPTER 18
COURT

Day 14—Greece

I have one millisecond to catalogue Hartley's watery smile before she launches herself at me.

"Yes," she says against my neck. "Yes, yes, yes."

My relief is instant but short-lived because there's a chance she might've misunderstood me. I pull back and frame her face in my hands. "Just to be clear, I want a relationship with you after the race."

"Still yes," she says with an emphatic nod.

Her confirmation is all it takes for my entire body to relax against her.

The idea for the stars came when we were sleeping on the airport floor in Cairo. It was getting harder to keep sex as only a physical thing, and then seeing Nefertari's ceiling and Gianna telling me to think about trying again . . . it felt like one of Hartley's nudges from the universe.

The original plan was to mail her some stars after the race, but then we won the Shortcut. Hartley had to use the bathroom when we got to the hotel, so I said I'd check us in. I used those few precious minutes to beg the front desk manager to switch us to a king bed and go shopping for me. As soon as I told her my plan, she called the concierge over and that was that. She wouldn't even accept my handwritten IOU for when I get home. She's totally getting a five-star review when I can get online again.

"I actually planned on talking to you later today," Hartley says.

"You did?"

"In addition to my epiphany at the Parthenon, I realized in the Jacuzzi that I was envious of a fake soap opera character named after a dipping sauce."

I bark out a laugh. "That's an oddly specific realization."

"It's true!" Hartley takes my hands and laces our fingers on top of the bag of stars. "When you said, 'My heart has always been yours' . . ." She shrugs. "I wished you were saying that to me and it brought a lot of things in focus."

I lift the bag between us and wait until she gives me her eyes to say, "Why do you think none of my relationships since college have worked out? You've had my heart since the first time we did this."

She releases a soft gasp as I drop the bag and claim her mouth, letting my tongue fill in the blanks to the rest of the words I haven't said yet. And there are so many words—hours of them, bottled up after six years, and I carefully place them on her neck, her jaw, the skin behind her ear. I slip her robe off one shoulder, then the other, and press more words on her nipples and her breasts, massaging them into her skin as I go.

The package of stars falls to the side when I untie her robe and toss it to the floor. I rise long enough to add my robe to the pile, then settle on top of her. Stunning green eyes blink up at me when I guide myself inside. I feel her nails press into my back as I fill her and then we're kissing again while I set a slow rhythm with my hips.

The more we move, the more my words scatter until there are only three left.

I.

Love.

You.

I leave them all over her body with my hands, my tongue, and finally with my voice. She repeats them as we tumble over the edge together.

———

Standings after leg 8, Greece

1. Us* Shortcut
2. Old Bay (Haylee and Kadeeja)
3. Kick Asspen (Treva and Boyd)

4. Bombshells (Gianna and Alexis)
5. Wise Guys (DeAngelo and Big Mike)
6. ~~A Team (Mitchell and Kennedy)~~ * Repeat

After starting strong leaving Greece, we came in fourth in Montenegro. It wasn't entirely our fault though. Our first taxi broke down, and later in the day, we got directions from a local who didn't know the difference between north and south . . . except we didn't realize that until we'd gone ten miles in the wrong direction.

What saved us is that despite Treva's speed on land, she's a weak swimmer, and we were able to overtake Kick Asspen in the team challenge. Thankfully, she promised there were no hard feelings and even let me borrow her essential oil roller in case my ankle starts hurting again.

We only saw the Bombshells for about thirty seconds in between our second clue and the solo challenge, which was long enough to make dinner plans for tonight so we can catch up. We're waiting in the hotel lobby with Justin, our cameraman and tonight's obligatory chaperone, when they come out of the elevator.

It takes them exactly four steps before they notice Hartley's hand in mine. Their smiles are immediate, with Gianna looking to the heavens, arms wide, saying, "Finally!" and Alexis shaking her head good-naturedly and adding, "Took you long enough."

Their questions come out in a flurry once we're seated at the restaurant across the street from our hotel.

"Tell us everything," Alexis says.

"Well, not *everything* everything," Gianna clarifies.

"When did it happen?"

"Where did it happen?"

"What made you two finally pull your heads out of your asses?"

"What did everyone else say?"

"What's your plan once the race is over?"

"When's the wedding?"

At this, Alexis rests her hand on Gianna's arm and says, "Whoa, slow down."

Gianna gives her an *oh, come on* look. "Tell me I'm wrong."

"Well, no, but . . ." Alexis cups her fingers and loudly whispers, "We don't want to scare the children."

"Valid," Gianna concedes, then to us says, "Sorry, guys."

Hartley waves off their worry with her free hand because I'm holding the other one. On top of the table. Because I can officially do stuff like this now. It's a heady feeling, and I'm trying to bank as much of it as possible.

"Let's start at the top," Hartley says with a mirthful smile. "The 'when' and 'where' depends on which part you're referring to. We agreed to try again during our break in Greece. But if you're talking about when I realized I had feelings for him . . ." She pauses to think. "It was probably after I bungee jumped in New Zealand."

"What about you?" Alexis asks me.

The answer rolls off my tongue without needing to think. "Dallas."

Two knowing smiles and one stunned gaze land on me.

"Dallas?" Hartley repeats.

"That tracks," Justin says from the table to our right.

She peers over at him. "It does?"

"I was your cameraman that day. Dude couldn't take his eyes off you."

She swings that stunned gaze back to me and raises her brows further.

"He's not wrong," I say.

"I thought you hated me at first."

"I've had many, *many* feelings for you." I lean in for a kiss since I can do that now, too. "But hate was never one of them."

Hartley's cheeks are pink when I pull away.

"Gah!" Alexis grabs Gianna's arm and squeezes. "I can't with the cuteness. It's too much."

Needing something other than Hartley to focus on, I give my attention to the Bombshells. "What was the next question?"

"What happened to change your minds about trying to make this work after the race?" Gianna asks. "Because the last time we talked to you in Egypt, you were both . . ." She spreads her hands apart to demonstrate her point.

"In a word, I'm an idiot," Hartley says with a self-deprecating eye roll. "The longer version is that I've watched Court's face light up throughout the race when he talks about history and geography. I already told him he should consider becoming a full-time teacher instead of a substitute."

Alexis glances at me. "I can definitely see you being a teacher."

"Exactly. But I couldn't tell him to consider switching careers and not be willing to do the same thing myself. I was only supposed to work for my dad's company for a few months until things settled down and we could hire some- one. Then I started feeling guilty about the accident and felt like it was my responsibility to stay and help. I worked through that part with my therapist, but I'd already been there a few years by that point and—"

"Wait, back up," I say. Hartley didn't mention the accident when we talked about careers last night, just that she was tired of feeling stuck and living someone else's life. "Why would you feel guilty if you weren't even there?"

"They were on the way to the airport to pick me up when it happened."

On the way to the airport.

My memory flips back to our interview with Wendell in Dallas when she said she didn't go to Italy because she had to go home.

Not *went* home.

Had to go home.

I force a swallow as prickles of icy heat climb my neck. Surely Isaac Newton wouldn't be this cruel, right? "Was this after you graduated?"

To my horror, she nods. "I'd already sold my car. I was going to spend a few weeks at home, then fly out to my internship."

Fuck.

Fuck!

This whole time I thought I was doing the right thing.

But they wouldn't have been there if she didn't need to fly home.

And she wouldn't have flown home if she had her car.

And she wouldn't have sold her car if . . .

FUCK!

"Court."

My lungs burn under the crushing weight of a reality I caused.

"Hey."

All I ever wanted was for her to—

"Courtland Everett Mueller." Hartley captures my face in her hands and blasts me with an authoritative stare. How can she stand to look at me right now?

"It's all my fault."

"It's not your fault."

"It wasn't supposed to happen like that."

"You didn't—"

"I did! I let you go so you wouldn't be trapped in a cage with me, and then forced you *and* your parents into a cage. A man is *paralyzed* because of me."

I'm going to puke. Or pass out. Why doesn't this room have any air? And when did the door get so far away? Maybe I can still make it. Maybe I'll just keep going until I'm in the street where the universe can right my wrongs.

I push up from the table to go, but Hartley's hands are right there pushing me back down.

I can't breathe.

"Court."

"I'm sorry," I rasp. "I'm so fucking sorry."

"It's not your fault." Her hands move from my shoulders to my face. I feel her wipe my cheeks, then rest her forehead against mine. "You weren't driving that truck. You didn't fall asleep at the wheel."

"But I made the decision that led them there. I swear I thought I was doing the right thing. If I would've known . . ."

"Look at me."

I shake my head.

"Please."

Her voice is filled with far too much compassion for someone who's responsible for ruining her father's life. Where's her anger? Her blame? Why can't she see I'm the literal reason she's been unhappy for the last six years?

She says something to the Bombshells, then lifts me by the arm and leads me outside. I spend our short walk picturing her face in the airport when she told me, Treva, and Boyd that she was running her dad's company. It was like someone took her colors away and gave her a palette of gray instead.

Well, not someone.

Me.

We stop abruptly and she pushes me onto a bench, straddles me, and takes me by the face again.

What is she doing?

"It's not like that," she says, reading my unspoken question about why she's sitting on my lap. "But I need you to see me right now and this is the only way I know how."

I release a heavy breath and reluctantly drag my gaze to hers.

"My dad wouldn't have gotten in his accident if I went to one of the other two colleges that accepted me. Or if I got that internship the first year I applied. Or if I chose the flight that came in two hours earlier. Or if, or if, or if. We make thousands of decisions every single day. Most turn out fine. Some don't. But you can't spend the rest of your life stuck in the domino effect of someone else's decisions.

"You are not responsible for that driver's decision to get in his truck knowing he was already tired, nor are you responsible for his decision not to pull off at any of the *seven* rest areas he passed before the site of the accident."

Damn. "Seven?"

She nods.

"What an asshole."

Shocked laughter bursts from her lips. "The biggest."

Despite the lingering heaviness, my next few breaths come easier. "I still feel awful though."

"I know. And I'll keep reminding you that it's not your fault for as long as it takes to sink in."

"How long did it take you?"

"Three years of therapy and thousands of dollars. You get the abbreviated version for a bargain price of twenty-seven dollars and twelve cents."

"You are something else," I mutter as the corners of my mouth quirk up. Only she'd be able to bookend this moment with something positive and make me smile in the process.

"And now I get to tell you the good part."

Of course there's a good part. I slide my hands around her hips and lock them behind her. "What's the bright side, Hartley O.?"

She unleashes a grin as she circles her arms around my neck. "My dad became paralyzed—"

"I thought we established that one as a negative."

She breaks her hold long enough to press a finger to my lips. "Stay with me here."

I lift my brows as if to say, *Proceed.*

"He became paralyzed, and I stayed home. Then I got stuck in a job I never wanted but couldn't get out of and I went stir-crazy. I desperately needed to do something for me, so I went for the biggest, wildest thing I could find and auditioned for this show. Which means . . ."

She pauses to let me fill in the rest.

"Without that accident, none of this would be happening."

CHAPTER 19
HARTLEY

Day 18—Netherlands

If you've ever wondered how it feels to be in the team challenge for the semi-finals of the biggest international reality television show, try wearing uncomfortable suits, perfecting specific techniques for holding trays, and remembering eight sets of measurements.

Oh, and listening to the Wise Asses talk about Big Mike's current bout of diarrhea and the travesty of their inability to find a McDonald's in the last two legs. I can't decide if I hope the editors keep that footage in to embarrass them or edit it out because literally no one needs or wants to hear about it.

Today's challenge took us to a butler academy in the Netherlands. I'd never heard of such a thing, and after today, I hope never to hear of it again. I bet in four months when this episode airs, I'll still be having nightmares where everyone keeps shouting, "Head up! Back straight! Don't forget to smile!"

"Wait, I think that one is supposed to be four centimeters," I tell Court.

"But isn't everything else two?"

"Except the dessert cutlery. I think." I frown at the place setting as I try to picture the example down the hallway. And when I say down the hallway, I mean the hallway of a 135-room mansion that's built like a square with a courtyard in the middle.

On its face, our challenge didn't seem that bad: go to the butler academy, do an obstacle course with crystal stemware on a silver tray, and replicate a place setting for two.

In reality, crystal stemware has a unique relationship with gravity and would rather be in small pieces on the floor. And the example place setting, the dining room, and the storage room of dinnerware are at three separate corners of the mansion. One team member is the place setter while the other acts as the runner to retrieve items from the storage room.

I felt more comfortable being the runner just in case Court's ankle decided to act up. I've probably run about two miles so far thanks to the other added challenge from our sadistic producers—the designs on the dinner plates are nearly identical and we can only bring out one design at a time.

As Court and I adjust the cutlery measurement, Big Mike sprints in from a bathroom-break-slash-storage-room run.

"How much you wanna bet he's not washing his hands?" I mutter to Court.

"I guarantee he's not."

"Maybe I can accidentally trip and spill a bottle of hand sanitizer on him."

"I'll give you bonus points if you get it in his eye while you're at it."

I snort a laugh and lift my hand for the instructor. "Check, please!"

He comes to our table for a whopping two seconds and says, "Incorrect."

"Ugh! Is it the measurements or the plates?"

I don't know why I bother asking. The only things they're allowed to say are "incorrect" and "correct," and so far, no one's gotten it right.

"Check!" DeAngelo's arm goes up.

His instructor approaches, takes a slow walk around the table, and . . . nods.

He nods.

"Correct."

Court and I exchange a stupefied look as the Wise Asses accept their clue and run out of the room.

"Tell me that didn't just happen."

I refuse to admit that my hope of going to the finals with the Bombshells and Old Bay is now dashed. "Maybe there's another clue and they'll get lost looking for it. At least now we can use their table as a guide instead of running all the—"

The instructor removes a folded tablecloth from the chair and covers their table.

"Dammit," I say on a long sigh. "They didn't do that with the puzzle in Egypt."

"That also wasn't the semi-finals." Court's voice is flat as he scrubs a hand over his face. "Anyway, are we trying new measurements or different plates?"

Before I can answer, Alexis runs in, immediately pulling to a stop when she sees the covered table. "They got it?"

"Yep."

"Dammit!"

I nod in solidarity. "Right now, I deeply regret not manifesting a sphincter prolapse."

She barks out a laugh and points at me with the wineglass in her hand. "It's not too late. Anything's possible on Xtreme Quest."

Thirty minutes later, we confirm this to be true—just not in the way we were hoping.

MEET PAUL BEHIND THE MANSION.
THE LAST TEAM TO CHECK IN WILL BE ELIMINATED.

"So much for the Wise Asses getting lost leaving here," I say. I shove the stupid clue in my fanny pack and sling my bag over my shoulder, pausing for one last look at Haylee and Kadeeja, who are still working on their place setting. "It's just not fair."

"I know," Court says, leading me down the hallway toward the exit.

With no need to rush, we take our time walking outside and around the building. Tears blur my vision the farther we get and eventually spill over when I spot the Bombshells waiting for us at the checkpoint.

Even Paul greets us with a half-hearted smile. "Team Hartbreak, you're the third to arrive at the checkpoint, and the last team that will be competing in the final leg of Xtreme Quest."

I should be happy. Ecstatic. Shouting from the rooftop because against all odds, Court and I made it to the finals. Instead, I'm standing here with a bitter-sweet lump lodged in my throat at the injustice of it all.

"Tell me what's going through your mind right now," Paul says.

I shrug and wipe my cheeks. "I was hoping for a different set of teams in the finale."

"What about you, Court?"

"What's going through my mind isn't suitable for TV."

There isn't much to do after that but step to the side and wait. Gianna and Alexis sandwich me in a hug, the three of us wiping our cheeks intermittently until Old Bay rounds the corner of the mansion.

In all the years I've watched this show, I've never seen Paul more apologetic than when he tells Kadeeja and Haylee they're the last to check in. To their credit, they have nothing but love and encouraging words for us and slide into their taxi with their heads held high like the badass women they are.

"You know what this means," Alexis says after they've left.

"What?"

"We need to destroy the Wise Asses."

———

Standings after leg 10, Netherlands

1. Wise Guys (DeAngelo and Big Mike)
2. Bombshells (Gianna and Alexis)
3. Us
4. Old Bay (Haylee and Kadeeja)

"You're going to run out of time," Court says.

"Just keep looking out the window."

Our flight from Amsterdam to New York City was about eight hours. We slept for the first half and spent the second half going over our notes for the memory challenge at the end of this leg. That's when I got the idea to give Court a souvenir to commemorate our journey.

"The buildings are getting bigger."

"I'm almost done." I cap the black fine-tip permanent marker and exchange it for the orange one.

"You'd better not be drawing a penis."

Ha! I roll my lips between my teeth because he's close in an abstract way.

"Don't worry, it's nothing the show will have to blur out."

I finish as the landing gears are lowered and stow my markers in my backpack. "Okay, you can look now."

I'm grinning my ass off when Court shifts his gaze from the window to the rubber duck on his right forearm. "Figured I'd leave you with a memory from the first time we were in an airport together."

His laugh comes out on a soft breath as he shakes his head and smiles. "You know damn good and well the Dallas airport is not what I'm going to think about."

I shrug innocently. "That's okay. Art's open to interpretation."

He mumbles something that sounds like, "I'm gonna open *you* to interpretation," which doesn't even make sense but is still sexy nonetheless.

And to think I almost murdered him that first day.

Really glad I changed my mind about that.

———

I've done my fair share of yelling at Xtreme Quest contestants through the TV.

"You're holding it wrong!"

"You just ran past the clue box!"

"If you stack them like that, they're all gonna fall!"

This is why I'm certain that when our season finale airs in four months, viewers will be yelling at me.

"The brush is at the wrong angle!"

"You forgot to turn the sprayer on again!"

"You're too far away from the curb!"

And I know, okay? But operating a street sweeper is a hell of a lot harder than it looks when you've had four hours of sleep after a six-hour time change, and you only get a five-minute crash course on how the glorified Zamboni vacuum works.

"I'm so sorry," I say to Court when I finally run back to him with our next clue. I've put us behind by about fifteen minutes, which isn't insurmountable, but also isn't a good feeling—especially when the Wise Asses have managed to keep their early lead on us and the Bombshells.

"Don't worry about it. We'll make up time."

He gives my shoulders a reassuring squeeze as I rip open our envelope.

Make your way to Ellen's Stardust Diner to receive your next clue.

This, we soon learn, is easier said than done thanks to traffic, detours, and one very angry bicyclist on a power trip. The sound guy uses our time as back seat captives to fire off a few questions for our confessional.

"Court, how is today different from day one?"

"There are a few obvious differences from day one." He catches my eye and rubs his thumb against the back of my neck. "But as a whole, I guess it's that I don't really care about winning anymore."

I snap my head in his direction because this is news to me.

"What do you mean?" I ask.

"I've spent most of my twenties feeling like a failure for not reaching the goals I set when I was nineteen. All I wanted to do was come on this show, win some money, and make a fresh start in a place that didn't represent all the things I'm not. But"—he shifts his hand from my neck to my shoulder and squeezes—"a few wise people from the race have helped me realize the things I *am* aren't half-bad and that I'd get out of my rut a lot quicker if I stopped digging and put down the shovel. So I guess that's a long way of saying the difference from day one to day twenty-one is that I'd like to win but I don't need to anymore."

His words trigger a rush of pride and love and admiration so big that I grit my teeth and fold my hands to keep from reaching over and squeezing him until his head pops off.

Ironically, I wanted to do the same thing in our first taxi ride but for very different reasons.

"How about you, Hartley," the sound guy says. "Would you change anything about the race if you could go back and do it over again?"

I could say yes, that I'd set aside my ego and my anger to have an honest conversation with Court on the first day so we could reach this point two weeks before Greece, but it's not that simple.

"I wouldn't change anything about the race if I could do it again because it would mess up all the layers."

"Is that a code word?" he asks.

I smile and shake my head. "Art is just a series of layers, and all of them play off each other. When I'm painting, I start with an idea and build on it. One layer may not turn out like I wanted, but it gives me an idea for something else I wouldn't have thought of without the one underneath. By the time I finish a painting, there are usually a handful of hidden layers that helped me get to the final image.

"I would've loved to have more time with Court when I wasn't stupidly hating his guts but skipping that layer could've changed the final image and I happen to quite like this one."

———

We catch up with the Bombshells at the next challenge because Gianna—understandably—is having a panic attack.

Our clue from Ellen's Stardust Diner told us to visit Edge, which touts itself as the highest outdoor sky deck in the western hemisphere at eleven hundred feet. From there, whoever didn't street sweep earlier would travel *another* nine hundred feet up to the apex of the building and lean out over New York City, arms and legs spread wide, for thirty seconds.

For reference, the jump pod in New Zealand was six hundred feet up and Alexis was the one who actually jumped.

"We got here about twenty minutes ago." Alexis points to the left where DeAngelo is sitting. "He was already here but I don't know for how long. I also don't know if we'll be able to finish this challenge. I can't get Gianna to even stand up."

Remembering how terrified I was in the jump pod, I walk over and immediately sink down to the stone floor beside Gianna, wrapping my arms around her. "You have every right to be scared out of your mind right now. I think the people who do this kind of thing voluntarily should probably have their head examined."

She lets out the tiniest of laughs between short, uneven breaths.

"Now, you see that guy right there?" She nods when I point to Court. "You're in luck because he also got the short end of this shitty stick. Believe me, there's no one better to be holding a short, shitty stick with than Court. He's literally the only reason I made it off that platform in New Zealand instead of taking a time penalty, and today he's going to be your personal guide on the staircase to Heaven."

Gianna pulls in a deeper breath.

"There you go. Do that one more time and I'll move on to the double whammy of good news."

She takes another breath.

"Fabulous. Okay good news number one: I read this clue about a dozen times in the taxi ride here and nowhere does it say you have to keep your eyes open. Number two: our taxi driver has already done this, and he said most people who do the leaning thing face the building and lean back instead of leaning forward while facing the ground.

"So you're going to take the hand of this incredibly handsome gentleman and stay with him every step of the way. When you get up there, you're going to keep facing the building and when you do the leaning thing, close your eyes and pretend you're a reasonable twelve inches off the ground."

After another series of steady breaths, she nods. "Okay."

I rise and pull her up, giving her a moment with Alexis while I turn to Court.

"If she starts freaking out up there, please offer your balls for kicking. That was a big help in New Zealand."

"You gonna make it up to me if she follows through?"

"Every day for a month, at least."

"Deal." He kisses me on the forehead, then holds his hand out to Gianna. "Milady, your chariot awaits . . . metaphorically speaking."

They get about ten steps away when I say to hell with it and throw Court to the metaphorical wolves.

"Gianna!"

She turns around, puzzled.

"Ask Court about his balls!"

———

Despite the short hiccup with Gianna's panic attack, we managed to leave for our memory challenge in Prospect Park about ten minutes after the Wise Asses.

"This is it," Court says.

We slow our jog to a walking pace as we approach three giant boards in a loosely shaped triangle with stacks of . . . something in front of each one. Big Mike and DeAngelo are already at work, but it doesn't look like they're that far into whatever it is we're doing.

No sign of the Bombshells though. Hopefully they get here soon because if we're going to lose to anyone, it needs to be them and not the Wise Asses.

Court takes an envelope from the clue box and reads the instructions for the challenge.

THE BEST PART OF TRAVELING IS MAKING MEMORIES. FIND YOUR BOARD AND

DOCUMENT EACH LEG OF YOUR TRIP WITH THAT COUNTRY'S FLAG, THE AIRPORT CODE, AND A PHOTO OF YOU AND YOUR TEAMMATE WHILE YOU WERE THERE. ONCE YOU HAVE EVERYTHING IN THE CORRECT ORDER, YOU WILL RECEIVE YOUR NEXT CLUE.

My head flinches back slightly. "Photos?"

"No idea."

We're in front of the #TeamBombshell board, so we jog to the other side. Our board has eleven columns, each with three sets of nails, and the stacks of wooden plaques are organized into groups. There's at least four times as many plaques in the flag and airport code groups than there are pictures. If teams don't know the codes or flags, they're going to have a hard time guessing.

Court rests his hands on his hips as he surveys the plaques. "How do you want to do this? We can work on each leg together, or we can each take a group and then do the last one together."

Part of our study session on the plane was flags so they'd be fresh in our heads, and I'm pretty confident the codes won't be difficult either. "Let's split up and see how far we can get. I'll take the codes if you want the flags."

"Sounds good."

As we head to our respective areas, a thought occurs to me and I snort a laugh.

"What's so funny?"

"This is another example of how today is different than the beginning of the race. In Costa Rica, that would've been a five-minute argument."

"I disagree. We made multiple decisions just now, so it would've been a ten-minute argument."

"Well, I disagree with your disagreement, so how about that?"

He mutters something I can't hear but he's smiling and shaking his head and looking all kinds of sexy and adorable. To avoid further distractions, I turn my back and focus on finding the three-letter codes I need.

By the time I get my row done, the Bombshells have arrived and have made great headway in catching up. Court hangs his last flag and after quickly double-checking our work, we get started on the photos.

"Hey Court," Alexis calls from her side.

"Yeah?"

"I meant to ask you at the last challenge—what's with the rubber duck?"

I cackle—CACKLE—as Court points at me and draws a finger across his throat. "You don't want to know, trust me."

She peeks around her board and eyes him with a skeptical smirk. "Somehow I don't think that's true, but I'll let it slide for now."

It takes me a full fifteen seconds to catch my breath. When I do, Court is staring at me with a murderous smile as he mouths, *You're gonna pay for this.*

I'm totally fine with that.

But anyway, back to the photos. "These look like still shots," I say as we lay them out.

Our faces appear in every image, but the overall picture has been cropped so much that we can barely see anything else.

"How are we supposed to put these in order if all we have are close-ups?" he asks.

I point my toe at the plaque closest to me. "I'm scowling at you in this one, so it's probably one of the first few legs."

"You look a little surly in this one too."

"Here's one where you're giving me the stink eye."

And so we sort our photos using the little clues in each one—the tree over Court's shoulder, the cloudless sky, the neck buff I'm wearing—and add them to our board.

The fifth photo is when it changes.

Court's looking out of the frame, but I'm wearing a tiny smile as I look at him.

In the sixth, neither of us are looking at each other, but we're both smiling.

By the ninth photo, Court's hand is on my shoulder while we're, presumably, reading a clue in Montenegro.

I don't know how they did it so quickly, but there's even one from the taxi this morning where Court and I have moved past looking at each other and are full-on gazing.

When Court hangs it on the final hook, we step back and survey the board. The challenge was simply to document our time during the race, but as we move through each of the eleven photos, we realize it captures our journey back together as well.

"I think we got everything right," he says.

Hell yeah we did.

CHAPTER 20
COURT

Day 21—New York City

We have our clue.

We have our final clue of the race and most importantly, we're the first ones to get it.

Hot dog, you did it! Meet Paul at the Wonder Wheel for your final checkpoint. The last two teams to arrive will be eliminated.

"What does it mean?" I ask.

"The Ferris wheel at Coney Island," Hartley says. She grabs my arm and we take off down the path, retracing our steps to the park entrance.

"How sure are you?"

"Positive. I went there during my Meg Ryan era."

"Your what? Actually, never mind. We can talk about that one later."

We save the rest of our energy for running and make it back to the street in good time.

"There!" Hartley spots a taxi at the curb.

As we pile in with our crew, the Wise Asses come sprinting out of the park.

"I don't see any other taxis," Hartley says. "Maybe we can get a head start on them."

DeAngelo approaches the curb and holds out his arm. "Taxi!"

"Please do whatever you can to stay ahead of those guys," I tell our driver.

He eases off the brake to merge onto the road when DeAngelo walks into the street in front of our car and holds his hand up higher. "Taxi!"

"Move, DeAngelo!" Hartley yells through the open window.

I know the bastard hears her but he stays put.

The cabbie lays on the horn, which never does anything for anyone in Manhattan.

"What the hell, man! Get out of the way!" I shout.

"Is there any room to go around him?" Hartley asks.

"Not without hitting him."

I meet the driver's eyes in the rearview mirror. "I can't tell you to hit him, but I won't be upset if you did."

A streak of yellow pulls up beside us, further blocking us in, and the Wise Asses load up.

"Dammit!" Hartley flips him off through the window.

We manage to pull out behind them but get stuck at the first red light while their car sails through the intersection.

"Come on, come on, come on," I whisper to the traffic signal.

"How long of a drive is it?" Hartley asks.

"Thirty minutes maybe? Depends on how many cars and red lights we have."

Is he seriously explaining the concept of traffic right now? Because if so, maybe I should introduce the concept of a gas pedal.

Hartley grabs my hand for moral support, or possibly because she knows it's harder to strangle a cabbie with only one hand. "There are tons of lights along the way. They'll have to stop eventually and we can catch up."

We do . . . then we don't. Then we do . . . and don't again.

It's an accordion of traffic all the way down Ocean Parkway, stopping and going with every other red light thanks to Brooklyn's most cautious taxi driver. My hope isn't restored until we reach Surf Avenue. Hartley says we can go the rest of the way on foot and tosses the last of our cash at the driver, telling him to keep the change. I follow her through parking lots and side streets while offering thanks to the mysterious Meg Ryan era.

We hit the boardwalk about a hundred feet behind the Wise Asses and it becomes an all-out sprint to the finish line. I don't think I've ever run this fast in my life. Actually, I know I haven't.

Almost there . . .

Keep going . . .

Don't quit . . .

And then two sets of arms go up as they cross the finish line.

"Dammit!"

Hartley and I get there about fifteen seconds later.

Paul gives us a moment to regain control of our lungs. I use the time to pull Hartley in and tell her I'm sorry because even though I said I didn't need to win anymore, I still really fucking wanted to.

"It sucks, but don't be sorry," she says between breaths. "We still get twenty-five thousand dollars and you're taking me to Italy."

I pull back laughing, despite our defeat. "Whatever you say, Hartley O."

"Team Hartbreak! After thirteen countries and more than thirty-one thousand miles, you have finally reached the finish line of Xtreme Quest . . . and you're both smiling."

I drape my arm around Hartley and tuck her into my side. "I promise, no one is more surprised by that than us."

Everyone laughs as he continues. "What are your plans now that the race is over?"

I know full well he's not talking about taking a hot shower, sleeping for a week, and returning to work. He's referring to the question he asked at the Parthenon checkpoint, except that was before Hartley and I officially got back together, and I sure as hell wasn't going to confess to hooking up in the meantime.

Before we left our hotel in Greece, we decided to keep things as they had been—teammates during the day and lovers at night—so we could enjoy our "bubble," as Hartley put it, until the finale. The only exception was telling the Bombshells because they were essentially our matchmakers.

But with the race complete and no more need for a bubble, I answer Paul's question by tilting Hartley's chin up and kissing the hell out of her. The cheering as we crossed the finish line is nothing compared to the celebration from our teammates now. Even Boyd joins in with a jubilant, "Way to go, Court!"

We're both laughing when I end the kiss and turn my attention back to Paul. "A lot more of *that* is what our plan is."

"I think I speak for everyone here when I say congratulations on an incredible journey to the finish line. We wish you nothing but the best for your future."

The crowd launches into another round of applause, first for us and then for Alexis and Gianna, who appear on the boardwalk. We turn and cheer them all the way to the mat, wrapping them in hugs after Paul officially checks them in.

"Did you win?" Alexis asks.

I shake my head.

"Damn."

"Yeah, but I got the girl, so . . ."

Hartley smiles up at me. "What I'm hearing you say is, I'm worth more than a million bucks?"

———

Boyd reaches the restaurant first and holds the door open for Old Bay, the Bombshells, Treva, and Hartley. When I bring up the rear of the group, he grabs my arm and pulls me aside.

"From one man to another, I'm just saying . . . you should look into a Prince Albert."

It comes out in the same tone he'd use to say, "I forgot my grocery list at home," so it takes me a few additional seconds to process his words. In fact, I'm still working on it when he continues with,

"We have four months before the NDA's up, right? That's plenty of time for it to heal and I promise, you'll both thank me."

Then he pats me on the back and ushers me inside along with the rest of our group.

"Why do you look like you just saw a jackalpottamus?" Hartley asks as she fits her hand into mine.

"Because I did, and his name is Prince Albert."

"*What?*" Her free hand flies to her mouth to cover a bubble of surprised laughter. "Do I even want to know?"

"Boyd said I should look into a piercing, but it's not happening no matter how much he insists we'd both thank him."

I shudder at the idea of a needle going anywhere near my dick.

Screw. That.

"If you were to get one, I'd probably think of Boyd every time I looked at it anyway." She scrunches her nose at the thought. "Also, as you may recall,

I'm a huge fan of the existing model. No need to install after-market accessories."

"Our table's ready," Haylee says, rescuing me from what would've been an epic boner in about thirty seconds.

We follow the hostess to the back of the Greek restaurant Alexis found a few blocks from our hotel. None of us is ready to acknowledge our flights home tomorrow, so we're pretending it's just another dinner on the race.

It's funny how only three weeks ago, everyone at our table but Hartley was a stranger. I wouldn't have been able to pick them out of a crowd. I wouldn't have known their strengths and weaknesses, their fears, their hopes. Now it feels like we've known each other forever.

If I'm being honest, it's nice to have fresh blood in my friendship pool. Part of what's been so difficult about staying in Green Valley is the barrage of reassurance I've gotten from my family and friends. It sounds backward, especially considering the fucked-up family situation Boyd's dealing with, but hear me out.

Ella told me a long time ago that she had to learn the difference between "true friends" and "truth friends."

True friends are your ride-or-dies. They're the ones you can call for encouragement or for help hiding a dead body. Truth friends are the ones who will tell you the things you need to hear, even if you don't want to hear them.

Basically, Ella said true friends will tell you that you look great in those jeans, and truth friends will tell you that your ass looks fat.

And for the last six years, I've been walking around feeling like my ass looks fat while my family and friends have told me how great I look in my jeans. I'm not searching for any ego strokes, but it's really nice to hear from outside sources that being the manager of a car wash instead of a school psychologist doesn't make my ass look fat.

Hartley said she loves my car wash ass but still thinks I'll look better in a new pair of teacher jeans. Her suggestion in Greece caught me off guard at first. The only way I'd ever envisioned myself in a school was in the guidance department.

The substitute thing was basically a favor to my mom several years ago when the high school lost a few teachers to retirement. They needed help, I was a living body with a college degree and no criminal history, and Rhett was able to man the car wash on days I was needed at the school.

She's right that I've enjoyed my time in the classroom. Getting a front-row seat to history for the last three weeks has been awesome too. Once I thought about it objectively, it made perfect sense. Technically that means I'm leaving the race with a new-ish girlfriend and a new-ish career and now I need the next four months to hurry up.

"Hey, how tall do you think that Athena statue at the hotel was?"

I shake off my thoughts and focus on what Hartley asked. "It was a couple of feet bigger than me, so eight feet maybe?"

"I can assure you there was not an eight-foot statue of Athena at the hotel in Greece," Treva says.

Gianna shakes her head along with Alexis. "We didn't see it either."

"How could you have missed it? It was right there in the center of the lobby in all its marble glory."

"I think we saw it," Haylee says.

"See? I told—"

"But it wasn't in our hotel."

Hartley's forehead creases as Kadeeja adds, "It was the one between the gas station and the fountain gazebo thing, right?"

Hartley nods.

"We saw it when we walked to the gas station from our hotel to get some snacks after we checked in."

"What hotel were you in?"

"I forget the name, but it was about a five-minute walk down the road."

Hartley slowly settles against the back of her chair. "Why would we be at a different hotel?"

"Hang on," Alexis says. "In Nepal, was everyone at the hotel with the row of huge chandeliers by the reception desk?"

We all nod.

"Then our upgrade was in the same hotel. What was your room like?"

"It was a corner suite with a wraparound balcony, a Jacuzzi, and an insanely nice shower."

Gianna lets out a soft laugh. "We had a nice room, but not *that* nice. Sounds like Wendell was rooting hard for you two."

"That would certainly explain why our room had one bed."

"Actually"—I lean in and give her a wolfishly unapologetic smirk—"that one was me."

"My man!" Boyd raises his arm for a high five but pauses halfway in. "Why do you have a rubber duck on your arm?"

———

After being together twenty-four seven for the last twenty-one days, our time is down to a matter of hours.

Fifteen to be exact, and I fucking hate it.

"I've never seen a man pout while he shaves."

"I'm not pouting," I say, even though we both know I am.

Hartley's been sitting on the bathroom counter watching me shave because apparently it's sexy? I don't know. Whatever keeps her close for now is fine by me.

"You are and it's adorable. Also, I have a small confession. Do you remember the morning we were in Costa Rica?"

I nod.

"I snooped through your toiletry bag and saw your razor. I couldn't believe you still had it."

I finish a pass on my cheek and rinse the lather from the blade. "It's the only one I've used since you gave it to me."

Her cheeks pinken as she pulls the corner of her bottom lip between her teeth. "Really?"

"Yep."

Still smiling, she goes back to watching me shave. I finish the left side of my face and move to the right while thinking about the private hell I'd been in that morning. How badly I'd wanted to touch her. To crawl into her bed and do all the things I'd thought about doing over the last six years. Well, maybe not all of them, but a good three or four at least.

"Since you shared your confession about that morning, I suppose it's only fair to share mine."

I glide the blade along my jaw for one final pass before rinsing my razor. "The reason I had to use the bathroom first was because I had a hard-on that wouldn't quit."

Her eyes widen.

"So I was left with no choice but to take matters into my own hands. Literally."

Those perfect pink lips part on a gasp as I wipe the remaining lather from my face.

"I came so hard that I nearly slipped in the shower."

She swallows. "You did?"

Nodding, I step between her legs and grab her ass, sliding her to the edge of the counter. "And the same thing happened almost every morning after that."

Her hands run up my bare chest and lock behind my neck. "So what I'm hearing you say is that I made things hard for you?"

I bark out a laugh at the sound of my words being thrown back in my face for the second time today. "It was the best and worst torture I've ever experienced."

Hartley's mischievous smirk becomes a determined grin and then she's using one finger to push me back. "That sounds like a challenge to me."

Before I can process what's happening, she hops down and tucks that same finger into the waistband of my shorts, pulling me out of the bathroom and toward the bed. Our one, singular bed, which really was Wendell's doing this time.

When the back of my legs meet the mattress, she removes her finger and reaches for the hem of her shirt, lifting it over her head. I knew she was braless because I watched her get dressed after our shower earlier, but I didn't know her nipples were already hard beneath that thin layer of cotton.

My hands move instinctively, seeking her flesh, but she steps out of my reach with a look that says, *No touching*.

As I start to protest, she hooks her thumbs into her shorts and panties and slides them down her legs in one sexy movement. But she doesn't stop there. No, this wonderful, devilish woman turns around and bends down, presenting me with the perfect view of her perfect ass while she retrieves her clothes and tosses them on the dresser.

My cock hardens instantly, catching Hartley's approving eye when she faces me again. I swallow thickly and clench my hands at my sides as she trails a hand down her stomach and slips a finger between her legs.

Her breath comes out in a soft sigh.

"Fucking hell, Hartley," I groan, desperate to touch her—or myself—at this point.

In response, she takes that damn finger and brushes it over my lips. I waste no time capturing it in my mouth and savoring the sweet taste of her. All it does is make me want more, though. I thrust my hips forward and then her hand is there, slowly jacking me over the thin material of my shorts.

"Damn, babe. That feels so good."

Continuing her relaxed pace, she kisses her way down my chest and abs until she's on her knees, pulling my shorts off. My cock springs free, thick and heavy.

"You have no idea how bad I want you right now."

Her gaze pauses at my dick before she meets my eyes. "I mean, I have *some* idea."

I breathe out a laugh that turns into a moan when she takes me into her mouth.

"What are the rules for your game of torture? Am I allowed to touch you yet?"

Her lips press against the head of my cock. "Do you want to touch me?"

"You know I do."

She massages my balls with one hand and slides the other up and down my shaft. "Hmm, after consulting with the referee, I must inform you that this game will continue with the no-touching rule."

The ache in my cock intensifies. "You're evil."

She smiles.

She fucking *smiles*.

"Hence the worst part of the torture game. But don't worry, we'll get to the best part soon and then you can decide if this round beats jacking off by yourself in half a dozen countries."

"I can already—"

She parts her lips and takes me to the back of her throat with an eager moan and what I was going to say is not important anymore.

"*Fuuuck.*"

I grip my ass to keep from touching her and watch her work me over, licking and sucking and—holy shit, whatever the hell *that* was with her tongue. I'm about to ask her to do it again when she releases my dick with a soft pop and leans back on her heels.

Locking her eyes on me, she spreads her knees, grabs ahold of one nipple, and sinks two fingers in her pussy. The air in my lungs evaporates. Gone. No exhales or sighs, just an instant absence of oxygen after witnessing the sexiest damn thing I've ever seen in my life.

"You're trying to kill me, aren't you?" I rasp.

She slides her fingers up to her clit and moans.

Yes. Death is imminent. Rest in peace to the man who traveled the world and died in a hotel room in New York City.

"I'm so wet, Court."

My cock juts out further, as if to say, *Hello, I'm right here,* and it takes everything in me to ball my hands into fists again so I don't break the rules.

"Are you thinking about my dick?"

Nodding, she moves her free hand to her other nipple, squeezing and twisting while she increases her speed below.

"Good girl. Play with that sweet pussy."

As I watch her do what I wish my tongue was doing, the muscles in my ass and thighs flex, thrusting my hips forward in search of anything that can relieve the building tension in my core.

She has so much power over me that if she so much as breathed on my dick, I'd probably come on the spot. "You've got me so goddamn hard right now," I say through clenched teeth.

Her gaze drops to my cock and her mouth parts on a series of low moans. "This feels so good."

My hips buck again and I'm back to grabbing my ass since I can't touch anything else. "I love watching you touch yourself and hearing the sounds you make."

She abandons her nipple in favor of massaging her tits. "I'm getting close," she whispers.

I don't know how, but it feels like I am too. "Keep going. I want to see you come all over your hand."

Her fingers move faster, and my cock bobs in the air as if her mouth is still there sucking me off. It's a physical impossibility, yet here we are.

"Court . . . I'm . . ."

I know the feeling—literally—because the sight of her on her knees staring up at me as she works herself to an orgasm sparks a familiar tingle at the base of my spine. "Shit, Hartley. I'm gonna come too. You're going to make me fucking come."

She sits up off her heels, giving me her tits, and for the first time in my twenty-seven years on this earth, I explode without anything touching my cock. She finds her release seconds later, and as far as I'm concerned, that officially ends the game.

"Now you're mine." In one fluid motion, I pull her up and toss her on the bed. She's still riding her first orgasm when I bury my face between her legs. "I love the way you taste."

"And I love your tongue," she says, breathless.

"Good because it's time for us to play a new game, and this time I highly recommend finding something to hold on to."

I glance down at the freshly touched up rubber duck on my arm. "I can't believe I let you do this. Rhett is going to give me so much shit for it."

"Come on, you know you secretly love it." She hits me with a cajoling smile, killing any attempt for a stern expression.

"Fine, but only because it'll be nice to have a little reminder of you."

"That's actually really sweet." She zips her marker bag and moves to toss it toward her backpack but stops mid-swing. When she turns back to me, her eyes are gleaming.

"I know that look. What's your brain cooking up?"

"Do you have to take your shirt off in front of anyone for the next week or so?"

"Not that I'm aware of."

"Good, because I just got an idea for something else I can leave you with, but this one's just for you."

"What is it?"

Again, she ignores my question and replies with one of her own. "Do you trust me?"

"Of course."

"Then take your shirt off."

"Bossy, bossy," I tease.

Once my shirt's off, she has me sit at the edge of the bed and sets her markers beside me. "No looking until I tell you."

"Since I escaped it the first time, will this one be a giant dick?"

She steps between my legs as the corners of her mouth quirk up. "Define, 'giant.'"

This fucking woman, I swear.

I pull her in for a quick kiss, then let her get to work on my drawing while I get to work running my hands on the backs of her thighs.

"What are you going to tell Rhett when he asks about the rubber duck?"

"I don't know. I'm debating between it being the European version of the swinger pineapple or a way to identify a fellow member of The Floating Society."

"What's The Floating Society?"

"I can't tell you. You have to be a member to know."

She covers her snort laugh with the back of her free hand and shakes her head. "Does he know you were on the race?"

"Only my parents. I told everyone else that I was going on a hiking trip with some college friends."

"Technically not a lie."

"And in two days, I'll go back to work and learn what great and wonderful things happened at Studs N Suds while I was away."

Hartley leans back, eyes wide and mouth hinging open. "Did you just say, 'Studs N Suds'?"

I don't even try suppressing a smile as I nod.

"Please tell me you have T-shirts."

"And boxers. Socks too, though I'll have to check our stock on those."

"Is your face on any of them?"

"Just the company logo."

"Damn."

We share an easy laugh that turns into comfortable silence as Hartley gets back to work. I quit trying to figure out what she's drawing about three minutes in. All I've felt is random horizontal and vertical lines and some swirls. Nothing dick-shaped, though.

"Court?" Her voice sounds smaller than it did moments ago, raising my concern.

"What's wrong?"

"Do you think Rhett will like me? And the rest of your friends and family?"

I almost laugh because that's the most ridiculous thing I've ever heard.

"First of all, Rhett already likes you."

Her hand freezes as her eyes meet mine. "He's never even met me."

"He's been my best friend since high school, and he was at the bachelor party that weekend. Until this trip, he was the only one who knew what really happened. His words were along the lines of, 'You're the stupidest son of a bitch in the history of sons of bitches who descended from the world's dumbest motherfuckers.'"

Hartley clamps her lips between her teeth to keep from smiling.

"He's also the only one who knows I tried to buy that print from you. When I showed him what you sent, that grown-ass man *giggled* and said it served me right."

Her smile finally breaks free. "Rhett's on Team Hartley. Got it."

"And my family will love you too. I just need to clean up some details with them as soon as I get home because I kind of let them think you were the one who broke up with me. Definitely not my finest moment and one I'll fix immediately."

I steel myself for whatever she throws my way, physically or metaphorically, because it was a dick move at best.

Instead, she says, "How are you going to tell them the truth without giving away the reason you're telling them?"

Ah yes. The damn NDA, because although I was allowed to tell my parents I was on the show, I can't tell them what happened while I was gone. They'll find out with the rest of America.

"This is the alumni season. I've spent a lot of time during the race reflecting on my time in college, so it's entirely plausible that I'd want to fess up to stuff I lied about. Plus, I'll be able to tell them the real reason in four weeks when the cast is announced. But I promise you they'll love you. In fact, I fully expect Ella to kidnap you for a while because she's wanted a sister for years."

"She won't be mad at me because of how I acted at the gallery?"

"Not at all." I squeeze the back of her thighs for reassurance and to get her to look at me again. "The only one she'll be mad at is me. There's a good chance she'll punch me in the dick. I'm already planning to repay her gas money because she was a broke community college student when she drove out to our campus."

This makes her laugh. While she finishes the rest of her drawing, I tell her about the things I want to do and places I want to take her when she comes for her first visit—Daisy's Nut House, Donner Bakery, Bandit Lake . . .

We could have *a lot* of fun at Bandit Lake.

"You're thinking about sex, aren't you?" she says with an amused laugh.

My smile is immediate and unabashed. "How'd you know?"

"You went from rubbing my legs to kneading my ass."

I flex my fingers and indeed find them digging into the gloriousness that is Hartley's backside. "Guilty as charged. I'm happy to discuss punishment options."

"We'll get to your penal code in a minute. I have something to show you first."

She tosses her marker on the bed and steps back. "No peeking yet," she warns. "In fact, close your eyes."

Doing as I'm told, she pulls me off the bed and guides me to what I'm assuming is the mirror.

"I need to preface this by saying I'm limited on supplies and colors and when I do the real thing, it'll look a hell of a lot better than this, but you'll still get the idea."

"Can I look?"

She releases a quiet breath. "Yeah. Go ahead."

I didn't know what to expect, but even if I had a hundred guesses, what I see in the mirror wouldn't be one of them.

"I did the lines randomly so you wouldn't guess the shape," she says beside me.

It worked. At no point did I realize she was drawing three boxes across my chest. The one on my right pec is blank. The one in the middle is a compass. The one on my left pec is a heart that's been stitched back together with . . .

I lean in closer.

. . . Stars.

Tiny yellow stars zigzagging across a mended heart.

I swallow past the knot of emotion in my throat and find Hartley's eyes in the mirror. "*The Evolution of a Lie*, but in reverse."

CHAPTER 21
HARTLEY

All I have to say is thank god for online dating, because it's the only thing that's making this NDA possible.

Before Court and I left New York City three weeks ago, Wendell pulled us aside and made sure we were crystal clear on the rules for the next four months until the season finale airs:

1. Don't disclose anything about the race.
2. Don't share any information about our relationship.
3. When in doubt, refer to rules 1 and 2.

He specifically advised us not to contact any contestants until after the finale, but there was no way Court and I were not going to talk for four months. This meant we needed a way to call and text each other without raising suspicion, particularly after the cast is announced next week. Enter "Thomas" and "Jessica," who we each met on a dating site a few weeks before we left for the race. Right now, Thomas is sending encouraging texts because I'm about to have The Talk with my parents.

Thomas: You got this.

Me: I hope so.

Thomas: I know so because of New Zealand and Greece. You're a badass.

Me: This is true. I'll keep you posted.

With a one last deep breath, I set my phone on my dresser and head for the living room. Mom's on the couch and Dad's in his chair beside the couch while they watch an old season of Xtreme Quest. It looks like a universe moment given the topic of discussion, but this is just a regular Saturday in the Billings house.

Before I lose my nerve, I claim an empty couch cushion and blurt out, "Can I talk to you?"

They exchange a glance and Mom mutes the TV. "What's wrong?"

"Nothing, I've just been thinking about a few things."

"Like what?" Dad asks, leaning forward in his chair.

My fingers twist in my lap as I work to figure out how to begin. "You both know I can't tell you anything about the race, but what I can say is it helped me realize that I've felt like I've been wearing a really great pair of shoes that don't fit me. Dad, your business has been your baby since before John and I were born, and after the accident, I wanted to do anything I could to make sure you didn't lose it.

"I don't regret my decision to move home and take over the company. I just figured if I kept at it long enough, I'd be able to turn your dream into mine, but I don't think that's going to happen."

My voice cracks on the last word. I hate having to tell them this, but I hate the idea of not having Court and feeling stagnant for the rest of my life even more.

"Over the last three weeks, I've thought a lot about my plans for the future, and they all start with . . ."

You can do this.

"What I mean is . . ."

Spit it out.

"I'm trying to say . . ."

God, just say it!

". . . I'm leaving the company."

They stare back at me in silence.

"It's not that I've been unhappy," I continue. "It's more like you got a new pair of shoes six years ago, I put one on, and never took it off. Now it's time for me to find my own pair of shoes."

More silence as they exchange glances, each of them wearing an expression I can't read.

I swallow and press on. "I'm really sorry for the burden this creates, but I'll handle the job posting and interviews and I promise I won't go anywhere until everything's settled with my replacement."

There.

I've said everything I can, short of telling them about Court.

. . . And they still haven't said anything.

Why aren't they saying anything?

They exchange another look, and this time Dad tilts his head at Mom. She nods, and then he nods, and they both turn to me.

"I guess this is a good time to tell you that I got an offer from a guy in Wilmington a couple of months ago. Why don't we all get some new shoes and sell the company instead?"

————

My college roommate Corrina was the first to text when the cast list was released this afternoon.

Corrina: COURT MUELLER?! ARE YOU KIDDING ME?
Me: I am not.
Corrina: What was he like? Did you murder him? Did you bang him? Is he married with nine kids?
Me: *zipped lips emoji*
Corrina: No fair!
Me: Tell that to the $500k NDA I signed.

The rest of the day was more of the same, but it's not until 8:32 p.m. that my phone finally lights up with the one name I've been waiting for. I set my notebook aside and sit up against my headboard to answer the video call.

"Heyyyyy . . ." My voice trails off when I realize the face on the other end of the line isn't Court's. The man is smiling though, and swatting at something off-screen.

"Hi Hartley, I'm Rhett."

Oh shit.

"Umm . . . Hi?"

"Give me the phone, asshole!"

That's definitely Court's voice. And his living room. What is happening right now?

"You'll get your turn in just a minute," Rhett says before turning his attention back to me. "Anyway, I figured out that you were 'Jessica' about thirty-seven seconds after the cast list was announced, so don't worry, Court's honor and bank account are still intact."

"But your balls won't be if you don't give me my phone!" Court hollers.

My cheeks already hurt from smiling. "It's nice to meet you, Rhett. I'm curious though—how'd you figure it out?"

"Because he's a nosy bastard."

"More like a man with a modicum of emotional intelligence who's watched your sorry ass mope for six damn years, and suddenly you're home from a mysterious hiking trip and halfway in love with a woman from the internet? *Please*. But don't worry," he says to me, "Court hasn't told anyone else about Jessica. He's actually a pretty private guy when it comes to his dating life."

"Are you done now?"

Ignoring Court, Rhett adds, "In all seriousness, I haven't seen him this happy in a really long time. I'm excited to meet you in person in a few months. In the meantime, my lips are sealed."

"I'm looking forward to it too, Rhett. I've heard great things about you."

"Not anymore you won't," Court says flatly.

"Don't mind him. He's cranky because Ella threatened to write him out of her will for not telling her about the show and he was really hoping to get her collection of vintage Barbie dolls."

I'm cracking up as Court battles for the phone again. A few seconds later, Rhett finally gives in and Court appears on the screen.

"Finally," he huffs, though his smirk reads more amused than annoyed.

"Bye Hartley!" Rhett calls.

"Bye Rhett."

After the front door closes, Court plops onto the couch with a grunt and scrubs a hand over his forehead. "I had no idea the cast announcement day would be so exhausting. I must've gotten at least three dozen messages from people I haven't talked to in years, along with texts or calls from just about everyone in my contacts."

"Same. Corrina and Megan say hi, by the way."

He breathes out a laugh and shakes his head. "I can only imagine what their text string looks like right now."

"Now that you mention it, Megan did say something about ordering a voodoo doll," I tease.

He rolls his eyes playfully, then returns his gaze to my face and releases a long breath. "I miss you."

Ugh!

I swoon.

I literally swoon, but can you blame me?

"I miss you too, and that brings me to this evening's good news. One"—I hold up a finger—"we made it through the first month and now there's only three to go, and two"—I add a finger—"my dad and the guy in Wilmington signed the paperwork today."

"He's really going to sell it?"

I nod. "He's ready to get a head start on retirement. We're no longer accepting new clients or booking anything after Thanksgiving."

"Wow, that happened a lot faster than I thought it would."

"You're telling me. I still haven't told them where I plan on going, but they know I'm heading out once we're done with the jobs on our schedule."

A smile slowly takes over his face. "If you're done by Thanksgiving and the finale is December seventh, that means—"

"I'll be there on December eighth."

CHAPTER 22
COURT

Leg eight aired last night, which means anyone who came to the PTA's weekly fundraiser-slash-viewing party in the gym watched me land on a drop zone and kiss Hartley on a forty-foot screen. Ella said the PTA chair had to pause the show to wait for the cheering to die down.

I watched from my living room with Rhett's moral support, which was mostly him clapping me on the shoulder while saying, "Atta boy!" and "It's about fucking time!"

It's not like I didn't know this episode was coming. I just didn't account for Blake Thompson's knee taking a crap on him in the dairy section of the Piggly Wiggly after the Argentina episode aired. That left his history class in need of a substitute for his two-month recovery from surgery.

Rather than continuing with my plan of hiding out in my office of Studs N Suds, I was dropped into the middle of the gossip mill otherwise known as Green Valley High School right after the New Zealand leg aired.

Here's the thing about high schoolers: When they're invested in something, there's no half-assing it. By the end of that first day, there was a #TeamHartbreak sign stuck to Blake's door and I'd been added to a "Protect Him At All Costs" list. Since then, my students have decreed Hartley to be my one true love. For the record, I've continued my I-can't-discuss-anything stance, but that didn't stop them from creating a mood board, whatever that is, to gather ideas for our eventual wedding.

The teachers have been just as invested. At lunch on Fridays, the lounge becomes a situation room to discuss the latest episode, and there's even a line item on the weekly staff meeting agenda where Janet Holstrom, an armchair body language expert in the English department, shares her analysis.

And the thing is, I really do appreciate their support. It's been fun to watch the show through their perspective, it's just getting harder to keep my expression in check while I dodge their questions and comments—which brings me back to today and the dilemma I'm currently facing: it's Friday and I need a microwave.

"I hear you get better results when you turn it," Nick Easton says of the doorknob for the lounge.

I breathe out a laugh. "With wisdom like that, we're sure to win the state championship this year."

"That's the plan. But seriously, are you going in, or . . ."

"Trying to decide if having hot lasagna is worth all of that." I circle my finger, indicating the lively voices on the other side of the door.

"You're telling me you jumped out of an airplane and you're scared of a few teachers?"

"No, but—"

"Exactly." He turns the knob and nudges me through the open door.

The lounge falls to a hush for a whole three seconds before Clara Hill, Ally Dalbotten, and Mari Mitchell launch into a round of applause.

"Thanks, Nick." I fire a mock glare at his back as he laughs his way to the vending machine.

"So," Clara says, leaning forward on the table and resting her chin in her hands, "that was an intense episode."

Smirking, Mari adds, "It looked like things were getting a little hot in Greece."

I uncover my lasagna and toss it in the microwave. "It was about ninety degrees if I remember correctly."

"Outside or in the hotel room?" Ally waggles her brows. "And was that your only kiss that day?"

I almost snort laugh, but instead, I respond with, "I appreciate your questions and I'm looking forward to discussing them—"

"—after the finale airs on December seventh at eight p.m. Eastern," they say in unison, laughing.

"One more month," I say with a placating smile.

I'm spared from further questioning when my phone buzzes in my pocket.

Jessica: My mom has apparently known who you are since episode two.

Me: She and Rhett should start a true crime podcast.

Me: What was her reaction?

Jessica: That as long as I'm happy, she's happy. And then she said I looked really happy.

Jessica: She also asked if I'd need any help driving my stuff to Green Valley after the show ends. *facepalm emoji*

Me: It's frightening how well she's connected the dots. On second thought, we should never introduce her and Rhett. They'd probably take over the world.

The microwave beeps. I retrieve my lasagna and pop the lid back on so I can eat in the privacy of my classroom while I chat with Hartley. When I turn for the door, everyone is staring at me.

"What?"

"Who are you texting?" Mari asks.

I feel the tips of my ears turn red. "A friend."

"Mm-hmm." Clara's amused smile tells me she's not buying it.

Apparently Nick isn't either, because he holds up his palms and says, "I'm not making assumptions, but I don't grin like that when I text my friends."

I clutch my chest on the way to the door. "Et tu, Brute?"

They laugh at my Shakespeare reference and wave me out, going back to what I'm sure will be a riveting discussion about my "friend."

I return to my classroom and shut the door for the last ten minutes of lunch.

Me: You free for a quick call?

In lieu of a response, my screen lights up. I accept the video call and prop my phone against my computer. Hartley's in her Billings Painting coveralls with her hair in a messy bun and a streak of light blue paint on her forehead. In other words, fucking adorable. Thank god we only have one month left.

"Did you see the email from Wendell that just came in?"

"No," I say around a bite of lasagna.

"They're flying us to LA the morning of the finale. They're calling it the Xtreme Reunion and we're supposed to watch the final episode with a studio audience and do follow-up interviews with Paul."

"Everyone or just us?"

"The whole cast."

"Weird," I say after swallowing another bite. "They've never had a reunion show."

"Mom thinks they're playing up the showmance between us since our season has had the highest ratings so far."

"That makes sense. Did you already respond?"

She smiles mischievously. "I told him I'd be there as long as they let us share a room."

————

You'd think after being filmed nearly twenty-four seven for three weeks that I'd be used to cameras, but knowing I'm about to be on live TV takes things to a whole new level. It doesn't help that the producers are playing up the tension as much as possible by keeping the contestants apart until the last minute.

That means I've been in the same building as Hartley for the last four hours, but I haven't seen her thanks to the merry-go-round schedule of hair, makeup, and wardrobe. Now I'm pacing the floor of my makeshift green room as I watch the last five minutes of the finale along with the studio audience and the rest of America.

Reliving it on the screen brings back all the emotions I felt that day, with anger rising to the top of the list because Big Mike and DeAngelo have talked shit about us and the Bombshells for the entire episode. DeAngelo was even impersonating Gianna's panic attack at Edge. What kind of asshole makes fun of something like that, especially knowing it'll likely end up on national TV?

At this point, it's a good thing they've kept us secluded from each other. Or maybe it's why they had to do that in the first place.

When the final commercial break ends, the show starts back with a clip of us running out of Prospect Park with the Wise Asses on our tail. The next sequence plays out like a bad dream with DeAngelo blocking our taxi, us getting stuck at red lights, and us sprinting down the final stretch of the board-walk only to cross the finish line fifteen seconds too late. The only solace I have right now is realizing that everyone was cheering for us in those final moments. When the Wise Asses got to the mat, the cheers dropped dramatically and picked back up as Hartley and I arrived.

Another thing I didn't notice that day is that when the Bombshells arrived, everyone pretty much ignored the Wise Asses. They keep moving from team to team to boast about their win but we're all too busy talking to each other.

"Serves you right, assholes," I mutter to the screen.

I hear a knock at the door and then the assistant I met earlier peeks her head in. "Ready?"

"Very." My stomach and heart do a weird high-five thing as I button my dark gray suit coat and follow her into the hall.

"One member of each team will be in the left wing and the other in the right wing. When Paul announces you, you'll walk to the center of the set and meet Hartley, then find a spot on the couches."

Easy enough.

After a few short hallways, I'm behind a curtain backstage with Gianna, Kadeeja, Boyd, Bobby, Mitchell, Ji-ho, Randall, Janessa, and Marcail. We exchange hugs and handshakes before lining up in the order of elimination.

I take my place at the end of the line behind Gianna, who gives me another hug. "How's your girl?"

"Fantastic and in a few days, she'll be Tennessee's newest resident."

She opens her mouth in a silent scream and squeezes my arm.

"Pretty much my feelings too," I laugh.

"Quiet please!" I hear from someplace on the set.

As the chatter dies down, I realize no one is behind me.

"Have you seen the Wise Asses?" I whisper to Gianna.

"No. I'm not sad about it though. They're gonna have to keep me on the opposite side of the set from both of them."

"Us too. Maybe they'll reconfigure everything after this segment to bring them out."

We hear Paul start his intro to the live portion of tonight's show, and then the backstage curtain parts and he's calling us up.

"My heart's gonna beat out of my freaking chest," I whisper.

Gianna laughs quietly and grabs ahold of my hand as we slowly move forward.

"Do I hug her or kiss her?"

"Yes."

"You're no help."

"In fourth place we have Team Old Bay, Kadeeja and Haylee!"

Gianna and I inch up and I can finally, *finally* see across the set. Hartley's in a shimmery, van Gogh blue dress that stops just above her knees and she's standing arm-in-arm with Alexis.

"She's beautiful," Gianna whispers.

I can only nod while I work to breathe properly.

"In third are the Bombshells, Gianna and Alexis!"

With a final squeeze, Gianna lets go of my hand and crosses the set, giving Alexis a quick hug before heading to the couch.

And then it's just me and Hartley.

Nothing standing between us.

Nothing keeping us apart.

Not intentional lies or misunderstood truths.

Not NDAs.

Not separate states.

"And now, for the team we've all been waiting for, Team Hartbreak, Court and Hartley!"

I briefly register the sound of cheering, but it quickly fades along with everything else that isn't her.

Five steps . . .

Three steps . . .

One step . . .

I pull her in, splaying one hand across her back and threading the other into her hair before lowering my mouth to hers. "God, I've missed you," I say through our kiss.

Her hands snake around my waist, drawing me in further. "Same."

"I should probably stop kissing you now."

She laughs and I gather the necessary willpower to turn her loose.

The crowd is still cheering when we take our seats next to the Bombshells. Hartley reaches over to do that hand-squeeze-hug-thing that women do, then settles into the crook of my arm.

"Welcome, everyone," Paul says after taking a seat in his chair. "We're so glad to see you again. I'm sure you've noticed the absence of our winning team, but we wanted to have a chance to chat with you all before we move on to them."

Translation: Everyone hates the Wise Asses and we didn't want them here either.

No one is saddened by this news.

In fact, it's pretty easy to forget about them altogether as we move into discussing the other teams, our strategies, our most challenging moments, and our favorite parts of the race. My nerves quickly subside and the conversation flows easily, because although we're on an immaculately decorated set surrounded by a live audience and a dozen cameras, this is basically a team dinner in better clothes and without the food.

But that mood changes when we return from the second commercial break.

"As I mentioned at the beginning of the reunion, the Wise Guys have not appeared on stage yet . . . and that's because they weren't invited. Here's why." The studio lights dim as Paul gestures to the screen at the side of the set. "As our editors were working on footage for leg ten in the Netherlands, one of them spotted something unusual."

The clip shows Haylee and Big Mike studying the example place setting for the butler challenge. She's going over the display with intense focus, but Mike just stands there for a few seconds and leaves. Then the footage zooms to his suit top, which was part of our costume.

"Our editor saw something sticking out of Big Mike's pocket. She began searching through other footage from that challenge and noticed a pattern— every time he said he needed to use the bathroom, she saw the same item in his pocket.

"We began searching through footage from other legs and saw the same thing appearing."

The clips move to a montage of him stowing something small and black in his pocket or his backpack.

"The Wise Guys brought a smartphone with them on the race."

There is a collective gasp throughout the studio as the lights come back up.

"How did they sneak it in? Our bags were checked in Dallas," Marcail says.

"They were, and our crew found no contraband in their backpacks. During our investigation, Big Mike confessed to having a friend in the crowd at the Giant Eyeball who followed their taxi to the airport and left the phone in a bathroom stall for Mike to retrieve. Throughout the race, he and DeAngelo connected to wi-fi at the airport, on airplanes, and at several McDonald's locations to gain information about each destination. During other legs, like the Netherlands, he recorded videos to assist him with memory challenges and watched the footage in the bathroom."

"Son of a . . ." Boyd catches himself before the last word and flattens his lips to a thin line.

"Needless to say, we're deeply disappointed in their behavior and have pursued legal action against them and their accomplice in Dallas, who assisted them in exchange for a portion of the prize money. Obviously, none of them will receive any money."

Now Paul's expression shifts from anger and disgust to . . . excited?

"With DeAngelo and Big Mike being disqualified from Xtreme Quest, the producers have updated the final standings."

The screen switches to a chart showing the results for the last leg of the race.

"Team Old Bay is now in third place and the winner of the ten-thousand-dollar prize. Team Bombshell is now in second place and the winner of the twenty-five-thousand-dollar prize."

Hartley's wide eyes lock onto mine as Paul finishes with,

"And Team Hartbreak is now in first place and the winner of the million-dollar prize."

We turn our focus to the screen, and everything happens in slow motion after that.

Hartley is in my arms, confetti surrounds us, the entire room is cheering, Boyd is leaping over the back of his couch to get to ours, I'm laughing, Hartley's laugh-crying along with the Bombshells and Old Bay, and now I'm somehow on my feet hugging Paul, who closes out our live event on national TV with me embracing him in a bear hug from the side.

It's an out-of-body experience to say the least.

After fielding more hugs and high fives from the rest of the contestants, I find my way back to Hartley and pull her against my chest. "So that just happened."

"This is not how I thought the race would end when I saw you on the lawn in Dallas."

"What did your version look like?"

"I was convinced there was an eighty-four percent chance I'd murder you before it was over."

I bark out a laugh because I can absolutely picture her imagining that. "How about we go with a different 'm' word and change that percentage."

Her eyes are gleaming when she says, "You mean 'marry' and a 'zero percent chance'?"

"'Marry,' yes, but you'd better add a one and another zero to make it a hundred percent."

She lifts her shoulders in a playful shrug and pulls my lips to hers. "I guess I can do that since we have all these extra zeros now."

EPILOGUE

HARTLEY, SIX MONTHS LATER

I watch with skeptical eyes as Court unloads two hundred hamburgers and hot dogs onto the conveyor belt at the Piggly Wiggly. "You're sure we'll be able to sell all of this in a four-hour fundraiser at the car wash?"

"The Winston brothers are stopping by, so that's easily a dozen each. Jackson said a bunch of deputies from the sheriff's office would be there too. Then there's the football team and the band parents, plus anyone else who comes off the street. Honestly, the bigger concern is running out before it's over."

If he's right, the Green Valley High marching band will get twelve hundred bucks just from food off the grill. If he's wrong, I guess we'll all be eating burgers and hot dogs for the next—

Hang on.

My attention snags on a tabloid headline to my right.

Caught! Xtreme Quest winner spotted with mystery man

The picture on the cover was taken from across a parking lot. I'm sitting in the passenger seat of a cherry-red sportscar smiling at the driver, whose face is conveniently blocked by the sun visor.

"Why do you insist on reading that trash?" Court asks when I pluck the magazine from the rack.

"How else am I going to know what I've been up to?"

While he continues unloading the cart, I flip to the exclusive article on page eight.

"Six months after the shocking Xtreme Quest reunion show, Hartley Billings was spotted car shopping in Knoxville with an unknown business-man," I say with an almost-straight face. "A source said Billings and her companion couldn't stop smiling as they signed paperwork together, and it was clear she wasn't wearing her engagement ring.

"As we reported in February, Court Mueller—Billings's ex-boyfriend and reality show teammate—popped the question with a one-carat blue sapphire and diamond ring. When asked about the upcoming nuptials, the source said Team Hartbreak has no plans for a wedding."

"Their source sucks," Court mutters as I return the magazine. "Wait, do you think it was one of the employees?"

I shake my head. "A customer recognized me and asked about the show and our wedding. I gave her our standard public response that we were still looking at our options and hadn't finalized anything yet."

The last part isn't true, but I'd rather the public not know we're getting married at Bandit Lake in two weeks. After the ceremony, we're flying our parents, my brother's family, Rhett, and Ella to Italy and Spain for a honey-moon-slash-family vacation.

As far as the tabloid goes, the only thing it got right was me being at the dealership in the first place. The man in the sportscar is the general manager and the paperwork he signed was the contract for me to paint a mural in their lobby. I got started that afternoon, which is why I wasn't wearing my ring.

Becoming a muralist was more of an accident than a plan. After moving to Green Valley, I had no idea what my future looked like career-wise. I was okay with that, especially considering most twenty-nine-year-olds don't get a chance to think about what they want to do without stressing about income in the meantime.

The day Court learned he'd be a world history teacher for the upcoming school year, I immediately knew I wanted to paint a mural in his classroom of the places we visited during the race. The only problem was having to wait until summer to get started, so I killed time by painting the school's mascot in the gym over spring break. A student posted a photo of it on social media, word spread from there, and now I'm booked through October.

I keep expecting to wake up from this crazy, amazing dream but it hasn't happened yet.

"Hey guys," a voice says behind me.

Court waves as I turn and smile up at Everett Monroe. He owns Twenty

Sides and Sundry, a gaming shop on Main Street, but still takes on small projects for his family's carpentry business. We met earlier this year when my parents moved to Green Valley and needed help making their home more wheelchair friendly. The day before they closed, Everett built ramps off the front door and back deck so my dad could have full access as soon as they got the keys.

"I'm actually glad I ran into you," he continues. "I have an idea for a mural at the shop that I want to run by you."

"I'd love to hear about it, but I'm not booking until after Halloween. Is that okay?"

"Yeah, that's no problem. Based on the one you did for Daisy's Nut House, you're worth the wait."

Court snorts a laugh and looks over at me. "He's not wrong."

———

Rhett pushes back from the table and stands. "May I have your attention please?"

"What's he doing?" Court whispers as our friends and family quiet down.

I shrug innocently while avoiding eye contact with Gianna so neither of us start laughing as she slips out of her seat at the contestants' table. Tonight is my rehearsal dinner at The Front Porch and the three of us have been plotting this moment for weeks.

"For those I haven't had a chance to meet, my name is Rhett and I'm the best man. Part of my duties include telling you how amazing this guy is . . . which I'm happy to do during my speech at the reception tomorrow. Right now, I think it's time for a little entertainment." He signals two servers, who move a curtained partition to reveal a TV on a high-top table. "I hope you all enjoy this unaired clip from the season finale of Xtreme Quest as much as I have."

With that, he plays a scene from Court and Gianna's challenge at Edge.

Positioning her back to the New York City skyline, Gianna wraps her arms around her waist and shakes her head. "I don't think I can do this."

"What if I gave you another option besides kicking me in the junk?" Court replies.

"Like what?"

"Hartley doesn't know this yet, but we're gonna get married. If you can

lean out from the building for thirty seconds, you can be a groomsman in the wedding."

"I'd take you up on that if she'd already said yes, but right now kicking you still sounds like the safer bet."

"Your lack of faith wounds me." He presses his hands over his heart for effect, coaxing a small laugh from Gianna.

"Are you ready?" the instructor calls from off camera.

"One second," Court says before giving his attention back to Gianna. "How about we up the ante? You do this lean and I'll wear a tutu and sing 'I'm a Little Teapot' at the rehearsal dinner."

She holds his gaze for several seconds. "Promise?"

He extends a pinky and hooks it with hers. "Promise."

"Court might've conveniently forgotten about that conversation," Rhett says when the screen goes black, "but Gianna didn't."

The room erupts into laughter when she joins Rhett holding a blue-and-orange Xtreme Quest tutu.

Court turns to me with a playful scowl. "Did you know about this?"

"Gianna and I might've hatched a plan with Paul after I invited him to the wedding."

His eyes flash with mischief as he leans in and nips my earlobe. "You're going to pay for this later."

"Is that another promise?" I tease.

He answers with a brief and surprisingly heated kiss before rising from his seat. "I hope everyone knows you're all signing an NDA before you leave."

"Worth it!" Boyd calls from his table, cueing another round of laughter.

While my co-conspirators help Court into his tutu, I'm hit with an overwhelming sense of gratitude for the irony of our lives this summer compared to last summer—Court's still in Green Valley and he's about to be a teacher. I'm marrying my college ex and I'm still painting walls. It's literally everything we never wanted a year ago and we couldn't be happier.

ABOUT THE AUTHOR

Hazel lives in Tampa Bay, Florida. She's a proud Army veteran, and her greatest loves include her family, lip gloss, Diet Coke, and the beach.

———

Website: http://www.authorhazeljames.com
Facebook: https://www.facebook.com/realhazeljames
Goodreads: https://www.goodreads.com/author/show/7264501.Hazel_James
TikTok: https://www.tiktok.com/@realhazeljames
Instagram: https://www.instagram.com/realhazeljames

Find Smartypants Romance online:
Website: www.smartypantsromance.com
Facebook: www.facebook.com/smartypantsromance/
Goodreads: www.goodreads.com/smartypantsromance
Twitter: @smartypantsrom
Instagram: @smartypantsromance

ALSO BY HAZEL JAMES

I'll Be the One
Chased
Saved
Checked Out
Guarding Shadows

ALSO BY SMARTYPANTS ROMANCE

<u>Green Valley Chronicles</u>

<u>The Love at First Sight Series</u>

<u>Baking Me Crazy by Karla Sorensen (#1)</u>

<u>Batter of Wits by Karla Sorensen (#2)</u>

<u>Steal My Magnolia by Karla Sorensen (#3)</u>

<u>Worth the Wait by Karla Sorensen (#4)</u>

<u>Fighting For Love Series</u>

<u>Stud Muffin by Jiffy Kate (#1)</u>

<u>Beef Cake by Jiffy Kate (#2)</u>

<u>Eye Candy by Jiffy Kate (#3)</u>

<u>Knock Out by Jiffy Kate (#4)</u>

<u>The Donner Bakery Series</u>

<u>No Whisk, No Reward by Ellie Kay (#1)</u>

<u>Dough You Love Me? By Stacy Travis (#2)</u>

<u>Tough Cookie by Talia Hunter (#3)</u>

<u>Muffin But Trouble by Talia Hunter (#4)</u>

<u>*Oh Brother! Series*</u>

<u>Crime and Periodicals by Nora Everly (#1)</u>

<u>Carpentry and Cocktails by Nora Everly (#2)</u>

<u>Hotshot and Hospitality by Nora Everly (#3)</u>

<u>Architecture and Artistry by Nora Everly (#4)</u>

<u>*Small Town Silver Fox Series*</u>

<u>Love in Due Time by L.B. Dunbar (#1)</u>

<u>Love in Deed by L.B. Dunbar (#2)</u>

<u>Love in a Pickle by L.B. Dunbar (#3)</u>

Passing Notes by Nora Everly (#1)

Band Together by Piper Sheldon (#2)

Ex Marks the Spot by Hazel James (#3)

Past Tents by Stacy Travis (#4)

Story of Us Collection

My Story of Us: Zach by Chris Brinkley (#1)

My Story of Us: Thomas by Chris Brinkley (#2)

My Story of Us: Grayson by Chris Brinkley (#3)

Seduction in the City

Cipher Security Series

Code of Conduct by April White (#1)

Code of Honor by April White (#2)

Code of Matrimony by April White (#2.5)

Code of Ethics by April White (#3)

Cipher Office Series

Weight Expectations by M.E. Carter (#1)

Sticking to the Script by Stella Weaver (#2)

Cutie and the Beast by M.E. Carter (#3)

Weights of Wrath by M.E. Carter (#4)

Common Threads Series

Mad About Ewe by Susannah Nix (#1)

Give Love a Chai by Nanxi Wen (#2)

Key Change by Heidi Hutchinson (#3)

Not Since Ewe by Susannah Nix (#4)

Lost Track by Heidi Hutchinson (#5)

Ewe Complete Me by Susannah Nix (#6)

Meet Your Matcha by Nanxi Wen (#7)

All Mixed Up by Heidi Hutchinson (#8)

Write or Wrong by Heidi Hutchinson (#9)